VILE BOYS
KNOT THEIR TOY BOOK 1

AJ MERLIN

Vile Boys

Copyright © 2022 AJ Merlin

All Rights Reserved

No part of this book may be reproduced in any form or by any electronic or mechanical means, including information storage and retrieval systems, without written permission from the author, except for the use of brief quotations in a book review.

Cover Design by Devon Kingsley

Paperback isbn: 978-1-955540-18-6

1

Would it be cheating to knock out my hearing aids so that I don't have to hear the dean of Winter Grove University keep going on and on about how *honored* we should feel?

Sure, it would take a bit of planning. With my hearing aids going over my ears and kept pretty securely in place, I might have to fake a bee in my long hair to shake them to the ground, or more preferably, into the black canvas bag between my knees.

In the end, I decide it's not worth it. Yet.

But still the dean goes on, voice rising and falling with a lull that makes me want to pass out. I take a deep breath, scents mingling to what amounts to smell-soup in my nose. Alpha, beta, omega, spicy, flowery, fruity...it's all there, and most of it smells like crap, thanks to the muddling in my nose.

The girl on my left glances over at me, eyes wide, when she sees me take a second deep, steadying breath. Her dark eyes dart around my face, then down to where my knee shakes impatiently, and a small frown appears on her face as if she's worried I'm going to get to my feet and riot until we can leave the ice hockey rink that poses for an auditorium here.

I may be one of the few incredibly lucky scholarship students, but I'm not a *heathen*. There's no need to worry when the worst I'll do is just stop listening.

She looks at me again, and this time I catch her gaze with my own to hold it. She's an omega too. Being close enough that her knee could brush mine if she wanted means that I can scent her just as clearly as the beta to my right, but this omega looks petrified. As if the dean is about to announce some cutthroat version of the Weakest Link to get a few students out of here and make room for the rich kids and all their money.

Personally, I've read the brochure enough to reasonably know that is not going to happen, but who can really be sure these days?

My eyes move from the girl's, going instead to canvas the chairs around me. For orientation, only the freshman have been cursed to show up and listen to this speech, but I'd thought there would be more than what there are. Don't most colleges have a few hundred students enroll each year? At *least*?

Frankly, if there are more than one hundred and fifty students sitting on the chairs in the covered hockey arena, I'll eat my Winter Grove brochure.

My eyes fall on a brunette boy who's leaned back in his chair, quite obviously staring at the ceiling instead of looking forward at the dean. His head tilts back, exposing more of his pale throat, and by the way the girl to his left keeps glancing at him and all of that pale skin on display, I can't help but think that he's an omega like me, and she's caught his scent strongly. Clearly, she wants to act on it, but I don't think she's about to go all vampire on his neck in front of everyone here.

A low, irritated sigh leaves me, and I drag my gaze back to the dean, away from the boy with his throat on display.

Or rather, the woman who slams the gate to the arena, her dress shoes making awkward scuffing noises on the cover of the rink. She bolts to the dean, her face white, and he pauses in what is probably the most heartfelt part of a truly rousing speech to bend down enough for her to whisper in his ear something I most certainly can't hear.

At least I'm close enough to see his face go white. *And* close enough to read his lips, being that I'm in the second row of students, and I lean forward enough to do just that, tuning out every muddy sound of muttering students to watch the way his lips move.

Are you sure? He asks, thankfully facing me enough that I can make out the words. The woman nods, but unfortunately her reply is said not facing me. I have no idea what it is she's told him.

He draws back, runs a hand down his face, and she continues to whisper in his ear. At last he shakes his head.

Where is the body? I'll keep the freshmen here until it's cleaned up so none of them see it.

Body? Maybe there is some kind of Battle Royale going on here that I hadn't expected.

"Can you tell what they're saying?" over the buzz of conversation, the girl's voice in my ear takes longer than it should to properly reach my brain. I look at her, blinking in surprise, and her confidence falters, though I'm sure I don't look *mean*. My resting bitch face is more like a resting anxious face on most occasions.

"Kind of," I admit with a shrug, leaning back and getting a good look at her once more. She doesn't look as nervous this time, though I'm not sure how she's going to respond to what I'm about to say. "I think they found a body on campus."

"A *what?*" She lurches away from me, as if I'm the one

who's committed a murder, and I fight so hard not to roll my eyes that they burn from the strain. "A *body*?"

"I think so? I guess, anyway. I guess they could be talking about an animal or something?"

"Nah, not an animal." The boy behind us leans forward, draping his arms over both of our chairs. I turn to look at him, my brows raised, and when I suck in a breath, his scent hits me. It reminds me of something tropical and alcoholic, and for a moment I think about calling him *Mr. Piña Colada.* Maybe not out loud. I'm not sure if he'd appreciate that. But in my head, that's what he is now.

It's also impossible to block out how incredibly appetizing that smell is. I almost want to lean into him, just for a better sniff, but again, I am not a heathen. I will not *sniff* the beta leaning on my chair, even though I could say it's compensation for where he has his arm.

"No?" I ask, brows lifting. "You're telling me there really is a dead body on Winter Grove grounds? The brochure never mentioned this."

"Brochure?" I lean forward and grab it out of my bag, lifting it with a flourish at his question.

"Oh." He plucks it out of my hands and looks it over, brows raising. "I see. One of *these* brochures. Guess you're pretty smart, aren't you?"

Irritation tickles my nerves, and I look at him as I slowly reach out and take the brochure back, to drop it back in my bag. I'd only kept it this long for the map, but now I'm feeling pretty judged about the whole situation. "Aren't we all pretty smart? Seems like it's a requirement to go here," I point out carefully.

"Money is the requirement to go here. Unless you're lucky enough to get a scholarship. Which you did." His words are confident, and he's not *asking* about my scholarship student status. He's *stating* a fact.

"What makes you think that?"

"Because you have the scholarship kid brochure. Not the rich kid brochure."

There are different ones?

Before I can remark on it, he throws me a knowing smirk from a handsome face, his light blue eyes set under long lashes glittering. "Anyway, it's a person. A student. My pack says that they've been mopping up blood for ten minutes."

"*Blood?*" the girl beside me repeats, her eyes back to being as big as saucers. "As in–"

"Looks like someone was murdered." The boy shrugs and sits back, just as the dean clears his throat.

"There's been an incident on campus. We'll let you know when there's more to tell. Unfortunately, we'll have to cut this short, and I'd like to ask all of you not to hang around the police as they investigate. You have three more days before classes start." He offers a wan smile. "And I'm sure many of you are anxious to explore the town. Remember that the lighthouse closes at dusk, and that the lake is much too cold to swim in during the fall. Congratulations on getting into Winter Grove University, and I look forward to seeing what you all do with this amazing opportunity."

When he dismisses us, I take my time. The boy behind me does not, instead tearing off towards two other students standing by the entrance to the ice rink. One of them grins, wrapping an arm over the boy's shoulders, but the other looks up, eyeing me balefully as I watch.

He doesn't look very friendly. With dark hair and dark eyes set on a pale face, he looks like he's trying his best to tell me to fuck off without words. Not that I've done anything. All things considered, his friend was the one who was rude to *me*.

Finally, the only students left are two girls talking to the dean's assistant, and the girl who'd been sitting beside me. She jumps up when I do, cementing her place in my mind as a truly nervous creature as her flowery scent washes over me.

At the end of the day, the only thing I can really ask for is to never be such a jumpy, nervous omega. It reminds me of a chihuahua, and the thought immediately makes me feel bad. Maybe something happened to her that I don't know about? After all, I don't even know her *name*.

"What dorm are you in?" I ask, trying to sound friendly.

The girl sucks in a breath. "Maliseet," she says, after a brief hesitation. "You?"

"I'm in Maliseet too, actually." I'm surprised to know we're going to the same place, so I add, "Want to walk there together? I haven't met my roommate yet, or anything. I just dumped my stuff in there earlier."

"What room?" She shoves her hands in her pockets and leads the way out of the row of chairs, taking the same gate out that the other students had.

"Four-eighteen."

A smile crosses her face for the first time since she'd sat down next to me. "Then…you've officially met your roommate," she informs me with a soft chuckle. "I've been out most of the day, and I've been here since last night. Sorry I wasn't there when you got in. I'm umm. Briella Navarro."

"I'm Mercy Noble." I smile and move to walk next to her, going down the hallway of the campus center the same way I'd come in. "I really wish I would've known there was a rich kids brochure and a poor kids brochure," I add, thinking back on the other boy's words. "Would've been great not to embarrass myself like that."

"He's just like that," Briella shrugs. "All three of them are?"

"You know them?"

"Yeah. Everyone here basically knows them. It's not a big deal that you don't." Her nose wrinkles. "They aren't worth the time it takes to memorize their names."

"What's *his* name?"

"Foster O'Dell." She shakes her head as we push open the doors of the campus center, emerging between the theater and one of the class halls.

Before I can ask anything else, or why she doesn't like Foster, my eyes fall on the crime scene tape that's placed around part of the courtyard in the middle of campus. Two cops patrol either side of it, and near a tarp that's long since had its occupant removed, two women talk in quiet voices.

"I don't suppose you can see what they're saying?" Briella asks, leaning into my shoulder.

I shake my head, not minding the physical contact from another omega. If she were *not* an omega, things would be different. But I've never been attracted to people of my designation, and physical touch is a pretty common thing for us. "Way too far," I tell her. "And they aren't looking this way." My eyes sweep over the crime scene, briefly finding the three boys that are on the other side of it, looking at what's going on with interest.

They don't look at me, and why should they?

"I guess this wasn't in the brochure, huh?" Briella's soft voice is amused, and she crosses her arms over her chest. "Or if it was, maybe it was in the small print?"

"Probably the small print," I agree. "I barely read any of it."

We stand at the top of the steps for a few moments longer, far from the only students watching the cops work. Finally, however, the dean comes tearing out of the building, and gives us a quick, warning look that's pretty obvious in its intent.

"Go somewhere else, all of you," he calls loudly, flapping his hands at the students gathered. "Let the cops do their work. We'll inform you all of what happened here the moment we know more, all right?"

"Sure he will," Briella snorts. "Because colleges are known for transparency with their students, right?"

"Oh, absolutely," I agree, catching sight of the three boys walking away. They don't go towards Maliseet dorm, however, instead finding a path that takes them towards the lake and the building perched on the edge of it.

The *fancy* dorms, as I've dubbed them. The ones that cost extra to take up space there.

"Hey, so uh...Welcome to Winter Grove University?" Briella turns that nervous grin on me again. "Since I'm sure no one's really told you that yet. And the dean didn't exactly get to, huh? I hope it lives up to every single one of your expectations."

"Yeah," I agree, rather unenthusiastically as I watch the dean do his hand-flapping in the faces of students who don't want to move. "Yeah, when I moved eight hundred miles from home to go here, this is exactly what I was expecting. I couldn't ask for a better orientation, actually. Let's do it again next week?"

2

Getting up for classes shouldn't be so hard. Not when I've only been out of high school for a little over three months, and here at Winter Grove I get to wake up two hours later than my usual seven a.m..

Not that I do, of course. Instead my brain jolts me awake at six thirty, the absolute silence pressing in on my ears. Without my hearing aids in, I can't hear the smaller noises of the room like the air conditioner, Briella's breathing, or anything else. If someone's walking around above or below me, or throwing a massive rager in the lounge at the end of the hall, I can't hear it.

Tentatively I reach up and press my hands to my ears, but the only thing it does is make the silence feel muffled.

And it does nothing to help me fall back asleep.

With eyes wide I stare at the dark mass of the ceiling above me, a frown tugging at my lips. *Why am I awake?* The thought echoes around my skull; the only imaginary noise in my noise-reduced world.

I'm *nervous*, I realize at last, though the revelation only makes the frown tug harder on my lips. I have no need to be, do I? It's college, not the marines or astronaut school. I'm a zoology major at Winter Grove and all I want is to be able to get a job at a good zoo. I don't need to rule the world like half these people do, I'm sure.

I just want to work with otters, lemurs, and maybe the odd maned wolf. In the scope of things, it doesn't feel like that much to ask for.

My hands fall back to the bed on either side of my head, fingers curling as I let out a breath to try and relax. My first class isn't until ten a.m., so there's really no need for me to be up at the ass-crack of dawn.

Slowly I drag the blankets up over my head, ignoring the way my heart rate speeds up just slightly at the thought of the death during orientation.

Or rather, ignoring the fact that the memory is tinged with the scent of tropical drinks and beaches.

When my eyes open again, I'm pleased to see that the sun is up. My alarm still hasn't gone off, and when I sit up, I see Briella up as well, flitting around the room in the nervous way I've come to realize is just *her*. She glances my way and says something, but she's not shouting and she looks away again before I can do more than read the word *morning* on her lips.

She looks back at me expectantly and I sigh, reaching out for the small case that holds my hearing aids and putting them in slowly, just so she can watch me do it. In case she *forgot* that hearing isn't one of the skills I was born with and needs the visual reminder.

Sure enough, as soon as I look up at her again, reaching once more for the box of migraine prevention tablets on my little bedside table, she looks embarrassed.

"I'm sorry," she tells me, pausing to toss her clothes into

the laundry. "I completely forgot. I didn't mean to. I *promised* myself I wouldn't—"

"It's fine," I assure her, popping the white, faintly mint-tasting tablet into my mouth and waiting for it to dissolve before swallowing. "I forget sometimes too."

"Really?"

I pause, my hand halfway to my brush, and fix her with a flat expression that makes her blush. A second later I soften it and sigh, grabbing the brush and proceeding to drag it through my long, auburn hair. "No." I'm not sure if she *needs* the confirmation, but I'm half-worried she's about to ask me if my migraine meds are related to my hearing as well. "It's definitely pretty hard to forget."

"Can you hear at all without those?" she gestures to the hearing aids that glitter in the light, their multicolored sparkles throwing off the light in a way I know can be eye-catching.

"Kind of," I say, thinking of how to explain it. "Things are muffled? If you shouted at me, I'd hear you. And I hear better in my left ear, than my right. So if you really do need me and they're not in and you can't, I don't know, shake me? Yell in that ear."

She snorts, then covers up the look until the smile is gone.

Does she think I'll be offended? My earlier assessment of *chihuahua* doesn't seem pointed enough, and it occurs to me that Briella is like a *mouse*.

And again, the thought makes me feel a little bad. I'm not trying to insult her. But she's the stereotypical omega, and looks like she's on the verge of slinking out the door like I've verbally or physically beaten her.

Doesn't it make it better that I'm an omega too? Or is she just like this with everyone and everything she encounters in the world? Her scent, a mix of flowers I don't recognize and earthy, has an almost-acrid edge to it, like she's been afraid for long enough for it to become part of her scent, and all that does is make me wonder yet again if she's always been this way, was taught to be this way, or had something happen to her long before I met her.

It's none of my business, either way.

"I'm up early," I complain, looking at my phone and turning off my alarm. "I wanted to get up in twenty minutes. Don't we...have English together first thing?" We'd compared our schedules, and as both of us had completed credits during high school, we're in some of the same general classes that we have to take as freshmen. "Why are you up so early?"

"Did I wake you?" she asks, in the way of answer.

I sigh, and shake my head. "A herd of elephants would have to have a band accompanying them on cymbals to wake me up," I reply teasingly, my voice dry. It occurs to me, belatedly, that she might actually believe me.

God, I hope she doesn't. Otherwise, I'll have to learn to watch what I say and how I say it around her.

I drag myself out of bed and pull on my clothes for the day, forgoing any ideas about dressing up for the first day of classes and instead opting for a pair of leggings, a long lavender hoodie, and my long auburn hair up in a ponytail so that I don't have to worry about how it looks. I hadn't expected to need a hoodie so early in September, being from the midwest where September is still *hot as balls* this time of year. Here, however, in Maine and on the lakeside, it seems that the heat is chased away much earlier in the year than at home.

Not that I can say I really mind. Hoodie weather is, in fact, the best weather. No debates accepted on the subject.

"Do you want to go to breakfast?" Briella asks, shoveling her books into her bag. "That's what I thought I'd do before class." The sour edge to her scent gets stronger, and it makes me wonder how she does anything at all without being terrified.

The thought of breakfast turns my stomach, but I nod anyway. "Sure," I agree, stomping the toe of my sneaker onto the hard floor to get my shoe in place. "I could eat." I don't think I can, actually. But if she senses the lie somehow, Briella doesn't say anything about it as I follow her out of the room, grabbing my own canvas bag and slinging it over my shoulders with a grunt. Though I only have two classes today, somehow my backpack is heavier than I feel it should be.

"Can I ask you something?" The words surprise me as we take the elevator to the basement, where the tunnel to the dining hall gives us direct access to food. According to the *scholarship* brochure, the tunnels were built because of how bad the snow is here, and serve to make sure we're never without meals even when classes are canceled. According to the campus map, all of the dorms are connected to a dining hall this way and by extension, a second dorm. The lakeside dorms are all connected to one another, thanks to the tunnels.

"Yeah, anything," I reply, running a list of questions through my head of what she might ask me. My ears is the topic I'd be willing to bet on, since she's tried a few times to ask me innocent questions that prove her curiosity about my lack of hearing ability.

But so far, she's kept her questions surface level and inoffensive. Though, in all honesty, I'd rather her just *ask* whatever she wants to know, instead of dancing around the subject with the grace of a hippo.

"What are the gloves for on your bedside table? I wasn't trying to snoop, or anything like that," she assures me, before I can even open my mouth to answer. "They just don't look like the gloves I would wear."

I open my mouth, intent on an answer filled with sarcasm

and half-truth, and instead close it to swallow my words and take a breath. If I did try something like that, I doubt she'd know I was joking. It seems my curse here is to have a roommate who takes me much too seriously.

Well, it could be worse. At least I *like* Briella, even though she's too shy and too quiet for me to really feel comfortable around her yet.

"Archery," I reply finally.

"Archery?" There's confusion evident in her voice, so I lift my hands and mimic drawing a bow back to my ear and release my fingers like I'm releasing an arrow. She watches me do it, only looking slightly less perplexed than she had before I'd shown her.

"I'm really into archery," I explain, dropping my arms to my sides again. "I'm trying out for the team tomorrow." Nervousness makes my heart flutter, and I take a deep breath to calm myself down as I have a thousand times before this week already. Being nervous won't do me any favors. I want to be on the team, and I know that I'm not a bad shot. But if I let myself get anxious, then I'm just going to wreck any chance that I have to do that.

"Are you good?" It's the most forward question she's asked me since yesterday.

"Uh, yeah? I think I am?" I can't be *bad* with all the practice and competitions I've done, surely. Still, nerves show themselves in the way my voice wavers as I add, "Though, I don't know how good the Winter Grove team is. Maybe I'm not good *enough*." I try to say it matter-of-factly, but it's definitely a worry I have.

The dining hall is surprisingly empty as we climb the stairs to the line, and when we give our IDs to the woman for them to be scanned and our unlimited meal plans registered, we both move into line for breakfast food.

Though, I can't help but do a bit of a doubletake when I see what's on the food line. I'd definitely expected eggs, toast, maybe french toast, maybe some kind of meat. But it seems to me like there's every type of egg imaginable, fresh fruit that *looks fresh*, and honest-to-god *crepes*.

What college serves *crepes*?

Well, other than this one, I guess.

I'm not going to miss this opportunity, and by the time we're at the end of the line, my plate is full of strawberry-crème crepes and poached eggs.

"You like poached eggs?" Briella seems surprised as I fill a cup with coffee and creamer, the mix turning light caramel colored.

"You know, I have no idea," I reply back with a hum, following her to a small booth for two in a corner against a wall of windows. Sitting down across from her gives me a good look out of the glass, and my eyes flick from building to building on campus. I can see at least half of them, including a few of the ones I have classes in. Only the new science center, with its shiny glass walls and modern architecture, is half-hidden behind the english building that houses creative writing, journalism, and film classes for some reason. In the middle of campus, in a large courtyard with fountains and benches and raised planters, is the campus center we'd had orientation at the day before.

In front of it, the crime scene tape flaps in the generous breeze, still taped in a square around where the body was found.

"Can you believe someone *died*?" I murmur, cutting off a piece of a crepe and popping it in my mouth. It, of course, is better than it has any right to be, and I'm suddenly even gladder that my academic performance, along with my extra-curriculars, was enough to get me into Winter Grove. Even if I never make enough money in my life to afford food like this on the daily, the next four years are going to be *so worth* all that hard work for the meals alone.

"No," Briella admits. Cutting up her fried eggs. She looks down studiously, all of her focus on the plate, and as I watch her, my mind drifts to Foster O'Dell.

"Hey, can I ask you about Foster?" I say, without really thinking about it. There has to be a reason she so clearly dislikes him, and if I'm anything, it's nosy.

"Why?" she looks up when she says it, brows raised. "He's not a zoo major like you. I doubt you'll see him or his pack that much."

"Because you don't like him, I'm nosy, and I like to know drama from afar?" I offer, dragging one leg up under me as I eat. "Mostly, I'm just nosy. I want to know *what's w*rong with him, and them?"

She hesitates, thinking about her words, before answering. "They're not nice," she says at last. "His pack, anyway. It's two alphas and him, and Foster's the youngest. Dorian Wakefield is the alpha in charge." she glances up at me, like I should know the name.

I do not.

"You haven't heard of his dad?"

"No, I really haven't."

"He owns like half the world's commerce?"

"Not ringing any bells."

"Created the *Connections* program for online shopping?"

"Oh, I totally used that once."

She stares at me, and I stare back. Finally she snorts, a genuine smile breaking out over her face. "Don't tell him that," she advises after a moment. "He's really *proud* of what his dad has done. And he's going to take over the business."

I blink, taking another bite, and shrug. "Okay, and? What's the problem? Is he anti-charity? Anti-female? Anti-omega?"

"He's anti-*friendly*," Briella supplies. "August Frost is the other alpha."

"Did he invent *winter*?"

I'm mostly joking, but it really does feel like the students here come from families with enough money to do anything with.

"Might as well have. Anyway I'm not trying to *Twilight* you. They aren't vampires, and you aren't Bella Swan. None of them are going to stare at you longingly from across the room or crash a car for you."

"Or bite me?"

"Literally? No. Metaphorically, but in just as painful a way?" She tilts her head to the side, meeting my light hazel gaze with her dark brown eyes. "Quite possible. Just don't think about them. Don't bother them. They don't bother anyone else who isn't in their social circle unless they're mad."

"Should I feel incredibly *blessed* that Foster spoke to me, then?" I can't help but ask, moving on to the poached eggs.

Briella waits, watching me take a bite and observing my scrunched nose and displeased noises.

"Yeah, I don't like them either," she says, tossing one of her napkins to me. "It's a texture thing, right?"

I nod, spitting the egg silently into the napkin and shuddering. "Definitely *not a fan*." Instead I gulp coffee, savoring the taste of it and wondering if I can dump out my plastic water bottle and fill it with enough espresso to power me through the day.

"He seems nice," Briella admits. "I guess, I don't know that much about him. Most of my info comes from my dad working for Dorian's dad. We met a few times before this." She shudders again. "I don't know what omega would *ever* want him, or August, for an alpha. Do you?"

I take my time answering, because I have a feeling our taste is very different. Still, I don't like cruelty, and I didn't come here to find it. "Not if they're everything you say they are," I agree, sitting back in my seat. "That's not really my thing." Though, I doubt my thing is hers. She looks like she'd need a teddy bear for an alpha.

But I don't break so easily, and I'd like a pack that pushed on my comfort zone, widened it, and helped make me more than I could make myself. As stupid as that sounds, even in my own mind. I definitely never plan to say it out loud.

Neither am I really *looking* for an alpha pack. Not now, anyway. I'm the scholarship kid at the most prestigious university in the world, and I don't think anyone here would look at me twice, when I don't have money or fame or prestige to back up my presence here.

I'm just Mercy Noble, and that's okay with me. Whether or not the other students here ever really take notice of me, I'm not here to become popular or get with a rich pack.

I just want to do the best for *me*, and I'm willing to do whatever I can to make that happen. If that means avoiding Dorian Wakefield and his pack? Well, I can't imagine why that'll be anything other than simple.

3

Sitting through two hours of biology is much easier than sitting through forty minutes of math ever was. In my opinion, I'd much rather do this, no matter the circumstance, though I can't help but dread the thought of actually taking my honors math class next semester.

I won't fail. I'm lucky enough that some of the numbers-stuff has absorbed into my skull after years of smacking a math book against my head, but that doesn't mean I enjoy it. If I'm a masochist, it's not of the academic kind.

Briella and I separate after bio, with her mumbling about how much she knows she'll hate it, and me moving to my first elective of the semester, and the one I'm both dreading and looking forward to. Astronomy has a lot of differing opinions, from what I've seen, and the few posts about it online I've found discussing the class at Winter Grove have all been… polarizing. Still, as I walk to the large, new science building that was just built in the past year, I can't help but grin.

Call me a nerd, but I *love* classes. I love learning new things, exploring my interests, and yeah, maybe I need a hobby. Another hobby other than shooting things.

That's not going to happen, and when my mind touches on the subject of archery, my fingers itch for a bow, and I take a deep breath to keep my heart from racing. Excitement for tomorrow's tryouts is an understatement. I also can't help but be incredibly glad classes started on a Thursday, so I can get a taste of things but then have the weekend to face-plant my bed and take stock of everything.

Looking to my left, I glance towards the small café in the middle of the first floor, framed by the glass above and lit by the sunshine that glitters through the panes. A few students sit at shiny new chairs, and tables with glimmering metal legs as the counter workers dish out bagels and smoothies.

I want a smoothie. But when I check my watch, I grimace and give a small shake of my head in irritation. I can *want one* all I desire. But I don't have the time. Besides, it would take me five minutes or so just to even–

A hand on my shoulder makes me levitate and I whirl around, eyes wide. My phone clatters to the floor, and the dark-haired girl behind me looks at me with confusion as I audibly gasp.

She'd snuck up on me, which isn't exactly difficult to do.

Judging by her face, however, I can assume that she'd been calling out to me. Especially with the way the people near us are giving me odd looks, like I'm something strange they can't figure out.

Like she's *definitely* been trying to get me to stop, and I've been looking like I ignored her.

Letting out a breath, I force my anxiety back and look up at her with what I hope is an apologetic smile. "Were you yelling for me?" I ask, dreading the answer. "I umm, can't hear it in open or loud spaces." It's probably more of an explanation than is necessary, and I gesture at my ear anyway to point out the hearing aids there.

"You couldn't hear me shouting? Even with those?" She holds out my black and red pen, the fanciest one I owned. "You dropped this."

"Oh shit—" I would've been incredibly upset to lose this, and I offer her another, wider smile. "Thank you so much. I *love* this pen." My eyes dart around the open space, and thankfully most people have walked away, instead of continuing to watch our conversation. "And no, umm." I clear my throat, trying to shove down my nerves. It's gotten better over the years, sure. But when things like this happen, when someone is yelling for me and it's clear I can't hear them or I'm not looking so I can see their faces, it reminds me how vulnerable I can end up.

And how *different* I am from so many of the other students here.

"You know how it's loud in here? And everyone's voices are echoing?" I gesture to the area around us, like we can somehow see sound. The dark-haired, golden-skinned girl nods, her almost-black eyes curious. "So, that kind of messes with me. With these." I flick my fingers towards my hearing aids again, and regret it. Clearly she would've known what I was talking about, anyway.

Don't get flustered, Mercy, I try to tell myself, repeating the words in my head. *It's not a big deal*. I will myself to chill out. Getting upset will end up triggering me into a migraine, and if there's anything I really don't need today, it's that.

"Oh." She smiles, all of the confusion melting from her gorgeous face. She's a beta, and belatedly I realize her scent is one of the calmest, least in-your-face I've ever encountered. Spices, maybe? Vanilla, nutmeg, and something spicier under that. But still, not overwhelming, and not at all clouding up my sensitive nose. "What class are you going to? And I'm happy I saw your pen fall, so I could get it back to you."

"Astronomy. It's...that way?" I gesture towards the elevator, and then flick my fingers up towards the ceiling. "Somewhere?"

Her smile widens. "I know where it is. I had a class beside it last year. And I'm actually heading there as well. Mind if I come with you?"

"Please do. I'll get lost," I assure her with a heavy, exaggerated sigh. She laughs and leads the way to the elevator, giving me a chance to look at her outfit that is all round more impressive than mine.

Her black hair falls almost to her waist in waves, and her plaid shirt that frames her figure perfectly is rolled up to her elbows. Her dark jeans, that also fit incredibly well, are frayed at the knees, and her backpack sports an assortment of pins and small patches.

One pin, in the shape of a small knife, glitters in the sun and catches my eye. At its tip is a drop of blood that might be an actual ruby, and I barely stop myself from whistling in appreciation.

The elevator door opens and we step inside, with me surreptitiously jamming the closed button so no one else can show up and wreck our good vibes.

She sees, and laughs. "You beat me to it. I'm Zara. You're a freshman. And you look lost. Not a legacy student, then? Most of them are carted around here by their alumni parents from birth. It's weird."

"I'm umm. I got in on a scholarship." I *refuse* to be embarrassed about it, or reluctant. Just because I don't have money doesn't mean I don't deserve to be here. In fact, in my silent opinion. I worked harder than any of these rich kids to get here.

All they had to do was be born into money.

I *earned* my way.

"I'm Mercy," I add, remembering that Zara had just given me her name. "Are you a sophomore?"

"Yeah," she sighs, leaning her back against the elevator wall. "Only three more years to go." She goes quiet, and I don't speak until the doors open and I follow her out and down the overwhelmingly off-white hallway. The only splashes of color are the gray accents on the walls, and even those aren't that interesting.

"You don't like it here?" I assume, keeping up with her longer stride. It hadn't occurred to me how much longer her legs were when I'd met her downstairs, but now I feel like I'm trying to outpace a damn track star.

"It is what it is." She shrugs one shoulder and turns down another hallway, onto a carpeted floor where the doors are further and further apart. At the end of the hall sits two double doors, and on a small gray plaque on the right I see *Astronomy Hall* in printed, white letters. "My mom came here, and it was always going to be where I ended up. Too bad for me, since she won't let me transfer anywhere else." Her scent gains a bitter edge, as if she really means what she says and wants to leave Winter Grove.

Why? I don't ask. This is the best school in the US, and probably in the world. Why go somewhere else, when this place can get you any of the connections you would *ever* need to make a good life for yourself in the working sphere?

"Oh," I say instead, wincing at the lame, non-committal answer. "I'm sorry you don't like it." God, I hope *I* don't end up not liking it.

Wouldn't that suck, after all the work I've put into it.

"It's not the school," she assures me, pushing the doors open and revealing a large, almost circular room with tiers of desks circling the desk and white board at the bottom. A large projector shines on the white surface, and an older man with thick glasses that I can see from here leans on the desk, chewing a thumbnail. "It's the people."

A student walks in as she says it, and Zara turns to offer the brown-haired girl a sickly-sweet grin. Had she heard her?

Dark eyes narrow at my companion, then at me, and the girl continues on to go sit by a red-haired girl on the far side of the room.

Judging by that reaction, she most definitely heard Zara.

We move in two separate directions, with Zara intent on taking a seat at the back, but me moving closer to the professor. When Zara looks at me in surprise, realization dawns a second later, and she frowns.

"Sorry, Mercy." Her crooked smile isn't that apologetic, and she shrugs. "I don't want to be that close to hear him *wheeze* at me with his smoker's lung. I'll be back here for moral support, though."

And there go all thoughts of this being the one friendship I'd hoped to make. Well, it's back to the Briella-drawing board, I guess. At least she seems like the kind of person who would sit at the front of the room with me no matter what, just as she had in bio this morning.

"It's fine," I say, shrugging like it doesn't slightly hurt my feelings. I'm disappointed, really. Nothing else.

But her refusal to sit with me, like we're at the cafeteria in grade school, stings a little as I make my way to the second-lowest row and sit down at the only still-empty table.

I sit, pulling out my iPad and my astronomy book and putting them on the table along with the pen I can use on my iPad to take notes. I prefer this, compared to a regular notebook, and I find it more forgiving. Especially when I stumble and inevitably get just a little bit behind.

When I sit down, a scent that cuts through the others in the room reaches my nose, and I make the mistake of sucking in a breath instead of holding my nose.

The result is that, when the black-haired boy descends the steps beside me to the left...I choke.

Literally, I nearly wretch up the crepe I'd eaten this morning, as the boy turns and watches me with cool, dark brown eyes.

Shit.

Shit. His face clicks in my memory a second later, and *Dorian Wakefield* raises a brow. Briella had pointed him out to me when we'd seen him across the courtyard this morning, and now here he is.

Probably thinking I'm making some kind of statement by choking on his scent.

Which, now that I can take another breath, is staggering. Cinnamon sinks into my lungs, followed by the sharp tang of leather and something undeniably sweet, like birthday cake. Fucking *birthday cake* and leather should never smell good.

But here I am. Choking to death on the best scent I've ever smelled.

I hate it here.

"You good?" His voice is soft and smooth and everything I've read about in a romance novel, only he's not the type of guy I'd find on a historical romance cover or anything described as *sweet* and *wholesome* romance.

Not with the way his dark eyes glitter. And *certainly* not with the way he grins so that I can see the flash of metal on his tongue.

In answer to his question, I am not good. Not at all. Certainly not with him staring at me with equal parts confusion, interest, and...yeah, that's definitely dismissal on his face.

"Yeah," I reply breathily, swallowing fervently in an

attempt not to cough in answer. That only succeeds in making my stomach turn over with nausea, and if karma were kind, the floor would open up and drop me back down to the smoothie shop on the first floor.

"I've got to say..." His voice trails off almost thoughtfully, though the undertone makes me dread whatever he's going to say next, and my breath catches in my throat. "There are a lot more subtle ways to make it known you don't like me, or my scent. If I hated cherries, should I have walked by you and started choking on air?"

I stare at him, and wonder if it's too late to play the *I can't hear you* card.

Or find a way to *make* the floor open up under me.

If my hearing were better, would I hear a chuckle from the other students in the room? The desks are almost full now, and when I look around, I see that Dorian Wakefield has the choice of three seats.

Across the room with the brown-haired girl, beside me, or directly in front of me.

It's a no brainer where he's going, and I simmer down a little knowing that I'm *safe* from him as soon as class starts.

"I choked on a peanut," I say finally, gazing up at him with baleful hazel eyes. "You just walked by at an incredibly bad time."

His mouth twitches, and a small part of me wishes he'd open it again so I could see his tongue ring better. He doesn't.

"What's your name?"

Uh oh.

Based on what Briella said, I don't think I want him knowing my name. With all the money in the world, I'm sure he could get me kicked right out for doing something so obscene as offending him.

However, I can't just sit here and stare him like I've lost my mind.

"I'm...Jessica," I say, grabbing the first name that comes to mind.

"Are you?" His eyebrows rise by increments, as if he doesn't believe me.

With my tone of voice, I wouldn't believe me either.

"Yeah, of course I am. Who lies about their *name*?" I try to laugh, knowing that I look less and less credible by the second.

Suddenly, he grins. A full, wicked grin that lights up his dark eyes. He chuckles, and it's just barely audible to me in the room full of other people talking.

Frankly, it sounds like more of a purr than a laugh.

"Yeah," he agrees, and the word throws me for a loop. "Who lies about their name, right, *Jessica*? It would be *so awkward* if I learned you were lying to me, huh? Who would *do that*?" Without taking his eyes off mine he points at the seat on my other side, and I lean away from his hand. "Is that seat taken?"

"Yes," I say, looking at the chair where I have my backpack.

"By your books, or by an actual person?" If his voice were any sweeter, I'd probably die of a sugar overdose.

I think about lying again, but instead I relent, sighing as his alpha-ness starts to creep up my spine. It's hard to sit here and do this, even though he is *not* my alpha. Slowly I reach out and snag my bag off the chair, dragging it under the table at my feet.

Surely he's not going to sit with *me*.

With pointed movements and almost exaggerated slowness, Dorian Wakefield proves me wrong. He moves across to the other side of the table, slips his backpack off his shoulders, and drops onto the seat beside me to sprawl out in it, kicking it back on its two back legs as the professor gets to his feet with a shuffle of papers and a wheeze of smoker's lung.

I take a deep breath to center myself, and regret it instantly. This time, at the very least, I don't choke, but still. Dorian's scent in my lungs is so *present* that it's difficult to right myself and tap the screen of my tablet to get to my notes app.

It's fine, I tell myself, glad that at least with the start of class, my humiliation and discomfort is almost at an end. Mostly, because he *is* still beside me.

"I don't know your names yet," Professor Belker grunts, picking up a tablet of his own with a sigh. "So we're going to do this the old-fashioned way. When I call your name, just raise your hand and say here."

Uh oh.

Oh no.

I don't *want* to turn and look at Dorian. I have a feeling I know what's on his face, and it isn't a blank expression.

But I can't help myself. As the professor starts going through the list, I sneak a glance at Dorian, hoping that maybe, just maybe, he's distracted enough that when my name is called, he won't really pay attention to what the professor calls me.

Instead, his arms are crossed and he's staring straight at me, as if waiting for me to look at him. His grin widens, lighting up his dark eyes again.

"You look worried," he says, and I realize distantly that Belker is on the 'D' names of the class.

I don't have a lot of time.

"Why would I be?" I ask, my heart racing in my chest. "Maybe you just make me nervous."

He can't smile any wider, but I swear he preens a little, like it's a compliment. "What's your name?" he invites, the words a challenge.

"Jessica."

"Is it?"

"Of course it is. Why would I lie about it?"

"Mercedes Noble?" I flinch as Professor Belker calls my name and lifts up his head, covering a cough as he does to look around the room.

I haven't raised my hand, but that doesn't stop Dorian from *staring at me*.

"Mercedes Noble?" the professor says again.

I don't *want* to lift my hand. I really, absolutely don't. But God, I don't exactly have an option.

Still looking at Dorian, I sigh and lift my hand into the air, albeit rather slowly.

Dorian's eyes narrow, and I swear I hear that same purring-chuckle from him that I'd heard before.

"Weird. Mercedes doesn't *sound* like Jessica," he comments, raising his hand when the professor calls his name.

"Maybe it's my middle name."

"Maybe I'll put you out of your misery, and say it's not." When I start to reply, he puts a finger to his lips, eyes dancing. "Can't talk anymore, Mercedes," he tells me *oh so sweetly*. "Can't you tell class is about to start?"

4

My heart pounds in my chest as I sit down in my last class of the week, and I take a deep breath as I settle back in the chair at the table near the front. A part of me *does* envy anyone who can go to the back of the room and still hear the professor clearly, but that's never going to happen when I need every advantage I can get to hear what the hell is going on.

Sometimes, when things get loud or there are rampant discussions and debates, I *still* can't hear everything I need to, and that's when things get incredibly frustrating. Luckily that hasn't happened yet, and I'm hoping that isn't going to change with *Diversity of Life* class. I don't exactly see how it could be that interactive, after all, and I'm definitely going to assume it's a seminar-style class.

A boy sidles by, sitting at a table in the same row as mine but not by me. I glance up at him, staring for a second longer than I mean to. He looks familiar, though when I take a deep breath of his scent that brings to mind lavender and storms, I almost have to take another deep breath just to catch it in my lungs. He's an alpha, I can tell. But he just feels so...mild?

And on closer inspection, I definitely don't know him.

Before I can turn away, his gaze catches mine and he gives me a half-smile before dumping the contents of his bag on the table and rifling through them to find whatever it is he's looking for.

The chair behind me skids back, drawing my attention to the boy sitting down gingerly in the chair beside me. He looks over with a quick grin, and then collapses in the chair and sighs heavily. "Are you a freshman?" he asks, after a few seconds of me surveying his features. He's thin and wiry, though just because he's an alpha doesn't mean he *needs* to be muscled like some bodybuilder. According to my best friend back home in Ohio, eighty-five percent of being an alpha is the mentality. Ten percent is the voice. Five percent is the ability to throw around anyone who pisses you off. Though, frankly, this boy doesn't look like he's going to be throwing *anyone* around. Ever. His bony arms are pale, and his brown hair lays lank against his forehead.

"Yeah," I reply, after a slight pause. "But I've completed a lot of my freshman credits already, so they let me throw this into my schedule." I don't know why I feel like I have to explain myself to him, but here we are.

"It's going to *suck*. Let me give you a preview. Professor Taylor is going to walk in, start class, and pass out a syllabus. He might ask a few questions, mostly so *Auggie* over there can show off." He nods his head towards the alpha on my left, and when I look his way, I see his head turn just enough towards us that I wonder if he can hear what's being said about him. "Then, mercifully, he'll end class early and we can all go home and enjoy the weekend. It sucks that Diversity of Life is so late on Friday this year. It's like a *test* for us, to prove we deserve the weekend or something."

"Is it really that bad?"

"The subject? No. Professor Taylor? Absolutely." He snorts and shakes his head, sitting back in his chair to fold his arms over his chest. "I'm Adrian," he adds, after another second of quiet.

"I'm Mercy." I don't know what else to really say to him that Adrian hasn't already breezed through, and thankfully the door slams behind an older man with red glasses and slicked back black hair before I have to say anything else. He not-so-gently drops a stack of papers on the front table with a muttered 'pass those around' before crossing to the desk and dropping his own bag onto it.

I already don't like him, and not *just* because I hate the smell of roses that exudes from his pores like he bathes in them.

God, isn't that a weird thought?

"Glad to see so many of you managed to pass your bio seminar," he says, not looking up from the tablet that his fingers dance over on his desk. He's thin, like Adrian, and from here I *believe* the man is a beta, though the disinterest in his scent and the stupid roses have me still guessing at what he may be. With his attitude so far, I could definitely see him as a beta or an alpha.

"Why don't we start with a few questions while those get passed out," he sighs, looking up finally and adjusting his glasses. Apparently, Adrian was right about how this was going to go. Though, just because class ends doesn't mean archery tryouts will come sooner. Still, I may be able to practice a little more than I'd originally intended on being able to do, which would be nice and hopefully might settle my nerves.

"Can anyone name a seedless, vascular plant?" His eyes go

straight to August, who raises a hand, but when I do as well, the professor looks at me instead. "What's your name?"

"Mercedes Noble," I reply, keeping my voice even. "A fern is a seedless, vascular plant."

He looks at August plaintively, and something curls in my stomach that I don't love. "Wasn't expecting that, huh?" he laughs, and August shrugs, not looking at me. So much for him seeming *friendly* when he'd walked in. "Let's try again. What is the first oxygen-producing organism?"

Immediately, both August and I raise our hands. Slowly, Adrian raises his hand as well, but Professor Taylor only has eyes for August and me.

"Let's give August a chance, shall we?"

But August drops his hand and shrugs. "She can answer," he says, turning to give me his full attention.

Professor Taylor looks at me as well, brows raised. "Autotrophic Cyanobacteria." He claps at my answer, slowly, like he's begrudgingly impressed.

August just *looks* at me, and it makes me want to squirm closer to Adrian in my chair.

"Why is it easier for a small animal to run up a hill, as opposed to a large animal?" This time, Professor Taylor stares me down, not bothering to ask the class.

I take a breath and say, "Because a small animal has a higher metabolic rate." I'm so, *so* glad I did so much reading over the summer, and even more relieved that I enjoy the subject of biology. I like learning things like this, and I'm good at having weird facts stick in my mind.

"And how do motile bacteria move?"

"...Flagella?" I guess having to think about the answer for a few seconds. Bacteria's aren't exactly my *favorite* area of study, and if he goes much more in-depth about them, then I won't be able to answer anything more.

But a rueful grin breaks out over his face, and he looks at *August,* yet again. Like he somehow has something to do with answering questions, even though it's been me this whole time.

August just shrugs, looking just as amused, and I suck in another deep breath as Adrian leans over to murmur, "Taylor knows August's dad. They always act like this, and it's not going to get any better all year." He takes a syllabus and passes it to me, and I toss it on the table next to me, where a blonde girl takes one and passes the rest to August.

"Let me know when you all have one. I hope you all can read, and I don't have any intention of starting class today. I think we all need an extra day off, frankly." Though the words are a relief, since I don't want to spend the next hour here, listening to him fawn over *Auggie,* I let out a sigh and sit back anyway.

I am looking forward to whatever he teaches. Whenever he decides to teach it.

"So that's it for the day." The last syllabi are passed back up to him, and he drops them on the desk and claps his hands. "Enjoy your weekend, and on Monday prepare for some real work. We also might not be staying in this room." He squints, and looks around the bright, medium-sized space. "I'd like us to be in the new building, if at all possible." With that he gets his stuff, and somehow manages to be the first out of the room as the students around me start shoving things back into their own backpacks.

"I think you surprised him. And you interrupted his love affair," Adrian chuckles, getting up as I do. I throw a look over to August, who's passing by our table and fixes Adrian with a look from bright green eyes. His lashes are longer than they have any right to be, and it's only this close that the scent of *alpha* washes over me, and his scent intensifies.

His nostrils flare, chin tilting in my direction like *he's* scenting *me*.

Well, I suppose I hope he likes what he smells, since we're going to be in this class together for the rest of the year. He looks at me but doesn't speak, and instead lets his gaze slide back to Adrian. "You're not quiet," he says flatly, his voice soft and even. He doesn't sound angry, or amused, or anything else.

He just sounds so....bored, really.

"I wasn't trying to be." Adrian grins at him, beaming like they're the best of friends. "In fact, I could be louder if you'd like. And it's not like any of it is a lie."

"It's not?" August raises his brows. "I can assure you, I'm not in any kind of affair with Taylor. You know he acts like that because–"

"Because your Daddy and him are such great friends? Yeah, I know. But he still doesn't have to act like you're God's greatest gift to mankind."

Suddenly, I wish I were anywhere but standing right here.

As if he can read my thoughts, August's eyes land on mine again. "Foster told me about you," he murmurs thoughtfully. "And Dorian mentioned you too. I guess we just can't help running into you, can we Jessica?"

Oh. Ouch.

I hate that my mistakes from yesterday are back to bite me in the ass, and my teeth grit together uncomfortably as I let out a long, unhappy breath.

"Jessica?" Adrian repeats, brows coming together in confusion. "I thought your name was Mercy?"

"It is," I grumble, slinging my backpack over my shoulder. "Look, it was just a...misunderstanding yesterday, okay?"

When I look at August again, his eyes are glittering with amusement. "Yeah," he agrees. "You misunderstanding how things work, and thinking you could get away with Dorian not knowing your name after you choked all over his scent."

Adrian makes a noise somewhere between a cough and a wheeze.

"Personally, I love the way he smells. But I can't fault you for having bad taste, can I?"

I should shut up and leave. It's clear August just wants to get a reaction out of me, for whatever reason. I should absolutely shut up and just go. The omega in me is all for this plan, and I don't want to embarrass myself by whining or acting like I need some kind of approval or his forgiveness for something I don't need to be sorry for.

Especially when he isn't better than me, my alpha, or someone who I want to be my friend. I don't care what he thinks of me. And frankly, it's probably better he thinks very little of me.

"Do you really love it?" I ask, instead of *shutting up*. "Or is it like, some form of Stockholm Syndrome? Maybe you've had your face shoved into his, well, *scent* for so long that you don't know what you like."

His head tilts to the side ever-so-slightly, and his emerald eyes darken. I can't tell what he's thinking, especially when he sweeps a hand through his curly, dark brown hair. "That's not Stockholm Syndrome," August says finally. Unexpectedly he steps forward, mouth close to my ear so much so that his lips brush the sparkly surface of my hearing aid. "But if you want, I'll take you back to my dorm room and *teach you* what those words really mean. How long do you think I'll have to keep you before you like me?"

Fear ignites a small fire in my chest, and I can't help the soft whine that leaves my throat at his words. He straightens, and the look on his face isn't as friendly as it was a few minutes ago. He looks...*dangerous*, for lack of a better term.

Like he really would follow through on his threat.

"Knock it off, August." Adrian's low, warning growl from behind me helps me regain some of my footing. "She's not into you, clearly. Fuck off."

"But that's the point of the conversation, Adrian," August hums, still much too close. "She doesn't like me *yet*. So I take her home and keep her. Then she wouldn't use those words incorrectly ever again, would you?" He pets me on the head like I'm a child and I instinctively knock his hand away.

I'm not expecting the grin that it brings to his face. But he does step back, which is nice, and without another word, turns and waltzes out the door, giving me room to finally breathe.

At my back, Adrian lets out a breath. "He's such an ass," he mutters, walking to the door with me after we've given August a few seconds to get some distance.

"This is where you add that he's harmless," I say, in a voice that's much too similar to a squeak for my preference. "Right?"

"Mmmm..." Adrian trails off, unsure. "This is where I tell you that compared to Dorian, he's...somewhat harmless."

"What's that supposed to mean?" I force a laugh into my voice. "You make it sound like Dorian is some kind of *serial killer* or something."

When Adrian doesn't immediately answer, my heart sinks.

"Just don't piss him off again," my new friend advises. "He doesn't normally hold a grudge, and I'm sure he'll forget about it once Foster shows up."

I want to ask what's so special about Foster, the beta I'd met at orientation, but before I can, Adrian and I part ways, with him telling me that he's meeting up with some friends across campus.

As I watch him go, my backpack over one shoulder, I bite my lip and hope I haven't fucked up too much for Dorian and his friends to forget that I exist.

Every time I shoot an arrow and it *thunks* into the target, some of the tension eases in my shoulders. Not only that, but it's easier to forget about Dorian's *pack* out here, when the only sounds are the light breeze, the lake at my back, and my bow.

I draw another arrow and nock it to the string, my old gloves that need to be replaced bending easily, having been worked in for years now. I loosen another arrow and it sinks deep into the target, right beside the other one in the bullseye. Can I go three for three?

"Tryouts haven't started yet." The amused, husky voice makes me pause, and the breeze brings a harsh fruity scent to my nose that I don't bother trying to sort through. "You're acting like you need the extra practice or something."

When I turn to look over my shoulder, I find a girl about my height, maybe an inch or so taller, leaning against the fence that's around the entire practice field that's set up for archery today. Her waves of dark brown hair stop just under her chin, and are almost a perfect match to her dark brown eyes that watch me from under heavy brows. She's gorgeous, in a 'choke me mistress' kind of way, and I stop to take another sniff of her scent.

No, I could never do it. I just don't love her scent, and I doubt I could move past it enough even to have her hand around my throat and cutting off most of my air.

"I just like to shoot," I shrug. "And my last class got out early. I wanted to come chill out."

"First week jitters? You look like a freshman."

"I am. Though, I don't know why it's so easy for people to tell," I admit with a soft, even laugh.

"The same way it's easy to tell you're a scholarship kid."

The words immediately push away any complacency I'd

felt, and I drop my bow to turn and look at her plaintively, a frown on my lips.

"Just means I worked *extra* hard to be here," I say finally, unsure of what else I *can* say. I am on a scholarship, and I worked my ass off to get into a school that's just as prestigious as fucking *Harvard*. I don't know why being on a scholarship is supposed to be an insult.

Even though it definitely feels like one.

She shrugs. "I don't care what it means. It's just a fact. You didn't have the money to get in, and you're a lot different than ninety-nine percent of the other students here."

"Mama always told me I was special," I tell her, keeping my voice flat and even. "Guess she was right."

Is that a smile on her thin lips? Her eyes narrow, so I can't be sure, and she studies the two arrows in the target. "I don't know why you're bothering to practice, either. With an aim like that, no one's going to turn you away from the team."

No matter how I feel about her earlier words, the sentiment makes me stand a little straighter. "Really?"

She shrugs and walks away, back towards the small outbuilding where the archery stuff is stored, and I notice for the first time that a few other girls are there, most of them looking nervous or unsure as they wait.

The girl, whose name I learn is *Eden*, is right. While she and two other students, two senior, watch the six freshmen trying out for the team, I'm surprised to see how bad four of the others are. Even the fifth, a girl with a steady arm whose face is impossible to read, can't shoot with the same consistency as me, and in the end only she and I make it onto the team.

It chases away more of the doubt I've been feeling, especially as I store my equipment back in the building and take a step out to see that most of the other girls are gone. Only one of the seniors is still here, talking to the other girl who made it, but I hesitate instead of walking over to them.

So far, everyone here is hit or miss, and I'm not sure how they'll act towards me. We could be the best of friends, or one of them could threaten to stab me.

Anything is possible.

The other freshman sees me hovering, and beckons me over with a grin. "I'm Amy," she greets, and nods to the senior. "This is my sister, Allison."

Something loosens in my chest, and I sigh. "I'm Mercy. You're a really good shot, and I love the wrist guards you were using."

"*You're a* really good shot," she counters with a laugh. "Have you ever shot a crossbow?"

5

The weekend is, predictably, much too short. I'd toyed with the idea of going out, just like Briella had decided to, but...

I'm way too chicken to really do it. When I do think about it, my movements become sluggish, and suddenly I remember all of the homework I should clearly do four weeks in advance, or something. It isn't that I don't want to meet people. Or *meet* people.

It's that I'm a chicken, and I've never been drunk.

"You've never drank?" Briella sits on her bed, lacing up her black boots as I watch. I tilt my head to the side with a frown, watching her, and wishing I looked as good in that much makeup.

"I've *drank*," I counter, just a little bit affronted by the implication. "I've just never been drunk."

"What have you drank?"

"Wine."

"Wow."

"At communion, before I stopped going to church."

She pauses and looks up at me, disbelief in her eyes. "Just come with me," she urges, though I'm unsure where this sudden bravery comes from, since she's been doing her best imitation of a mouse since we've met.

"Why do you want to go?" I reply, drawing my legs up under me. "There's literally so much to do *here*, so why go? And it's *Sunday*."

"Yeah, and the semester just started. So what? I don't have class until noon, anyway."

Her logic doesn't make me want to go any more than I already don't.

"Why do you want to go?" I ask again, enunciating the words.

She just shrugs and looks back down at her boots. "I just…I want to meet someone, you know? Eventually. Maybe I'll connect with someone's scent. Or a pack's scent and they'll…" She trails off, but I don't need her to continue. In fact, my heart breaks for her a little. Briella wants a pack just as much as she's afraid of them. Or at least *someone* to treat her like she matters and give her the kind of love she's clearly aching for.

I just want to stuff myself with nachos, watch a movie, and pass out. My brain sticks for a moment on the nachos part, and my mom's voice in my head about me getting fat and grabbing my arms to show me how 'ugly' I am tries to invade my thoughts.

But I push it away, not breaking my focus from Briella.

"Have fun? Call me if you need me. I don't know why you'd need me, but you know." She offers me a thin, wan smile and I again consider calling her out for how much she may not want to go, even though she tells me the opposite. Still, I'm not her mother and I don't have any say on what she will or won't do. So I smile, wish her good luck, and wait for Briella to leave before rummaging around the mini fridge for a few moments.

There's nothing really appetizing in there, apart from the crepes I'd stuffed into a small cup from breakfast. Bringing out doggy bags is fine, so long as they're in the cup that they have for 'takeout' at the dining hall. It seems like a weird concept, but after watching Briella pull apart a grilled cheese and stuff it into one, I'm not going to ask questions.

Especially not after watching a student slowly pour a jar of mustard into a cup nonchalantly, like he had no care in the world for what he was doing, and no shame.

Rich kids are so weird.

With nachos on my brain, I pull my light, pink hoodie on over my tee and running shorts, then toe on my sneakers before leaving the room with my ID and keycard in hand. I'm grateful for the short walk to the dining hall, and contrary to Briella's normal attitude, I *enjoy* eating alone.

I like doing a lot of things alone, honestly. It's how I grew up, and now that I'm a few days into my life at Winter Grove, I feel like I finally, *finally*, have the chance to decompress and just consider everything so far.

Overall, things aren't awful.

I hadn't had a lot of expectations, truth-be-told. I hadn't known what to expect, and as I sit down with my plate of chicken nachos to stare at them and their queso goodness, I sigh.

The only problem with Winter Grove is that I feel...lonely, kind of. Sure. I have Briella. I have the archery team, thankfully. And I hopefully have Adrian for the classes we share. Even Zara isn't awful, though something about her just feels too cold to me. Like she's willing to ice me out whenever it's convenient for her to do so. Like maybe I'll never make it past arms length with her.

But it isn't friends, exactly, that makes me feel lonely.

It's that I really *am* the odd one out here. It's subtle, sometimes. Occasionally I can barely tell that I'm the scholarship kid in a sea of rich kids. But a lot of the time...it's not subtle. Even with Briella. And it's the little things that make me take notice. The things she and the others take for granted.

Absently I press my hands over my ears, though if I really wanted a break from the light noise in the dining hall, I'd take my hearing aids out altogether. I've been lucky so far that I haven't had a migraine yet, though I know that it's just a matter of time, and since normally I have a few a month, I'm sure there's one just around the corner waiting to fuck up my day.

My mom's voice comes swimming back at me, and I take a bite of the nachos before I can think *not* to. There's nothing wrong with me. I know that, rationally. I'm a healthy weight, a healthy size, and I *am* healthy, save for the migraines. And my mom had meant well...mostly.

And she probably didn't know what years of yelling at me and guilting me over my food choices would cause, right? Otherwise, I like to think she wouldn't have been so nasty when she grabbed my arm, or my stomach, and asked me if I was choosing food over being *pretty*.

Like pretty is the be all and end all in life.

I'd rather be *smart* than a pretty omega who bats her eyes and hunts for her pack or her alpha. I'd rather be *smart* than a pretty, comfortably middle-class girl who never could've gotten into this school without the intelligence I've worked my whole life for people to notice.

I'd rather be me than my mother.

I'm so caught up in my swirling, ugly thoughts that I almost miss it when the boy sits down in front of me, though I'm still aware enough that I look up in time to see him looking me over, like I've done something specifically to attract his attention.

He's an alpha, my brain registers instantly, a moment behind the cloying scent of grass and blueberries that serves to clog up my nostrils. It's overpowering, awful, and I've never smelled anything so dreadful, quite frankly.

This time, I manage not to gag, but it's a near thing. I take in breaths through my mouth as I look over the broad-shouldered blonde, wishing he'd tell me what he wanted so he can *leave*.

"You're the scholarship kid." It isn't a question, and I'm so tired of hearing it that I want to hit him.

Instead I sigh and roll my eyes before picking up another chip and crunching it in my mouth, eyes still on him.

"You know, it's pretty cool that you're smart enough to get here without money." He leans closer over the table, and I abandon my nachos in favor of trying not to wretch. He smells *terrible*, and even the omega in me is leaning away, wanting to punch out a window so that I can get some fresh air.

And normally, I feel some itch to submit to an alpha when they're this close, giving me this kind of attention. Lord knows I felt that way with August and Dorian.

Don't even go there, I tell myself, dragging my attention away from the boy for a few seconds. *Bad Mercy. Bad.*

"It's not a big deal," I say finally, not sure what he even wants. "So...?" I raise my brows, hoping he'll *tell me* so I can get back to my nachos and my impending horror movie marathon.

"You don't seem to have a lot of friends, huh? I guess that's to be expected. You're not even from around here, are you?" Those aren't questions I want to answer, and I'm absolutely not about to. He shifts in his spot, blue eyes bright, and a fresh wave of his scent hits my nose and triggers an automatic nauseous response.

"I do have friends. And I'm not from around here, but so what? I feel like *most* people aren't?" It's pretty stupid to assume everyone lives within driving distance of Winter Grove, Maine. I doubt *anyone* does, actually.

But I don't say that part out loud.

"I have a pack," he goes on, and suddenly I have an idea of where this is going. I don't like it, and I wish I could fake a heart attack to get out.

Jumping out the window is looking better and better every second.

"Okay?" I raise my brows. "That's cool, I guess."

"You should come over to our suite sometime."

I want to vomit. Hard. All over him. Though, I suppose it would be a waste of tasty, tasty nachos.

"Oh, no, I don't think so. Thanks for the invite, though."

He doesn't move. Even though I'm *pretty sure* I just told him *no fucking thank you.*

"Why?"

I look up at him, frowning.

"Why what?"

"Why *not*? You don't have any better options. And we're not so bad." When he tries to lean across the table a little more, I lean back into the booth behind me.

"I..." I trail off, not willing to just give him another answer that he'll ignore. I need a *real* answer. And unfortunately, being a man and an alpha with this charming personality, I doubt another *I don't want to* is going to suffice.

No, he needs to think I have someone backing me up.

Adrian? My brain heads there first, though I shy away from the thought immediately. He seems like a safe option, but not an option this guy would leave me alone for.

No, I need something better.

"I've already been approached by a pack," I say, still scrambling to figure out what I can use. "And I'm really interested in getting to know them."

"Who?" Because of course he asks. *Of fucking course.* He couldn't just leave it there, that I've *met a pack* or something.

God, sometimes I hate pushy men. Especially when they smell as bad as him.

"Does it matter?" I shoot back, crossing my arms over my chest. "You're not *my* alpha, or my family." It's pretty easy to keep a tone of assured confidence in my voice, even when I'm lying like this. "So why does it matter *who*?"

"Because, omega, I'm so sure I could change your mind, if it's anyone that I'm thinking of." He purrs at the end of his words, though it sounds a lot more like choking to me. How embarrassing for him.

"No, I don't think so." God, I need to figure out what to say. Adrian *definitely* won't work here from the little I know about him. And neither would Briella or Zara, obviously.

But that only leaves one other pack. And I don't want to lie about them.

"Because you're lying to me, aren't you, little omega?" His purr turns to an almost disapproving, condescending growl, and if he leans any further his face is going to be in the sour cream. Part of me wants to help him along.

But a small part of me has her heart in her throat, and my natural instincts are to admit that he's right, I'm wrong, and just *submit* to him. That's not on my list of things to do tonight, though.

So I don't.

"Dorian Wakefield asked me to consider *his* pack," I say, leaning forward and letting my voice soften. "So I think you'll see why I didn't want to tell you."

Immediately the alpha sits up, eyebrows knit together in surprise. "*Dorian?*" he replies, disbelievingly. His gaze darts away, then back at me, but I don't move. Instead I raise my brows, looking unimpressed.

Looking like I'm telling the damn truth.

Still my heart pounds in my chest, reminding me with every beat that I'm a *liar*.

But it's just a little lie. Just a small, white lie to get me out of trouble, and I doubt he's going to find out about it.

How would he? It's not like I need to go tell everyone in the school the same thing I just told this boy.

He doesn't have the balls to call me out on it. I can see that in his face as he slides to his feet and frowns. "Whatever," he mutters, rubbing the back of his neck. "You should've just told me—"

"I tried to," I interrupt, pressing my advantage to drive home the lie. "Because I don't need the whole school knowing. I don't think *they* want everyone to, either. At least not yet." I might throw up. The words are so untrue that I'm surprised they come out of my mouth with any kind of confidence, but here I am.

"Whatever. Have a…good night, I guess." He shakes his head and walks away, disappearing towards the stairs that lead back out of the dining hall.

I gaze back at my nachos and sigh, thumping back in my booth once more. "He won't find out," I tell them, picking up a chip and gazing thoughtfully at it. My heart pounds in exhilaration like I've run a mile, and I put the chip in my mouth and chew while pushing my unease away. He won't find out, because I have a feeling this alpha won't have the balls to tell him.

I just need to stop worrying about it and get on with my plans for the night.

6

As my teeth sink into my bagel and I curl my fingers around the cool cup of my peanut butter smoothie, my eyes fall on the shape of Briella making her way across the courtyard, relative panic on her face.

Worse, she's looking at *me*. I slow, unsure how much I want her to catch up to me with that look, though the other part of me is wondering what in the world has her speed walking towards me with that kind of look creasing her brow and widening her eyes. Is she in trouble? Did something happen at her party that she hadn't told me about this morning when we'd parted from breakfast? We have no classes together Monday, Wednesday, or Friday, but it hasn't been more than a few hours since I've seen her.

Not long enough for something earth-shattering to have happened, right?

She gestures for me to follow her when she's close enough, head tilting to the side towards the benches that line the walk around the fountain. They're packed, and I don't know why she wants to gaze romantically at a fountain with me, but I have no more classes today, nothing to do, and all of the curiosity of an about to get killed cat.

So I follow her.

Briella walks quickly, passing the fountain and instead ending up behind the campus center, on the stairs that wrap around the building, before she stops and whirls on me.

"What were you thinking?" she hisses, before I can do more than swallow another bite of my bagel. "What were you–do you *want* to get kicked out of here, Mercy?"

A thrill of terror shoots up my spine. What had I done?

"I didn't do anything," I tell her, setting my smoothie down on a low wall that frames this side of the stairs as I look at her. "You live with me. If I'd killed anyone, you'd know about it Bri."

"I don't mean today." She rubs a hand over her eyes. "Shit, Mercy. I was there when Foster found out about it from Rhett."

I still have no idea what's going on, and it's frustrating.

"Found out *what*?"

"That you name dropped Dorian's pack like you're *friends!*"

I blink, then blink again. My brows rise, though I look around our secluded little area before I say again, "Okay, and? I guess I'll say sorry for using his name to get some creep from being pushy? I couldn't get rid of him any other way, Bri. He was in my space, in my *face*, and I didn't know what else to do. I didn't think anyone would find out, either, but whatever. I'll just say sorry–"

She lets out a strangled laugh, cutting me off. "Sorry?" she repeats. "You think they'll care about sorry?"

"I think you're overreacting way more than any reasonable person would. They can't be that upset."

She looks at me again, and I can't stop myself from rolling my eyes. "No one can be that upset over it. C'mon. It's not a big deal. *I'll apologize.*"

"They're not going to care," she snaps. "And of course it's a big deal. Yeah, okay, you didn't kill anyone. But you're going around school saying they want you as *pack* when that's not true."

"Thanks, Briella. Rub my nose in it. Make it hurt more that I'm alone," I reply without thinking, and she stops mid-rant, as if she can't decide if I'm being truthful or not.

"You don't want them as pack," she says quietly, but with conviction ringing in her words. "You don't want them anywhere near you. They're awful, Mercy. And they're going to be pissed as fuck that you're pretending–"

"That I said *one thing* to get me out of a bad situation. Got it. I've done the worst thing imaginable." I finish my bagel, though it tastes like cardboard in my mouth and I almost want to vomit. This shouldn't be happening, and I replay the scenario in my mind, even though I can't come up with anything else I could've said to the alpha in the dining hall. I suck in a slow breath, trying not to hop on the freak out train with her.

"And they can't be *that* mad, right?" My voice takes that unfortunate moment to waver, and I hate it. "I'll explain what happened. I'll *whine*." Especially if I can catch either Dorian or August. They're alphas, and if I give them a wide eye, fluttering lashes, *whiny* look, they surely won't be that upset. It's worked before in tight situations, and it's one of the few nice things about being an omega.

Once in a while.

Distantly I calculate the weeks from my last heat, though it's not my main priority right now. I just prefer to stay on top of it and dump suppressants down my throat when the time gets closer. It won't be bad, obviously. With no pack and nothing to trigger it into being worse, it's normally just a few uncomfortably *warm* days, once I take my suppressants. And, according to my brain-math, I have until the beginning of October before it hits.

"You better make it a good apology." I'm tired of Briella's alarmism, and I force myself to sigh.

"It'll be a great apology. It'll be *fine*. I'll find, umm..." I trail off, thinking which of the three of them would be best. "August—"

"That won't work," she says, cutting me off instantly. "Dorian makes the big decisions. And it's Dorian's name you dropped. You'd have to get *him* not to be mad."

"Does he even *know*?" I'll have class with him tomorrow, though I'm sure he'll know by then.

"If he doesn't, then he'll know the second Foster gets back to the dorms. It's got to be where he's headed now," Briella replies.

"Okay, well...okay then." I take a deep breath, once again trying to convince my heart to stop pounding so fast. "I'll figure it out. I'll go find them. It won't be a big deal. Do you know where they live, by chance?" I know it's probably a long-shot, and Briella hesitates before shaking her head. "I know they live in the Fallbarrow dorm by the lake," she shrugs. "But I don't know what room, or anything. And I doubt it would be a great idea to just stroll on over there and start knocking on doors."

"Yeah..." I sigh. "I'll figure it out. Worst case scenario, I'll talk to Dorian tomorrow. We have Astronomy together."

"Do you want to get dinner later?" She eyes the smoothie in my hand. "If you're hungry? If not, we can just do something else."

"No, we can get dinner," I assure her. "You have one more class today, right?" She nods at my words. "I'm done. But I'll see you when you get back. Honestly, I'm going to just take a nap, so that's probably where you'll find me when you're out."

All day I've felt the tickles of a migraine coming on, and all day I've been ignoring it as best I can. Hopefully if I go sleep, I won't have to deal with it for the rest of the night, or the next couple of days.

"Think of an apology," she advises, shouldering her backpack with a frown. Nerves prickle my insides, but I try not to let that show on my face as she goes towards the doors of the campus center.

"I'll write them a letter," I assure her. "A really sincere letter. Then you can tell me about the girl you said you met last night." She gives me a quick glance over her shoulder, then pushes the door open and lets it fall closed behind her, disappearing from view a few moments later.

"Well fuck," I murmur, rocking back on my heels. Now that she's gone, it's harder not to be anxious. It's harder to pretend I'm not worried. But I refuse to let her panic infect me like this. It's *not a big deal*. There's no way they're going to think it is.

...Right?

Rounding the corner of the building, my eyes flick around the courtyard of the campus center lazily, not looking for anyone. She's right. I *won't* find any of them if I go knocking on doors in Fallbarrow, so there's no point in trying. And I don't know their schedules, or anything else about them. They could all be done for the day. Or they could be in class now.

Or, Foster O'Dell could be taking the path down to the lakeshore, phone in hand and head bowed.

I barely hesitate, though Briella's words about approaching *Dorian* instead of the others ring in my ears. Surely if I explain things to Foster, he'll tell Dorian and it'll be okay. He's a beta, and out of the three of them, he's the least problematic. The one I'm least afraid is going to growl and drag me off to some dark corner to be murdered or something.

He's also the one I've managed not to insult.

"Foster!" His name is out of my mouth before I can think that this might not be a good idea, and I take off down the path towards him. Breaking into a jog, it still takes me a good thirty seconds to catch up to him, and by then we've left the crowd of the courtyard behind. He's halfway to the lakeshore dorms, though he still hasn't looked up.

This time, I falter, even as my hand goes up with the intent to touch his shoulder.

Then again, what other choice do I have?

Ever so lightly, I touch his shoulder, and when the brunette-haired beta with sharp, blue eyes turns to look at me, there's not a lick of surprise in their depths. Almost as if he *had* heard me calling, and knew I was following him. That sends a wave of nerves through me again, but I push them down as he stops and looks at me with raised brows and a slight-smile on his full lips.

"It's Mercy, right?" he asks, still walking. I fall into step with him, wondering why he won't *stop* so we can talk.

"Umm. Yeah." My fear flutters like butterflies in my throat, intent on choking me before I can say what I need to. "Look, Foster, I–"

"Why Jessica?" his amused words cut me off before I can finish, and when he looks at me, it's with a sly grin that curls his lips and makes him even more attractive than he was a few seconds ago. He really might be the most gorgeous beta I've ever seen, with tousled brunette hair and eyes like the sky. He's just a few shades darker than my own almost-ivory complexion, with very light freckles decorating his nose and cheeks. Under light any less bright than the afternoon sun, I never would've seen them.

"What?" I ask, my brain not working well enough to figure out what he's asking me.

"Look, I've heard the *Jessica* story like three times now.

When you choked on Dorian's scent and lied about your name. I'm just curious why you picked Jessica, is all."

"...I have no idea," I reply, bewildered.

"Was it a Jessica Rabbit thing?"

"It was a 'this is what came out of my mouth for some reason' thing." I'm still confused as to why this is what he's interested in, and unsure why it matters, but my brain also registers that we're still on the path to Fallbarrow, which is closer than I'd thought it was, and I stop.

Foster does as well, his smile turning a little less friendly.

"What's wrong?" he asks, head tilting to the side.

"I'm. Umm." I glance at the dorm, then back at him, and realization dawns in his eyes.

"Oh, you're afraid of what he's going to do, aren't you?"

"No! No, not at all. I want to apologize. Actually."

"To Dorian?"

"*No*. I mean yes, obviously. I used his name, so he's...obviously the one I should apologize to." I let out a soft, nervous laugh, and drag my fingers through my hair that's still up in a ponytail. "Is he, umm....here?" *God I hope he isn't.*

"No." I'm sure the relief is plain on my face, and his humor grows. "If you're so afraid of him, why use his name?" He takes another step towards Fallbarrow, but I don't move. "Come on, Mercedes. I'm not going to stand here all afternoon. I want to take a shower."

The idea of Foster taking a shower has no place in my head, so I sweep it away like autumn leaves on the kitchen floor.

"I'm. Umm. I'm trying to apologize to you," I point out, scuffing my foot on the sidewalk. "And, you know, explain what happened."

"So walk and talk."

"But my dorm is the *other* way," I point out, trying not to whine. I don't want to follow him to Fallbarrow. I want to go home and nap away the beginnings of this migraine.

"And *you're* the one with an apology to make." He looks down at his phone and types something quick before pocketing it, earbuds still in. "So, you get to walk with *me*." His grin is fierce, and not as friendly as I'd like it to be.

"...Whatever," I murmur at last, and fall into step with him when he starts walking once more. When I do, he looks at me triumphantly and with every bit of sarcasm in his body says, "Good *girl*."

I hate it.

Well, I want to hate it, but his scent is washing over me and invading my nose in the best way while he speaks. Not to mention his voice is a great combination of a purr and a tease.

But, again, Foster O'Dell has no place in my brain in a *sexy* way.

"Okay. So, I was alone." I need to play up the danger I thought I was in, to make him see it really was a last resort. I still haven't lost hope that he can pass this on to Dorian and save me the trouble in doing so. "Briella, my roommate, was at a party. I was in the dining hall." As if I need to set the scene for him.

But, judging by the way he's looking at me and the way he nods his head, he's not *bored* at least. "So, I was just eating, and–"

"Eating what?" he asks blithely.

"Umm...nachos."

"What did you get on them?"

"What?"

"Well, there were chicken nachos and beef nachos. And veggie-chili nachos, if you count that. What did you have on yours?" His voice is mild as he speaks, though he's looking towards his dorm instead of at me.

"Does it matter?"

He shrugs, smile touching his lips again. "Maybe? I don't know."

"Chicken. I had chicken on them." *Though I really don't see why it matters.* "So I was eating, and this guy sat down across from me. He—"

"Rhett," Foster interrupts again.

"What?" I feel like a broken record today, and his weird reactions aren't doing anything for my nerves. Butterflies still flutter uncomfortably around my insides, and I sigh to try to relieve some of the tension.

"That's his name. *Rhett.* It's a weird name, right? Like his parents forgot the B, or something. But go on."

"Okay. So umm, *Rhett* sat down and invited me to uh, hang out with his pack."

"That's sweet of him."

"It wasn't, though." Frustration rises to the back of my throat, and I chuck my half-empty smoothie into a trash can we pass with a sigh.

Foster eyes the can, then me. "Didn't like it?"

"No I...I loved it, actually." I *had* loved it, up until everything had started tasting like ash in my mouth, thanks to Foster.

"Then why throw it away?" When I don't answer, he sneaks a sidelong glance at me. "Oh, Mercy, don't tell me *I* make *you* nervous. I'm not Dorian or August. I'm not alpha."

I want to reply, to dismiss his claims, but I can't. He does make me nervous, even without having any of that. There's something about him that puts me off my game. Like there's something under the surface that isn't as easy-going as he seems.

I don't trust him, but I just shrug. "I'm just nervous about the situation, I guess."

"Oh yeah? So it's not me?" He slows, eyes catching mine like he already knows the answer, but I just shake my head slowly and stare at him without breaking eye contact. "Good." He picks up the pace once more. "I'd feel so bad if I were making you nervous."

I doubt that. I doubt he feels bad about anyone being nervous or unsure or anything else around him like I'm feeling now.

"So he wouldn't leave me alone," I continue, dropping the line of conversation about how he makes me feel. "And dropping your pack's name wasn't my first resort or anything." I pause when he pulls the glass door of Fallbarrow dorm open, staring into the lobby like it's a funeral home and I'm the dead girl.

"Come on," he urges. "I told you, I want to go back to my suite and your story is taking forever. We're not standing here forever."

"Dorian isn't here, right?" I know he gets some small joy out of my insecurity about his pack's alpha, but I don't care.

Sure enough, he grins. "He's in class."

"What about August?"

"He's swimming. That's who I was texting on the way here."

He could be lying to me. I look into his face, feeling slightly nauseous. I don't know him well enough to know if he *is* lying. Though I'm not sure why he would. What does he have to gain by doing so?

"Come on," he chuckles, ushering me into the dorm. "I'm not spiriting you away off campus, or something. You're literally ten minutes from Maliseet." He may be right, but ten minutes feels like thirty when I'm standing here at his dorm with no one to tell me if I should trust him or not.

7

I walk inside close behind Foster, but pause with a frown before I've gone more than a few feet. "How do you know where I live?" I ask, as the glass door closes almost noiselessly behind us.

"Oh, it's not that hard to figure out," Foster assures me, going to the elevator behind the security desk and pressing the button a couple of times, seeming impatient. He bites his lip, though his grin tries to widen anyway, and suddenly, I don't feel so safe.

Not that I'd felt that safe in the first place.

"Maybe I should go home." This is seeming like a worse and worse idea, no matter how I spin it, but when Foster looks up at me with wide, confused eyes, I doubt myself again.

"Why? Look, I know I'm not Dorian, but..." He lets out a breath, and offers me a much kinder smile as the elevator dings softly and the doors open. "Just tell me what happened, and I'll tell him. That's what you want, right? To not have to say this to *him*?" He walks inside the elevator and holds the door open while I hesitate.

He's right. He's so incredibly right, though my heart pounds in my throat and my fingers twist in the hem of my hoodie as I step into the elevator with him. My breath catches in my throat at his scent, though his own nostrils flare at mine. I'm sure that I must scent terribly, with the burned tinge of fear on the edge of everything because of how nervous this makes me.

"Sorry," I murmur, and scuff my foot on the floor. "I know my scent must be–"

"Fine," he assures me. "It's totally fine." As if to prove his point, he takes a deep breath of the elevator air, like he somehow *enjoys* the scent of my fear.

What a good actor.

"So umm, anyway, I–"

"I didn't know you could get glittery hearing aids." I don't understand why he keeps interrupting me, and irritation builds in my chest as he does it yet again. "Have you always had them like that?"

"What?" I press my fingers to one of them. "Yeah, I mean… no. I've switched colors a few times. I just–"

"Have you always been hard of hearing?"

"Does it matter?" My words are sharper than I intend to be, and the elevator doors open as he glances back at me with a small smirk and steps out into the hallway of the third floor.

"Guess not," he shrugs. "I was just curious." He sets off down the hallway, winding past a lounge where four people sit on their laptops, the TV hanging on the wall playing something that might be a reality show.

"I haven't always been. I got sick as a kid," I explain quickly. It's not like there's an exciting story to go along with it, so there's no reason for me to go in depth.

"Okay." he shrugs again, and stops at the very last door to

swipe his key in the lock. It beeps and he pushes it open, gesturing for me to walk inside.

But I don't.

I don't *trust him*, for one. Though I don't know why I feel so nervous about going into his room. He's told me the others aren't here, and he has no reason to lie, does he?

"Come *on*, Mercy," he sighs. "We go in, you finish this story, you're out before your scent gets on anything and Dorian doesn't learn you're here. Easy."

Somehow, this doesn't feel as easy as he says it is. But I follow him inside, letting the door close behind me and taking a deep breath.

Their combined scent is...something. It hits my nose hard, and for a moment I feel as if I'm drowning in lavender, leather, and a tropical island. I've scented a pack before but this is something else entirely. Embarrassingly, I realize I've taken another deep breath, and turn to look at Foster expectantly, only to see that he's looking at me the same way.

"I'll be right back," he says after a second of silence. "I'm going to throw this in my room. Take a look around, if you want. It's a lot different than Maliseet." Without giving me a chance to reply, he walks down the hallway to the left, pushing open the door at the end of the short hallway.

He's right. It *is* a lot different. The room I'm standing in has two couches and a large TV mounted on one wall. Under it, on a long shelf that's attached to the dark blue wall, sit a few game consoles. The couches look more comfortable than anything I've ever sat my ass on, and there's a little kitchenette with a sink and a microwave to my right. An ajar door looks like it leads to a bathroom, though I'm not going to move from my spot.

That is, until another door to my right suddenly creaks open a few inches, and I jump.

That's definitely not the room Foster had gone into, and my heart jumps to pound in my throat.

"Foster?" I call, fighting not to sound like I'm nervous.

"Yeah?" he calls back lazily. "I'm almost done."

"Are you sure no one else is here?"

"Of course I am." He appears in the doorway, seeming confused. "Why?"

"That door just shut." I nod at the door at the other end of the suite, and look back at the door that'll take me *out* of here. "Hey, you know what? I think I should leave." I try to keep my voice light, for all the good it does, and Foster just shrugs.

"Yeah, okay. If you want to, *I'm* not going to stop you."

I try for a nervous laugh and release the hem of my hoodie. "When you say it like that, it sounds like someone else might."

He just shrugs, watching me with keen eyes as I move to the door. "I'll umm. Look, I'm really sorry and I guess I'll talk to Dorian...tomorrow?" I don't *want* to talk to him, but anything feels safer than being in this slightly too cold dorm room with the possibility of someone else being here.

If Dorian really is mad, I don't want to be here when he finds out.

"Are you sure?" My hand lands on the knob, but Foster doesn't make a move except to lean on his doorframe with his arms crossed. When I look at him, his eyes dance and his smile isn't exactly nice. "Because you could just tell him now."

The doorknob twists under my fingers, though I haven't tried to turn it, and I gasp as it's pushed open to admit the person I want to see the least.

Dorian Wakefield.

"Oh my god," I mutter, taking a few steps back. "I–" I look at Foster, then at the door that opens on the other side of the suite to show August, who leans on his frame as well. "He told me you weren't here."

"Yeah." Dorian blinks and steps inside, closing the door behind him. His hair is messier than the last time I'd seen him, and his dark brown eyes look black in the absence of direct lighting. "He lied to you, Mercedes."

"But—" I turn to look at Foster again, taken aback by the anticipation and thrill on his features. "You tricked me! Why would you trick me?"

"Because he wants to see *this*," Dorian replies, taking another step forward so I have to move back into the living room of the suite. "What? Did you think he was really going to hear you out and help you out of the kindness of his heart?" Dorian snorts. "He brought you back here while we were all home just to see that look on your fucking face." When his nostrils flare, I get a sense that he's scenting as much of my fear as he can, and I *hate* that I'm giving him—giving *them*—exactly what they want. I try to get a handle on myself, and when Dorian steps towards me again, I don't move. Instead I hold my ground, catch his gaze, and hold it.

"Oh, little *omega*," he purrs, looking a lot less impressed and a lot less amused than I'd hoped. "You don't want to play this game with me. You're not going to win."

"You're not going to hurt me, no matter if we're in your suite or *not.*" It's certainly a bold thing of me to say, especially when I feel like I'm going to vomit all over his sneakers.

He trades a look with August when the latter snorts a laugh into his palm, and looks back at me. "That's certainly a bold statement from you."

"It's just realistic," I shoot back. I force myself to keep as calm as I can, though I'm not sure how well I succeed. "Do you want to hear my apology and explanation, or not?" Foster's right in that regard. I really can get this over with right now so that we can end whatever this is.

"Not," he replies easily.

"Then like I...said..." My voice trails off as my brain registers what he's just said, and I stare at him with hurt and confusion on my face. "What did you say?"

"Not. Because I don't want to hear your apology, or your explanation." He's grinning as he says it, eyes never leaving mine.

"But it was an *accident*! And if you just let me explain–"

"I said no–"

"I don't care!" As I say it I step forward, invading his space so we're almost nose to nose.

It's definitely the wrong thing to say. Foster makes a noise like a snicker from his side of the suite, and August whistles quietly. I don't move, though, and my nails dig painful crescents into my palms as I meet his eyes.

Would it be too late to whine and try to appeal to his alpha nature?

Judging by the soft growl that's building in his throat, I'd say so.

"Okay. Umm. This isn't...this isn't how I wanted this to go," I whisper, still not moving even though I drop down to my heels instead of balancing on the balls of my feet to be closer to him. Why had I tried so hard to get in his face?

Why had I followed Foster here in the first place like an idiot?

"I'm sorry," I say softly.

"I told you I don't want to hear it."

"Well I...I don't know what else to say," I whisper, my eyes wide and locked on his. This close, they're still so incredibly dark that I could drown in them and never find my way out again, if I were to keep staring at him.

"You really want me to forgive you? Want me to forget this, and pretend that you didn't use my name, my pack's reputation, and other people's opinions of me to get yourself out of an uncomfortable situation?"

Slowly, I nod. It seems almost too good to be true, maybe, but if he's offering...

"I'll even throw in forgetting that you choked on my scent and lied to me the other day."

I wish he wouldn't remind me of that, or his scent. This close, it's all I can smell and it smells *amazing*. Too bad it's on him, and not someone sane.

"...Yes," I breathe, when he doesn't continue. "I'm sorry for that too, I–"

"Then beg."

I'm sure I've heard him wrong. There's no way he just said that. No sane person wants someone else to *beg*.

"What?"

"I'll give you the benefit of the doubt this once and assume you really didn't hear me," he tells me after a moment. "I said...*beg*." He lifts his voice slightly, his chin rising as he stares down at me. "But not like that. It's not believable if you're just going to stand there when we have a perfectly good floor for you to get on your knees."

"I'm not...going to do that," I say, though my words come out as uncertain. "I'm not going to *beg* for–"

"I'm going to say this *one time*, Mercedes Noble." His words are slow and clear, and surprisingly even. "You're going to get down on this floor and *beg* for me to overlook what a bad impression you've made on me this week."

"Or what?" I ask, challengingly. "Are you going to try to keep me here until I do?"

Raising his brows innocently, he shakes his head and steps away from the door so I have a clear shot to it. "Not at all. You can leave whenever you want. I can't *hurt* you here, right?

That's what you said?" there's a note of goading in his voice that I don't like, but I'm not in a position to challenge it.

"I said I was sorry. I offered you an explanation. I'm not giving you anything else. I'm sorry that I upset you—" he cuts me off with a laugh.

"I still don't want that. I want you to *beg* or to get out. But if you don't get on my floor on your knees right now until I believe you're sorry?" When I go to the door and put my hand on it, he reaches out suddenly to grip my wrist, drawing my gaze once more as my stomach twists painfully. "Then you're going to regret it every day for the next year."

I suck in a breath, my hand tightening on the knob before I jerk my hand to shake him off. "I'm not afraid of you," I lie, and pull the door open harshly.

"That's okay," Dorian assures me, not moving as I walk right on out. "You're going to be. I promise. See you in astronomy tomorrow, Mercy Noble."

I don't give him, or any of them, the satisfaction of an answer. I let the door slam behind me and walk down the hallway, not stopping until I'm at the elevator and I can collapse against the wall and let out the gasp I've been holding in my lungs while I try not to cry.

8

I don't know how I don't wake up Tuesday with a migraine. Instead I feel it receding, and about an hour after I take my medicine, it goes away completely. At least that's one less thing I have to worry about. And I'm *trying* to not worry about the other things, either.

Unlike Briella, who's doing enough worrying for the both of us. She paces the floor in between our beds, and I watch her with some concern.

"You know…it's me they're threatening, not you," I point out calmly, and she looks up at me with wide, concerned eyes.

"Yeah, but…I don't know, Mercy. This is *really bad*. You know he meant what he said, right? That he'd make the rest of your year hell?" She shakes her head. "Don't hate me, but you should've dropped to your knees and begged."

Absolutely not. I shake my head as I watch her, and sigh. While I am incredibly nervous about what Dorian and his pack are planning to do, it isn't going to help for me to break down and freak out about it. That just gives them more of a victory, and I'm unwilling to do that.

"Tell me about the girl you met the other day," I say instead, pulling my blanket up over my lap and keeping my phone in my hands as I tap the screen absently. "You never got a chance to."

"Hmm? Oh." A blush tinges her darkly tanned face, and she ducks her head before sitting down on her bed as well. "She was really nice. Umm. A sophomore? Yeah. Black hair, really dark eyes. A little bit taller than you, I think."

For a moment, it sounds like she's talking about Zara. But *dark hair, dark eyes,* and *taller than us* isn't exactly a way to pinpoint who she means. I'm sure there are a hundred other girls here who fit the description.

"She had all these pins and stuff on her purse. It was cute."

Oh. Well, that's a better detail. And one that *does* point towards the girl I share astronomy with.

"Zara?" I ask, tilting my head to the side.

Briella nods enthusiastically. "You know her?" She sounds hopeful, nervous, and knits the blanket between her fingers as if she can do more than twist it up. I agree with a nod of my own.

"She's in astronomy with me. She's really nice." Well, she's moderately nice, but still. At least she's not nasty like Dorian. "And she *likes* you?" I wiggle my eyebrows, not at all shocked that Bri isn't hooking up with an alpha. I know for a fact most of them make her nervous. Even Adrian probably would, though he's the most mild-mannered alpha I've ever met. Not to mention, she always stinks of residual fear, and I can't think of anyone that would enjoy that.

Well. Almost anyone.

"I don't know. Maybe? I like her. She's really sweet," Briella goes on. "We're hanging out tomorrow, actually. Around five, I think." She looks up at me again, with worry on her features. "What if I make an idiot out of myself? What if she's secretly an asshole who gets off on begging and humiliation?"

I snort at the pointed jab. "Definitely don't think campus is big enough for more people with that specific kink." Is it a kink? Personally, both sound intriguing to me, under better circumstances that don't involve Dorian's pack. "And she's not going to think you're an idiot." Though, honestly, I feel like Briella could be a little less terrified if she wants to make a good impression on Zara. Not that I have any intention of saying that. "You'll be fine," I assure her, finally getting to my feet. I need to go pick up my medicine from the pharmacy tonight, as much as I don't want to. Especially since it's time to give myself a shot in the leg that I really won't enjoy. "Want to go grab some breakfast?"

I drag my feet as I walk towards Astronomy, hoping against hope that somehow, Dorian came down with a cold. Or the flu. Or scarlet fever. Really, I'm not picky. The longer he's out of class, the better. I'm just early enough that the classroom is only half full, and when I stare down at my seat that I'd claimed on Thursday, I hesitate.

What if I move? He's not going to *follow* me. That would be petty. And while there are only a few other seat options, including the table right in front of mine, at least it would put me a little further away from him. On the other hand, he'll see it as a victory. He'll gloat, I'm sure, and think he's won.

Then again, he probably already has. I'm terrified of what he'll do when he gets here, and worried that he'll somehow announce to the whole class what happened.

That's stupid, Mercy, I whisper to myself silently. *He's not going to do that. We're in class.* I waver, but sit down in the spot I'd claimed for myself last time and sigh. It is what it is, and I'm not going to make this worse.

His scent is the first thing that lets me know he's coming. Birthday cake and *spice* with that after-scent of leather that makes me take a deep breath. Thankfully, I don't choke this time. I'm also glad that he doesn't know *why* I'd choked when he came in here the first time.

It's even more embarrassing now that I hate him.

When he stops beside me, I rest my head on my chin and level a glare up into his cocky expression, and his smirk grows. "Oh, someone's cocky today," he murmurs, surprising me by leaning down over the table so his face is inches from mine. My heart speeds up in my chest, banging against my ribs like it wants a way out.

I don't respond. I simply eye him reproachfully and watch his expression never change.

"I can change that," he assures me. "I'll have you getting on your feet whenever I walk by soon enough."

"Why? Because you feel like a high society damsel and want to live out your dreams?" I murmur, keeping my voice just as quiet as his.

"Knock it off, *omega*," he purrs, though there's only a note of warning in his tone, not a threat. "Don't make me discipline you in front of all of our classmates. Only think of how embarrassing it'll be for you if I make you cry."

"You can't do *shit* in front of anyone," I reply, forcing myself not to shrink away from him. "You don't own this school."

"I might as well. And you know what? I changed my mind. *Get up.*"

"Why? There's plenty of room for you to walk past. Or walk the fuck around." My voice falters, however, and I hate the way he looks like he's won.

"Because I said so."

"Go fuck yourself." I don't know why I say it. Well, I do. I didn't come here to be pushed around. I thought if anything my money status would be what got me ostracized or treated poorly. Not an accidental decision I'd made to get myself out of a shitty situation.

God, I hate Dorian Wakefield.

"You could still beg, you know." he doesn't move, and his hand on the table starts to move so he can tap his fingers on the surface of my iPad. I try to shoo them off, but he doesn't move. Instead, my only option is to grab his hand and *make* him move.

But I don't have the nerve for that.

"I'm not begging you for anything."

"I won't even make you do it in front of anyone. We can go back to my dorm and you can get on your knees for me right there in the door way. August and Foster would watch, of course. They'd *love* to watch you grovel for me."

"Because they're looking for tips?"

I swear his grin twitches a little wider, but instead he just sighs and stands straight. "Remember that you got yourself into this all on your own. There's no one else to blame, little omega." He walks behind me to sit down, lounging in his chair the same way he had before. He tilts it back on its back legs, though I stop watching the moment Professor Belker descends the stairs and claps his hands once to get our attention.

"We'll be starting our first project this week," he says to everyone, looking around the room. "It's a relatively simple one, and I think you'll all agree. We're picking a constellation and doing research on it, and the stars that make it up. I'll allow you to work by yourselves or in pairs, but pairs must either do a large constellation or two smaller ones. There's information for you all on these papers. Especially for all of you that've never had a class with me." He smiles in a way that makes it seem like he's not that happy and hands the papers off to a red-haired girl, who passes them around the room. I watch, and when they get to Dorian I hold my hand out for one.

Only for him to hand it off to the person behind us. The girl looks at me, confused, and when I reach out to her, Dorian shakes his head slightly.

"She doesn't need one," he murmurs, and the girl shrugs and hands them up and out of reach.

I freeze, and take a breath. "I'll just get one after class," I mutter under my breath. "This isn't elementary school, you know."

"Of course it isn't," Dorian agrees breezily. "If it were, he wouldn't be ready to yell at anyone who doesn't grab a paper to read from here in a few moments."

Glaring his way, I sit back in my chair again. There's nothing I can do, other than look at *his*.

My eyes follow the papers as they make a circuit back to him, but before I can ask for one, he drops them on his desk and faces us again. "I know it sounds immature, but I want to make sure you all understand," he says, looking between us. "I'll call on someone to read a paragraph, and then when that's done I'll call on someone else. So on and so on, until we've read the whole thing."

There are only ten paragraphs or so, front and back. And there are twenty-six people in the room. There's an incredibly good chance he won't call on me.

Blinking, I try to force my heart to beat at a slower pace while coaxing my insides to stop doing their best impression of an origami swan. It'll be *fine*.

"Miss Noble, right?" My head jerks up as Professor Belker squints at me. "Why don't you start us off."

"I, umm." I swallow hard. "I can't." Yet again I wish the floor would open up and just *swallow* me on the spot.

"You can't?"

"No I umm…" I look wildly at Dorian, as if he's going to give me some kind of *help*. "I don't…have one."

The professor sighs heavily, disappointment on his face as he snatches a paper off his desk and hands it to me. "Next time, follow directions," he reprimands, and I'm sure my cheeks are burning red at his words. "Now could you *please* read the first paragraph for us? Unless there's some other kind of problem here?"

I shake my head and start reading, stammering over the words. Every time I make a mistake I can feel myself getting more and more flustered, and when the paragraph is finally over, I let out a relieved, soft sigh.

I hate Dorian Wakefield.

"Mr. Wakefield? Why don't you keep it going for us?"

Dorian flashes a brilliant smile towards the professor and does as he's told, a direct contrast to my stammering, stuttering mess of a read with his smooth, easy voice that never trips up on anything.

After class ends, Dorian is out of his seat before me. He doesn't even *look* at me as he leaves, just brushes past my seat while I sit there and seethe, watching him go say a few words to Professor Belker before he makes his way to the doors at the top of the room. We'd been told to pick a partner before next class, should we want one, but that's not something I need to worry about since I have no desire for a partner in this. I *like* doing projects alone.

Just as I like it when teachers like me, instead of thinking that I'm an idiot. So far, Belker probably thinks I don't give a damn about this class, which couldn't be further from the truth.

With a sigh I get to my feet, sliding my iPad into my backpack before shouldering it and trudging to the center of the room where our professor gets his papers together and prepares to leave. "Professor?" I call, my voice shier than I intend it to be. I want to apologize, and I don't want him to be mad or think badly of me. It wouldn't look good for my scholarship, should that be the case.

He looks up and adjusts his glasses, looking me over with a creased brow before nodding and setting down his bag. "Miss Noble," he nods. "I hope you're feeling all right. You seemed to be struggling earlier."

"Oh, yeah. I am so sorry about that," I say, trying to keep my tone apologetic. "There was a miscommunication between Dorian and me. I meant to get a paper and it's totally my fault I didn't. I'm so sorry." I offer him a soft smile, trying to look as remorseful over the stupid error as I feel. Though in reality, the error isn't *mine*.

"That's all right." He flaps a hand at me. "I figured it had to be something like that, judging by your academic record. You know, I might say you're the most deserving of that scholarship as I've seen in a while. Though I suppose I might not be able to convince you to pick up an astronomy minor." He chuckles and my smile relaxes. I sigh out a breath.

"Maybe," I reply, just as lighthearted. I'm so happy he doesn't find what happened something to stay worked up about. In my opinion, it's a victory for me, and not one for Dorian.

Take that, asshole. Part of me wishes he was still here to witness how his plan didn't work. Unless it really was just to embarrass me.

"I'm surprised to hear that you'll be working with Dorian on your projects this semester," Professor Belker goes on, and the smile falls from my face instantly. My stomach tightens and I look at him, nonplussed and no idea what to say.

"...What?" I ask politely, fingers tightening on the strap of my bag.

"Don't worry, I've already made a note of it. Mr. Wakefield told me before he left. He said you'd asked for his help in getting settled here at Winter Grove. I know he's not the most well-liked around here, but I think you've made a good decision in having him be your, oh, mentor of sorts, I suppose. Things can be difficult when you don't share the same background as most of the students here."

He goes on, rambling about Dorian's great qualities, but I'm too busy staring at him and hoping that my brain is now unable to process sound at all and I'm hearing things.

Finally I realize he's staring at me, concerned, and I try to smile again. "Yes," I say finally. I can't just stand here and deny Dorian's words, can I?

Not when it's clear Belker really likes him.

"Yeah," I agree finally, nodding again. "It was so great of him to offer. Really, I'm incredibly grateful to him for...everything he's helped me with so far. And I'm happy to know he's going to, umm, help me for the rest of the semester."

9

I release the arrow and let out a breath, watching it sink into the target near the middle, yet slightly to the side. The migraine I'd thought was gone is back to teasing at my temples, promising me that I'm to going to enjoy things when it does hit, but I ignore it in favor of nocking another arrow and aiming down its length. I take a breath and let it out, holding the pose for a few seconds longer than usual before I let it go and the arrow whistles through the air.

This time, it hits the center of the target and I let out a sigh of relief and tilt my head back. It's rare that things are bad enough for me to be off my game at archery, but not impossible. I shouldn't be shocked, with how worked up I am at Dorian's *shit* and the migraine that's going to take me by storm soon.

But that doesn't mean I have to be happy with it.

I stomp to the target and grab my arrows, taking more time than I need to, but when I look back towards my spot at the end of the line, I see that Eden is there, leaning against the fence closest to where I've been shooting from and eyeing me with something like amusement clear on her face. Beside her leans a red-haired, fair-skinned girl who watches me as well, though her green eyes are a lot less amused and a lot more curious than her companion's.

"I thought I was being set up when I heard," she says, as if we've been having a conversation and she'd just paused in the middle of it. I glance at them both and re-count my arrows, sliding my fingers through the feathers as I do, just out of habit. "But I guess he's not joking." She looks me over and sniffs derisively, like I've done something wrong.

"Do I know you?" I ask, glancing at Eden in case she can give me any clues as to who her friend is. I'm pretty sure Eden and I aren't *friends*, exactly. But still. At least I know her *name*.

"I'm Cecily," the girl replies, draping over the fence and watching me lazily. "We haven't met. And I don't think we have any classes together, but I doubted we would. I don't like astronomy, and I'm a business major like Dorian."

Like Dorian.

The words put me on guard instantly. Is she a friend of his? Maybe *her* dad works for his too, like everyone else's seems to. I sigh and she catches the sound, her eyes narrowing slightly. "You don't like him. I suppose I wouldn't either if I were you, but I would've worked harder not to piss him off."

"I didn't mean to," I snap, hand tightening on the fiberglass of the bow. "I didn't even really *do* anything."

"I agree."

Even Eden looks at her with raised brows, as if she's surprised by the answer. "You do?" the brunette asks a second later, confirming my suspicions of her reaction. "But you heard what she did."

"And I know Rhett," Cecily points out. "He's pushy. Especially with omegas he thinks he can make submit." She offers me a smile that's as caring as it is cruel. "If I knew you, I would've let you use my name. He would've left you alone, and I wouldn't be spending my free time looking for ways to make you squirm or cry."

"That's so unsettling. And I doubt he's spending *all* his free time obsessed with me," I point out, giving up on the idea of shooting again while they're standing here. They make me nervous. Especially both of them together.

Cecily shrugs, her red hair falling back over her shoulders from the movement. "Not the time he spends fucking Foster, I guess."

That's way more than I need to know, and I close my eyes against the unbidden, unwelcome, yet still sexy image. It's none of my business who Dorian fucks, or how great Foster probably looks *getting* fucked.

"I don't see why he's so *mad*," I say, walking forward to decrease the space between us. Eden's earthy scent hits me first, though Cecily's floral, gentler scent is close behind. I can smell the alpha on her, and it's nothing like the gentle presence of Adrian. "I didn't think it was that big of a deal."

Cecily's cold smile widens. "It wouldn't have been to me, little omega." When she calls me that, the words slide over me in an unpleasant way, like cold rain, and I offer her a smile in return.

"Mercy Noble," I introduce, hoping that she'll never call me *little omega* ever again in my lifetime. "Any idea on how I can get him *less* mad at me? If that's possible?"

"Give in?" Cecily suggests. "Find someone that upsets him more? Hmm. If you give him what he wants enough, he'll get bored eventually. He likes to work for his amusement." I hate the way she makes it sound. Worse, I hate that his current *amusement* is making my life hell. "He's usually willing to bargain, though. He gets it from his dad. Did he not give you some kind of out for him to leave you alone?"

I can feel the way my face reddens, and I grit my teeth in frustration. "No," I say flatly. "Not a real one."

Her eyes sharpen curiously. "There's a fake one?" she prods, and I know I shouldn't have said *anything* to her about it. I should've just shrugged, looked dumb, and hoped she'd go away.

"He told me..." I take a deep breath, and try not to let my embarrassment get the better of me. "He told me I could *beg* and he'd forgive me. That if I begged him on my knees, then he wouldn't be mad." There was obviously a lot more to what he'd said, but I definitely don't feel like I need to go into that.

"You should've begged." Her words are simple, but her smile isn't particularly friendly. "It would've sucked in the moment, but it would've gotten you out of this in the long run. Embarrassing you in front of Becker is child's play. He could hurt you, Mercy."

I hate the way her words sound too ominous for me to ignore.

So I shrug one shoulder, noticing that practice is wrapping up. "I don't beg," I tell her, trying to sound as unworried as I *don't* feel. If anything, surely I can create some kind of front for her to believe. "And I'm not afraid of him. I just don't like him, or being embarrassed."

Cecily tilts her head to the side, studying me. "I guess I see it," she says finally.

"See what?" Both Eden and I ask, though her question is much sharper than mine.

"Why he's obsessed. Just be careful with how far you're willing to let your pride take you. I can promise you. Dorian will take his obsession further." She pushes off the rail with a brighter grin. "Are you hungry?" she asks Eden, who frowns at her words.

"I guess," the dark-haired beta shrugs. "If that's what you want to do."

"Do you want to come?" The invite is unexpected, and when I look into the redhead's face, I know immediately that I don't want to go. She makes me nervous. She's too nice, with an edge of sincerity that isn't real.

She reminds me of Dorian in the worst way possible, though I suppose that's to be expected.

"No, that's okay. I have to finish up and I have homework," I lie, with a quick, appreciative smile. "It was nice meeting you, though."

She walks away without a word, though when Eden hesitates, my eyes flick to hers.

"She's not your friend," Eden promises quietly. "So don't think for a moment that she is." With that she turns as well, leaving me with my bow near the fence as she catches up to Cecily with long strides and disappears around the corner of the shed.

I don't know how I let Briella convince me to go to a party.

My hands are tight around the plastic cup of beer that I've only taken a sip of, and the other is wrapped around my stomach like I'm about to lose my insides. Or at the very least, like I might *vomit*.

Taking a deep breath, I look down at the pale amber liquid in the cup and set it down. There's no drinking it for me. I don't want to get drunk, and I don't particularly enjoy the taste of it. Not at all. Briella is nowhere to be seen, though I'm sure I saw Zara somewhere around here, so that's not really surprising.

I just wish she hadn't left me alone. There's no one else here that I know, and now that I'm huddled up in a corner, trying my best to be unnoticed, I realize how much I want to go back to my dorm room.

Without anyone to make this less terrifying, it's no fun whatsoever. The noise levels cause everything to sound like a mess in my ears, and I'm pretty sure a volcano could be erupting and I wouldn't be able to tell. I can't hear voices, only *noise* and music that pounds against my ears like a stray drummer using them as instruments.

I should've known it would be like this. I just hadn't expected Briella to ditch me to *moon* over Zara. Besides, when she'd told me she'd 'be right back' I'd expected that to mean she'd be gone for maybe 10 minutes. Not 15, or 17, or however long I've been standing here doing my best impression of a column.

The frat house is the first one I've ever been in, though it's not exactly an accomplishment I was looking to achieve. It's nice, I guess. Though with beer cups and trash littering the floor, it's not really that impressive now with the lights low. It just looks...sketchy.

Yeah, that's what I'm going with. This frat house is undeniably shady and sketchy.

I blink, looking around the room, and then pause. My eyes do another sweep, landing on three familiar shapes that I don't enjoy seeing.

But, thankfully, none of them appear to have seen *me* just yet. It gives me enough time so that I can slip away, and in my mind I have a plan to go out through the kitchen, to the back yard that I'd been to when I got here, and back to campus one way or another. If Briella wants to hang out here and 'chat' with Zara? Great. Good for her. But I'm going *home*.

That is, until I turn and see that two guys are blocking my path, both of them giving me what they might consider friendly grins.

I, in fact, do not agree. I sigh and rock back on my heels,

considering throwing my beer in their faces just so I can walk away.

Though with my luck, they own the continent of North America or something and if I do, they'll place a thousand year blood curse on me. I can't handle more than one pack being mad at me at once, so I try for a friendly, inoffensive smile as I look back at them.

I don't think I succeed, though.

"We have biology together," the blonde on the left says, taking a step closer to me. "I'm Andy." I don't like him. I don't *know* him, to be fair. But I'm not in a position to think positively of anyone right now since I'm trying to leave.

"Oh, yeah, umm..." I can barely hear him, even though he talks loudly over the crowd. Even turning my right ear towards him a little, it's still hard to catch what he says.

And it doesn't help that he almost seems to barely move his mouth when he talks.

"I have to go," I tell them both, hoping I'm not shouting. "It was nice meeting you here." I flash them another smile and try to walk past them, only for Andy's friend to reach out and grip my arm tight enough that I have no choice but to come to a halt.

"Don't you want to talk? We could hang out. It's a *party*, and..." The rest of his words are inaudible, so I try to turn and look at his mouth instead. My own lips part, and I'm about to ask him to repeat himself so that I can try and *see* what he says, when all of a sudden he kisses me.

It's *awful*. His scent, a mix of weeds and freshly mown grass, is overpowering as he tries to coax my lips open. My stomach twists, and I jerk my arm free just as I tip my cup of beer over on his shirt, causing him to take a surprised step back and curse.

"What is *wrong with you?*" I spit, wiping my forearm across my mouth like he's infectious. "I never wanted–"

He says something that I can't hear, and I'm too aggravated to read his lips. With my heart pounding in my ears and the music up too loud, I can't hear *anything* either of them are saying. Anxiety drives a spike through my chest and I step back, trying to get control of myself. Andy recoils, catching my fear-scent in his nose most likely, but I'm too overwhelmed to notice.

The only thing I *do* see as I wheel around and stride towards the kitchen, Is Dorian's face and the concern that's plain on it as he looks at me.

Which is how I know I'm clearly hallucinating, since Dorian Wakefield has no concern for *me*. If anything, he'd be cheering on these two, I'm sure, and doing whatever he could to make things worse.

God, I just need to get out of here. My hands shake as I slam the empty cup down on the counter, my ears pounding from the noise level in here. This had been such a bad idea, and I can feel the migraine at my temples that I'm sure is going to make the rest of my night dreadful.

I shove at the back door, opening it up into the yard that's emptied out since we got here. That's *fine*. I'd rather that no one is here anyway, and as I make my way around the bushes and onto the sidewalk that'll take me back to a main road so I can wait for a bus, call a cab, or fucking *walk* back to campus, I suddenly slip.

With a gasp I go down onto the cement, cracking my hands against it and yelping in surprise and pain. Something warm and wet sinks into my leggings, and I scramble for my phone in my pocket so that I can figure out what in the hell made me slip and what's on my hands.

When I find it and turn on the light, I immediately wish I

hadn't. The liquid on my hands is dark, and smeared into my phone from my fingers. At first, I think it's oil.

Until the light catches it and I realize it isn't black at all.

It's red like blood.

My hands tremble as I move the phone around, finding the puddle on the cement that I'm *sitting in* and moving the small, barely effective light to the bushes. For a moment the only thing I see is leaves...until something pale catches the flashlight. I move the light along it, gritting my teeth together until at last the pale shape takes form.

It's an arm.

And deeper in the bushes, staring out at me like he's just as surprised as I am, is a man's body.

10

I know that I'm screaming, but the sound in my ears seems distant. Like it's someone else screaming in another room, instead of *me*.

Fingers grip my upper arms, digging in hard enough to almost bruise and yanking me backward, out of the pool of blood. Looking up, I find *August* standing there, worry and concern plain on his features.

It does nothing for my panic, or my racing heart, though some part of me that's disconnected from the dead body and the blood notes that there's a small scar on his upper lip, slightly pulling his mouth up on that side. Though I'd never notice if I wasn't this close to him. I suck in a breath, probably to scream again, and the scent of lavender and storms overwhelms me, distracting me for an instant so that I can catch my breath. He looks from the body to me, lips parting, just as a shape barrels into him and knocks him away from me, nearly making me fall over again.

August stumbles and turns, a snarl on his lips as Zara strides towards him. "What the fuck are you doing?" she sneers, as Bri bolts to my side. She kneels beside me, only to pause as she sees my blood covered hands and phone. "It's not enough that you bully her during the week? You have to–"

"Zara!" Briella's voice is full of panic, and shakes when her eyes find the body in the bushes. "Zara there's–holy *shit* there's a body!"

Both Zara and August whirl around again, but when August tries to take a step back towards us, Zara blocks his path and shoves him *hard*. "No," she spits, anger in every line of her body. "Fuck off, August."

Finally he turns to look at her, the expression on his face unfriendly at best. At worse? He looks like he wants to hurt her. But instead August raises his hands in surrender, the light illuminating smears of blood on his palms.

"Whatever," he sneers. "But if you cared about her so much, you wouldn't have left her in there to get cornered by Andy." Before either of them can reply he wheels around and leaves, shoving his hands in his pockets with one last glance at the dead body in the bushes.

The one that I'm still staring at, my heart pounding in my chest. "I need to get up," I mumble, feeling nauseous. My hands still shake, and as I stumble to my feet, I drop my phone onto the cement of the sidewalk with a wince.

Briella helps me, though tries her hardest not to get blood on her skin as I reach down and pick up my phone that's thankfully still in one piece.

"That's a dead body," she murmurs again, as Zara steps forward to shine her own light on it.

"Yep," I agree, swallowing back the bile in my throat. "That is definitely....*yep*." I don't know what else to say, though I suck in a deep breath and close my eyes hard for a second to try to catch my breath. "We have to call the cops," I state, more stability in my voice than I feel.

Zara sighs, gesturing to her phone that's on speaker, and I see that she's already dialed 911. Well, at least one of us is able to think clearly. With blood on my clothes and smeared into my skin, that person sure as hell isn't me.

Her words are rushed as she tells them where we are, and it feels like only a few seconds before lights are flickering in my peripheral vision and sirens come blaring up the street.

"I want to go to bed," I murmur, folding my arms and shivering in the cool night air. I hadn't worn a jacket, and now I'm really regretting it.

"I don't think that's going to happen for a while," Zara replies, bumping my shoulder comfortingly with hers. "But hey, we'll stay as long as you need us. Right Bri?" My roommate nods her head in enthusiastic agreement. "And maybe *Dragonfly China* will still be open by the time they let us all go."

"You really think so?"

"On a Sunday? No. Not at all."

As my head pounds and my eyes burn at the hint of any kind of light, I can't help but think back to my discussion with the cops.

Zara had been right, of course. By the time they *had* let us go back to campus, the sun was almost up and I'd decided then and there that I was skipping class for the day.

The cops had looked surprised, and uncertain. Like murder in the small town of Winter Grove was an impossibility, and none of them had been trained for it. A woman who smelled like gardenias had been assigned to talk to me, since I had been the one to find the body, but even though the woman was a beta and seemed pretty okay, Zara had insisted on staying.

"We'll stick together," she'd promised me, nudging my shoulder. "And then we'll go back to the dorms together. It would be shitty to just leave you here." The cop hadn't really liked her saying that, but Zara made certain they understood the three of us were a package deal.

Which, admittedly, I'd really appreciated. Especially as my headache got worse and after I'd repeated my story for the third time without it changing at all.

No, I don't know who he is.

No, I don't know how long he's been there.

Yes, I called for help the moment I found him.

By the end of things, I'd wanted to cry with how frustrated, tired, and upset I was.

A soft knock on the door pulls me from my memory, and I don't open my eyes as Bri walks in. "I brought you something," she tells me, causing me to crack my eyes just enough to see her sit down one of the dining hall cups and two napkins wrapped around food that she unearths from her jacket pockets.

"They don't have crepes today," she goes on, her voice teasing. "But I thought maybe you'd appreciate the sugar."

Sitting up feels like the hardest thing I've done all day, and makes me dizzy. My stomach twists, and when I unwrap the donut, the first thing that hits me is *nausea*.

But I really need to eat. Going so long without my medicine last night hadn't been smart, but it also hadn't really been my choice.

"I have to go to the pharmacy later today," I sigh as Bri sits down on her brightly colored bed. My own is much more muted, and above it sits my shelf of crystals that I've spent the past year collecting from live sales and random shops I find when I'm out walking. Unfortunately, if there's somewhere to buy crystals in Winter Grove, however, they're hiding from me.

"Why? What's wrong? Other than your migraine?" Briella folds her legs under her, and when I glance up at her I can't help but notice the small, half-covered mark on her neck that's evidence of just how much she and Zara are getting along.

Good for them.

"No, it's just that. But I have to jam a needle into my thigh like a zombie movie heroine fighting off impending infection once a month so that the migraines don't take over my life, and it's about time to do that." When Bri just stares at me blankly, I sigh. "Shot. I have to give myself a shot in the leg." Though, my other explanation seems like a better one to me. At least it's more interesting. Reluctantly I tear a bite out of the donut and put it in my mouth, forcing myself to eat first one, then two bites, then the whole donut. I know I'll feel better for it. The sugar will help more than I want to admit, and I haven't eaten in a *bit*.

Which, doesn't do any favors to getting over my migraine. Sometimes, though, the act of eating is just too much and I want to try and sleep it off. Not that it normally works if I haven't taken medicine and eaten before falling asleep.

Briella carries the conversation for a few minutes, though with the combination of the meds I've taken and how much my head hurts, I barely respond. This time I fall asleep *after* taking my hearing aids out, not caring that there are donut crumbs in the bed and cherry kool-aid getting warm on my dresser.

I need to get over this headache before I deal with that, or the fact that I *saw a dead body* last night.

Knocking on the door wakes me up again, though this time I'm glad to find that I feel somewhat better than I did before. I'm still achy, and my eyes still hurt, but the pain that had me here in the first place has vanished.

Though, judging by the light of the setting sun coming

through the window, it did take almost twenty hours for that to happen.

"Briella?" I murmur, sitting up, I'm still wearing my sleep shorts and a tee, with my clothes from the night before somewhere out of sight until I can sanitize them.

Which somehow reminds me, I still haven't told my mom. She'll overreact, for one. Not to mention, we haven't been on great terms for the past year and a half or so. Ever since she'd learned I intended on coming here to Winter Grove instead of any of the other schools I'd gotten full rides to.

Though, why she's disappointed that I'm at the *best school in the country* is beyond me, unless it's because I'm harder to bitch at when I'm this far away.

No more policing the food I eat, the times I take my meds, or my friends. A shame. A tragedy.

Another knock on the door pulls me to my feet and I sigh, stumbling to it and pulling it open with narrowed eyes and my hearing aids only half in.

The student outside doesn't look familiar, but she stares at me with wide eyes and holds a notebook in her hands. "I brought astronomy notes for you," she tells me, looking anywhere but at my face. "Since you, umm, couldn't come to class today." She presses her lips together like she's trying not to smile, and my eyes narrow.

"Do I know you? And whose notes are these?" I reach out for them and she hands them over gingerly, like they're more than just a notebook full of scribbles.

"No, you don't." She stifles a snicker. "Sorry. Not really, but it *is* kind of funny."

My brows jerk upwards towards my bangs. "*What's* funny?" I suddenly have a very bad feeling about these astronomy notes, and I'm not sure that I want them. I also don't think I want to know what she finds so funny, but it's too late to stop her now.

"Look, it's no big deal. Lots of freshmen don't know how to hold their alcohol and end up getting blackout at their first party. It's just...always really funny. Especially since you *cried* when Foster wouldn't kiss you."

I did...what?

I blink once, wondering if this is some kind of headache fever dream but knowing I can't be that lucky. My eyes flit from one side of the open door to the other, and suddenly the notebook in my hands seems to burn.

Is it worth telling her that's a lie?

"That's not what happened. And who even told...you...?" I trail off, closing my eyes with a sigh. "Whose notes are these? And how did you know where I live?"

"I live on this floor too." She gestures down the hallway and pushes her long blonde hair back over her shoulders. "Dorian told us, after Becker left. He said he didn't want to embarrass you, but wanted someone to take you his notes since you're partners. He went on and signed you up as that, by the way. It's really nice of him, since you went after Foster."

"I didn't–I would *literally never–*" Bile burns at my throat as the girl tries to hide another laugh.

"Whatever. Everyone fucks up. Just...not normally so publicly and with Dorian's pack. Maybe find an alpha next time to help you not be so desperate, huh?" She gives me a half-sympathetic, half-amused smile and walks away, not looking over her shoulder as I step back and slam the door in my own face.

I drop the notebook on my desk and sneer at it, grabbing my longer hair in my fingers and tugging on my scalp until it burns. What the fuck is *wrong* with him? I didn't do anything, and it isn't my fault he's too much of an asshole to accept my apology for something I shouldn't have to apologize for in the first place.

Tears burn at my eyes and I squeeze them closed, unwilling to start crying. Not only would it be a victory for fucking *Dorian*, crying always makes my headaches worse. I'm not willing to risk it now.

Absently I walk back to my desk and flip open the notebook, half-wondering if there are actually notes worth copying in here.

Unsurprisingly, there aren't. The notebook looks old, like it's been used for another class, and there are maybe half the pages remaining. All of them are blank it looks like, except the front page, which has his neat cursive on it.

You make this too easy, little omega.

But you could still beg.

I tear out the page and shred it summarily, closing my eyes again and trying not to cry as I try and fail to think of ways to get him to leave me the fuck alone and for everyone to stop thinking that I want anything to do with Dorian, Foster, or August.

11

"Have you been to *Video Valhalla* yet?" Adrian packs as he talks, though my eye is still on August to my left. Though our professor had looked at me multiple times to answer one of his many, many questions, I hadn't. Not for lack of knowing the answers, though.

But because August makes me nervous, and my head still aches. The migraine has been gone since last night, sure. But that doesn't mean everything else is gone. Luckily, a box with my injector full of migraine prevention medicine sits in my backpack, along with a new bottle of ibuprofen and a box of tablets that should also help with my migraines not being as bad as they could.

"What's *Video Valhalla*?" I ask, as August breezes out the door without a look in my direction. He hasn't looked in my direction all class, which is great. And I would know, since my eyes feel magnetized to him just in case.

"It's a store in town that has a lot of old movies. I remember you mentioned liking old horror movies the other day, so I figured it was something you'd like." He catches sight of the black, scratched notebook that half falls out of my bag as I shovel my iPad and book into it, and snorts. "I thought you were against paper notebooks. That one certainly looks well used."

"Hmm?" I blink, looking down at it, and grimace. "Yeah, it's…" *Not mine* is what I should say, but I shake my head. "I don't know. I'm sentimental sometimes." I don't know why I'm carrying it around, though I definitely would love to beat Dorian in the face with it. "Anyway. *Video Valhalla*? I'll have to check it out. I *do* love old horror movies. Though, if everything they have is literally on *video*, I doubt I'll be able to watch any of it." I trade a grin with him as my phone rings, and answer it as I'm walking out the door, not bothering to look at who it is.

"Hello?" I ask, happy that class is over for the day.

"*I thought you'd decided to have no contact with me since you got into your fancy new school.*" My mother's voice is sour and unfriendly, causing me to close my eyes and sigh.

"No, Mom. It's not that. I've just been…" Getting bullied. Finding a dead body. *Busy*. "Really busy with schoolwork. Like, it's insane how much work they give us here, actually." I put a chuckle into my voice, though I'm not sure she believes it.

"*You could've just gone to school around here.*" She's told me this so many times that I'm sure I can repeat the rest of her speech word for word. Not that I have any desire to. "*You wouldn't be miserable, or so far away from me. Though, I suppose that's what you wanted.*" Yeah Mom, exactly what I wanted.

Though, to be fair, it is somewhat of a bonus. Ever since Dad died, she's been more miserable than any woman really has a right to be. Especially when she turned most of that bad energy on me, trying to make me into the *perfect* omega.

Which is absolutely not a philosophy I subscribe to. I'm my own person. With or without a pack. And unlike her, I'm not under the impression I need a *pack* to get me anywhere.

Besides, the way my mom tells it, all I should have to do is let any alpha pack fuck me until they decide to keep me, and I'll be set for life. But in reality, I'd like to be more than a glorified fuck toy.

"How's your eating going?" Of course she'd go there next. It's so very like her that I can't help the loud sigh that I know she hears. *"I know, I know. You don't like when I say it. But if you aren't careful, you'll gain weight like you did when you were little. And being 'chubby' as an adult isn't cute like it is when you're a kid."* She laughs at the unfunny joke, but it just makes a stab of hurt go through me, and brings up the thoughts she'd worked hard to instill in me back to the surface.

That I'm ugly. That I'm fat. That I'm *not enough*.

"I'm in between classes, Mom," I say, trying my best to sound amicable. "Can I call you back another time?"

"I'm leaving for the lake with Declan tonight," she informs me, almost reproachfully. *"Didn't I tell you that?"*

"Oh. Umm. Maybe?" I have no fucking clue if she did or not. "Text me when you get back. I know your service is shit at the lake." I secretly hate that she's going there with her new boyfriend.

That was *our* place. Back when we were a happy family, and Dad was still alive. Back when Mom wasn't so problematic, and she and I had a good relationship.

But things are different now, and I suppose I should get used to her going there with someone else. Taking a deep breath, I add, "Tell me how the campground is? I miss the cabins."

"I'll let you know," my mother assures me, with something like affection in her voice. *"Good luck on your homework, okay? I love you."*

Sometimes, I'm not so sure if she really feels the love for me that she swears by. "Love you too, Mom," I tell her, and hang up before she can do the same.

The side effect of talking to my mother is that any desire I'd had for food is suddenly gone. I *want* to eat, sure, but her words echoing in my head have my appetite sliding off into a dark corner to be ashamed of itself. I could work out, though? Not that I enjoy working out in any capacity, but if I do then I'll maybe feel better about everything. Food and my mother included.

Besides, it isn't like this day can get much worse after the week I've had so far with...well, everything.

The secondary campus pool is *glassed* in. Which I did not think was possible outside of a millionaire's vacation house. Clear, clean glass arcs above the shifting water, and I stare at it for a few moments with my hand hooked in the strap of my bag. After a quick stop by my dorm, I'd decided to just exchange my ipad for my swimsuit and bring everything else with me for a quick swim. I'd invited Briella as well, but she'd very directly informed me that she was not about to do laps for 25 minutes before going to dinner, but she *would* meet me at the dining hall.

Which was good enough for me.

I shake my head at the pool before heading towards the locker rooms, glad that there's no one else here right now. It isn't that I have an issue with swimming when other people are around. Not really. Though, it does make me nervous sometimes when I feel like *I'm* the one being judged or looked at, but...

Noise like a locker being slammed makes me jump, and I nearly gasp as the sound happens again. Looking up, I find that I'm just outside of the boy's locker room, and it sounds like someone's beating one of the lockers with a backpack, or a beef shank.

Realistically, probably a backpack.

It's none of my business. Especially since if I tilt my head just right, I can see in the zig-zag hall and slightly into the boy's locker room, which is *definitely* none of my business, since I am not a guy.

Except, movement catches my eye when I do it, and a body clad only in swim trunks is *slammed* once more into the locker, while the person responsible lunges forward to cover the taller body with their own and lets out a *growl*.

I can't not look. Not when both of their hands are on each other, and they're making lewd noises loud enough for my hearing aids to pick up. My eyes slide up along with the shorter boy's hands, going up over his partner's chest, up his shoulders and–

My brain short circuits when I catch sight of the face of the boy being kissed against the lockers.

It's *August*.

Fucking *August* is about to get railed against the lockers, and when I cock my head forward, I'm able to see that it's *Foster* doing the railing.

Holy shit.

I need to leave.

Their motions slow the second I move, and I pray I'm quick enough to dart into the girl's locker room. For safety, I bolt into one of the stalls and lock the door, standing in front of the toilet as I listen for movement.

Not that I can hear a damn thing outside of the sounds of the pipes in the walls that vibrate with the insulation around them. Softly I take a breath, then let it out. I take another one, still listening, and it's not until I've let out a fifth breath that I ease out of the locked stall, my heart pounding in my chest as I go over what I'd seen in my mind.

Over, and over, and over.

Foster's hands. August's open-mouthed kisses against his jaw. The *looks* on both their faces.

I can't get any of it to stay out of my brain as I change into my swimsuit. While it's nothing special, I'm sure, to rich kid standards, it is one of my favorite I've ever owned. To compound that, I'm happier with myself than I *ever* was growing up, now that my mom isn't here to make me feel like crap every time I put a cookie in my mouth.

The swimsuit itself is two-piece, though the bottom looks more like boyshorts than a bikini. The top has thicker straps, and crisscrosses at my back. They match, both pieces being black with lime-green marbling on them that I couldn't pass up when I'd seen it at the store, and it's the only swimsuit I brought. Hell, it's the only one I care about owning, even though I have two others at home that I don't care for even half as much.

But that could be because whenever my mom saw me in them, she'd never had many nice things to say. The good thing about *this* swimsuit is that she'd never seen me in it.

I check once more, making sure they aren't in the pool area and hover by the door to the boy's locker room. Glancing back at my bag, I consider putting it in a locker or somewhere else, but I'm not going to be here long and I can't imagine why anyone would steal anything here. Especially anything of mine. So I leave it, letting it sit on the bench as I toe off my shoes and leave them by the wall next to the locker room. My medicine is still inside it, and I swear to myself that after I swim I *will* get in touch with my inner zombie movie heroine fighting off the impending infection and actually inject myself. Not to mention, my hearing aids are in it too, in the little case that I keep them in whenever I need to take them out and I'm not home.

Without them, everything is much quieter. Sound is muffled, if audible at all, and the echoing noises I know must exist in the room are simply...gone. At this point, someone really would have to scream for me to get my attention, or set off a bunch of fireworks near me so that I turn around.

But I don't hate it. In fact, I enjoy the break. Things sometimes feel less crowded in my head without my hearing aids, and this is one of those times. Without sound, I can simply just exist with myself, swimming laps around a pool encased under glass.

Taking a break, I glance at the clock and see that enough time has gone by that I won't feel bad about myself for *eating*. Not that I should anyway, but sometimes my inner voices that sound too much like Mom win out, and it takes giving in and working out like this before I can really eat again. That, or I'll just feel miserable and go days without having something I actually *like* for a meal. Today, I don't intend to repeat the process.

Still in the pool I turn, and immediately freeze in the water.

Foster stands at the edge of the pool, my backpack dangling from his hand. My heart speeds up in my chest at the victorious, arrogant grin plastered on his features, and I belatedly take in his wet hair and the way his tee is stuck to his chest.

Had he waited around for me to get in the pool, just so he could get my backpack?

I realize too late that he's saying something and backing away, still grinning, and I blink while trying to figure out what in the world he's saying to me.

"Wait!" I call, scrambling to that side of the pool and grabbing onto the lip of it. "Wait, *Foster!* I can't hear you–I can't fucking *hear!*" My heart pounds in my chest as my slick hands try to find purchase on the edge of the pool. He has my medicine, my phone, and my hearing aids. I can't afford more of *any* of them, and I want to cry.

What if he does something with them? What if he comes back and decides to dunk them in the pool?

Finally I make it out, gracelessly climbing up from the pool though the moment I try to take off after him I slip on the wet tile and hit the floor hard enough that I cry out as my knees throb in time with my panicked heartbeat.

Shoes. I need my shoes if I'm going to chase after him. Quickly I find and pull them on, slightly grateful that he hadn't taken those too, before taking off at a dead run down the hallway as I look for him.

The gym complex is huge. He could be anywhere. Literally anywhere. Still, I run down the hallways, tears burning at my eyes as I pray to whatever God is listening that he won't do anything to my backpack. Muffled sound hits my ears, and I hate myself for not putting my backpack in a locker, or somewhere that it would've been hidden. Something rings in my ears, but I brush it off. If someone is questioning why I'm running through the gym complex, they can wait. They can absolutely wait until–

A hand grabs my arm, pulling me around *hard*. I gasp and lose my balance, ending up on my ass on the tile floor and staring up into *Dorian's* face.

But more importantly than the look on his face, is the fact that he has my backpack in his hands.

He kneels down slowly in front of me, not bothering to say anything, and sets my backpack in my lap almost gingerly. It's probably the nicest thing he's ever done, but at the moment I couldn't care less. Without hesitating I dive into it, pulling out the small case with my hearing aids and fumbling to get them back into my ears. My hands slip, wet and shaking, and I feel like I'm going to *cry* by the time they're both finally hooked over my ears and in place.

Only then do I look back up at Dorian, eyes narrowed.

"What is *wrong with you?*" I sneer, diving back into my backpack and pulling out all of my medicine to make sure that it's dry and that I'm not missing anything. He reaches out, as if to grab the box for my injector, but I snatch everything back and throw it back into my bag. My eyes burn with tears and chlorine, but this time I don't bother trying not to cry as relief and terror wars in my chest. "Why would you do that?! I can't afford–" I swallow the words, knowing he won't care, but Dorian just fucking *watches* me.

"He didn't know," he says finally, tone even. "He didn't even think about it. He didn't know about your medicine, and didn't think about your hearing aids being off while you were in the pool."

"That's not a fucking *apology*," I sneer, too angry to be afraid of anything he might say.

"I know. I'm not giving you one." He doesn't move to get up, and I'm sure to anyone else it would just appear like we're having a conversation in the middle of the hallway.

Wordlessly I reach into my backpack, trying to ignore his scent as my trembling hand pulls out his stupid notebook so I can slam it against his chest. The action causes him to fall back on his heels, and his brow raises as he catches the notebook before it can fall. "Careful, little *omega*," he warns. "While I'm willing to admit we made a mistake taking your backpack, that doesn't mean I forgive you–"

"I didn't do anything wrong!" I want to punch him. I want to *hit him* in his stupid fucking face, but I have a feeling that he won't only catch it, he'll make me regret it almost instantly. "I didn't do *anything*–"

"We've had this discussion before," he reminds me mildly,

getting to his feet and offering me a hand up. I don't take it. Instead I knock it to the side, aware of the look on his face that morphs from lingering concern to derision and arrogance. God, I hate him so fucking much it's unreal.

"I hate you," I whisper, hopefully too quietly for him to hear.

Apparently not. He swoops down, hand going forward so he can grip my chin and tilt my face up to his. "Tragic," he purrs, not looking at all put out. "But just for that, I don't think I'll accept you begging anymore. I'll only accept full and total surrender, little omega."

I have a name, not that he seems to want to use it.

I stare at him, unwilling to look away, as his sweet yet musky scent and the touch of *alpha* surrounds me. My hands tighten on my backpack, and it's too many seconds by the time he straightens with a sigh. "They won't take your stuff again," he says, already walking away. "But that's the only *nice* thing you'll get from me this year."

"I don't want *anything* from you," I sneer, getting to my feet. "I've never wanted anything from you! I wish I'd never met you, and I wish I never knew your name! Rhett's pack would've been miles better than you, and I regret ever knowing who you *are*."

He stops, turns, and puts a hand over his heart with a mock-grimace on his face. "Ouch," he murmurs. "Sticks and stones, sweetheart. Sticks and stones."

"I hope you fall out of a helicopter into the Pacific ocean to get eaten by sharks," I respond with a snarl, and when I hear the laugh from behind me, I whirl around just in time to see Foster duck away from the door, giving me a small wave before walking away with August at his heels.

I've never hated three people more in my entire life.

12

"We're...dating now." Briella looks away, nervousness in every line of her body as she stares down at her hands. "I've never dated a girl before. And she's not an alpha."

I blink twice, the anger and humiliation from the pool still draining out of me as my hair dries. I sit on my own bed, cross-legged, my hands draped over my knees. I'd told her as little as possible about the pool, and now I'm holding the injector in one hand, rolling it over my fingers. I *hate* giving myself shots in my thigh, but it absolutely can't be put off anymore. Especially if I have to worry about my stuff being stolen just to humiliate me.

Though of course, Dorian had *said* they wouldn't take my stuff anymore. Not that I believe that. Not with how they are. He's lying to me, obviously, and it means I'll have to be more careful with my things. Already I suppose I should count myself incredibly lucky that he'd seen fit to give it back at all.

"That's really great." I uncap the injector as I look up at her, trying to keep the slight tremor out of my voice. My stomach twists and does a little flip, but I push it away. I hate needles. I hate doing this, and it makes it worse somehow that I'm inflicting this on *myself*. "I think you guys are a really sweet couple, actually."

Taking a deep breath, I press the injector against my thigh and hit the button on the top, wincing at the *click* of the plunger and the sting of the needle as it goes into my thigh. My stomach tightens. This is the worst part, though not the most painful. When it clicks again I pull it away, hating that even after months of doing this, my hand still trembles.

Briella watches me, looking mildly horrified. "That seems painful," she observes, as I rub my leg to disperse the medicine and wince. *This* is the most painful part. The sting of the medication under my skin will throb for a few minutes yet, and if I'm unlucky it'll form a knot and I'll be sorry tomorrow. To avoid that I rub a little harder, gritting my teeth against the discomfort.

"It's not my favorite time of the month," I admit begrudgingly. "But it helps with my migraines, so I can't really say I don't appreciate it." But that doesn't mean I like it. Not to mention, it would be easier if I had someone here to help me with the injection. Sure, I can do it. Obviously. And it isn't difficult. But I always hesitate as long as possible, my nerves getting the better of me every single time. "And who cares if she's not an alpha? That's so nineteen fifties to think we need an alpha or a *pack*." I scrunch my nose up in distaste. The conversation does remind me that I'm three weeks out from my heat, and my suppressants are one medicine that I will not be late on. Though they're pills, rather than a shot. But even if it were an injection, I'd force myself to do it on time one way or another.

I've only gone through one heat in my life, and that's enough for me. At least until I figure out what I'm doing and who I want to do it with. And so far, no one here at Winter Grove fits the bill. Not even for something casual.

"It's just not how I was raised," Briella goes on, scratching at the blanket beside her leg. "Anyway. Do you want to do something tonight? Other than dinner, weird cartoons, and passing out at four am?"

"Have you ever heard of *Video Valhalla*?" I ask, unable to help being curious and a little bit interested about the store. "A friend of mine, Adrian, says that they have a lot of classic movies. And I really like classic movies."

"I've heard of it," Bri admits, looking thoughtful. "My cousin who went here went all the time. I'm not sure exactly where it's at, but that's what GPS apps are for, right?"

"You want to go?" I perk up, finally done rubbing my leg. "I didn't think you'd be into it. But you *really* want to go?" She nods and gets to her feet, stretching as she hunts for her shoes and giving me time to figure out where exactly we're going.

As luck would have it, *Video Valhalla* is right next to the *Winter Grove Tea Shop*. I stare in the window, ogling the fresh bread, small gifts, and extensive array of teas. Unfortunately for us, the tea shop is only open until three or so, and only open Thursday through Sunday. It seems weird to me, but Bri assures me it's a *thing* and that the tea shop has been open for almost fifty years.

Good for them, I suppose. Apparently, their weird hours are working for them.

I push open the glass door of the video shop, mouth slightly open as I take a breath and stare at the wooden shelves that march down the shop, creating three different aisles. At the back is a wall of video games and memorabilia, and I'm happy to see that, while *Video Valhalla* lives up to its name with videotapes, it also has quite the selection of DVDs on the shelves.

"I don't like scary movies," Bri informs me, giving me a quick, apologetic grin. "But I like old romance movies?" She gestures to another part of the store, and I nod enthusiastically. "So I'll be over there. Try not to throw *every* movie in your backpack, okay?" We walk past the sensors in the front of the store, which are surprisingly high-tech for the vintage feel of this place. But good for them, though I wonder if they actually have that much of a theft problem on *old movies*. Not that anyone has anything to worry about, since it's certainly not my intention to use my backpack as more than storage for after we've bought the movies we want.

A woman behind the counter smiles, looking over both of us with interest for a moment before going back to her magazine. "Everything's thirty percent off," she tells us in a hoarse smoker's tone. "And buy four, get the fifth free."

"Oh?" Suddenly it looks like I'll be heavily expanding my DVD collection. Sure, it's a little outdated since anything can be streamed for the most part. But there's something about having a shelf of my favorite movies on display that I can't help but want more than anything in this moment, though I'm sure I've never really cared about it before.

I leave Bri, going to the horror movie section to browse. There isn't anything new there, which is to be expected, but when I come across the entire *Texas Chainsaw Massacre* collection on DVD in pristine boxes that are wrapped in plastic, my heart melts a little. Those, plus a collection of *Scream* DVDs, would be better than any other kind of decoration that I could ever buy with all the money in the world.

I need them.

"I would've thought you were into, I don't know, rom-coms." The drawling, lazy voice makes me tense, my fingers only inches from grabbing the movies I want to buy. It takes my brain a moment to catch up, but when the tropical, coconut scent invades my nostrils, I let out a breath and clench my jaw hard.

"Come to take my stuff again?" I ask, turning to look at Foster. With the shelves being taller than me, I'm not exactly surprised I hadn't seen him when we'd come in. But it's an absolutely unwelcome surprise all the same. "Are you going to rip my backpack off my shoulders this time?"

He rolls his eyes like I'm boring him. "I didn't know what you had in it. Why didn't you put your stuff in a locker and *lock it* like any other sensible human? You were just asking for it, especially after you spied on us."

"Spied on you?" I repeat, watching as he rolls his light blue eyes dramatically. "When you were moaning like you were in porn right in front of the door to your locker room? Yeah, okay Mr. Exhibitionist. I was totally spying on you." I shake my head at his words, only half believing even he takes himself seriously.

A grin curls on his lips before evaporating. "I'm not apologizing," he adds, just in case I wasn't clear. And did you hear what I said when you were in the pool?"

"No, you asswipe. Of course I fucking didn't." He brings out the worst in me. They all do. And this was supposed to be my evening to recover from them, not deal with them again.

He doesn't reply right away. Foster tilts his head to the side, and it hits me for the first time that we're almost the same height, with him being maybe an inch or two taller than me. He's certainly shorter than Dorian and August, and a lot less intimidating.

"You're just so arrogant with me today, aren't you? Is it because August and Dorian aren't here? Or is it just a *Dorian* thing, hmm?" He takes a step forward, invading my space as his hands rest on the shelf behind me on either side of my face. "Because I promise you that I can be just as scary as they can."

"I'm not afraid of any of you," I lie, not looking away from his gaze. He's not an alpha, and nothing in me wants to submit to him, or feels the need to back down. "Get out of my *space*, Foster. Unless you're going to hit me. But I'll break your nose if you do." While none of them have physically injured me, I don't consider it off the table, with how they've acted so far.

Something flashes in his eyes, and he shakes his head. "I'm not going to hit you, Mercy."

"Why? Because someone might see and think that you're less than perfect?"

A grin hitches across his lips, though there's nothing friendly about it. "Because I really want to see you cry, and that seems like too easy of a way to do it. Tell me...did you cry for Dorian today? He didn't say you did, but maybe he missed it. Maybe he just couldn't tell. If it were me, I would've made you cry before I gave your things back to you."

I try to jerk away from him, my heart suddenly beating rabbit-fast in my chest. "Get away from me," I murmur, reaching up but stopping just short of touching him.

"But we're having such a nice chat. We're practically friends, Mercy Noble–"

"We're not friends," I hiss, before he can finish. "We'll never be friends. I don't want anything to do with you."

"Then you should've gotten on your knees and *begged* that day I brought you back to our suite."

I can't help it. I bark out a harsh laugh, the sound seeming to surprise Foster. "Is that your fucking *kink*, then? Do you like to put girls in bad situations and drag them back to your *alphas* so they beg? Do your alphas just not get enough of it from you, Foster? Maybe you're looking for tips on how it's done." I finally work up the nerve to shove him backward, and he takes a few steps back more willingly than I'd expected.

"Maybe you're right," he shrugs, and the words take me by

surprise, though they're full of humor and sarcasm. He doesn't mean them, but I'm still shocked. "I'll have to tell Dorian and August *exactly* what you said and get their input."

"Whatever." Suddenly, I don't want to buy anything anymore. I just want to go back home, or anywhere else in this town. "Thanks for ruining this for me."

His eyes narrow, like he wasn't expecting that, and he opens his mouth to say something before closing it and sighing. "You shouldn't have used his name," he says quietly, while I'm walking away from the movies.

I stop and turn, surprised that he isn't looking as confident or nasty as he was only a few seconds ago.

"What?"

"It's happened before. Maybe that's what got him so riled up. Maybe you didn't know, I guess." He doesn't look too concerned about the possibility. "But you shouldn't have done it. Dealing with Rhett would've been better."

"Fuck you."

The smirk is back a second later. "Nah, I don't think so. I don't think you'd enjoy what I'm into, pretty omega."

The 'pretty' comment throws me off, but I look away and sigh. "Anything else before I go? Want to, I don't know, insult my ancestors? Remind me that I fucked up? You could try to force my backpack off my shoulders, I guess, but there's nothing in it I care about this time." That's a lie. My medicine is still in it, but the doesn't need to know.

Foster smiles brightly. "No, you keep it. Really, I insist." With that he raises his hands in surrender, taking a step back like he really means to just let me walk on out. Not that he could really stop me with Bri and the lady behind the counter.

Bri catches my eye as I walk and sets down the movie she'd picked up, catching up with me at the counter. "You okay?" she asks, looking back and seeing Foster. He waves sweetly at her, and I flip him off without a thought.

"No," I mutter, smiling tightly at the counter lady. "I just want to go home. I want to go—"

The sensors at the front of the store go off suddenly, surprising me into nearly levitating. I gasp loudly, looking at Bri, only to see the same panicked look on her face, along with the confusion in her eyes that I'm sure we share.

"Really?" The woman at the counter gets up with a sigh, hefting herself up and around it with irritation and frustration in her eyes. "Movies are five bucks, and you feel like you have to steal something?" She rolls her eyes, then looks us over before her eyes stop on mine. "Give me the backpack, young lady."

My hands tighten on the straps as I look at her, bewildered. "*What?*"

"Backpack. Now."

"Okay, okay, I—"

"Or I call the cops."

That has both of us moving, and Briella helps me give the woman my backpack that she takes to the counter and dumps the contents onto. "There's nothing in—" I stop talking as a DVD of *Nightmare on Elm Street* clatters to the surface from the depths of my backpack.

Briella looks at me, worry on her face, but all I can do is stand there and stare at it. I *hate* this movie, so I know theres no way it got in there by my hand.

"Oh man, Mercy." Foster leans on the counter at my other side, his arm brushing mine. He whistles, then grimaces in false sympathy. "Were you really just going to walk away with that? You don't seem like that kind of person."

I can't help it. Tears burn in my eyes as the counter lady reads me the riot act about stealing, and threatens the cops again. I would never steal anything, though whenever I try to say something to that effect, she just cuts me off and keeps going.

"You know, if you're short on money, I can buy it from you," Foster offers sweetly.

It's the last straw. I take a deep breath, hands still clenched, and try to count to ten with my eyes closed. There's no use explaining that I wouldn't steal, obviously. But I don't know what else to do, other than buy a movie I have no interest in.

"I'm sorry," I whisper finally, staring up at the woman. "I really don't know how it happened. I'm so, so sorry. And I'll absolutely buy it–"

"Don't bother," the woman grumbles, swiping the movie off the counter. "You two can just go on and leave. And don't worry about coming back for a month or so." She glowers as I step back, unsure of what to say. "I'll remember. And it's *my store*. Got it? A *month*, or next time it'll be forever." She makes a motion towards the door, and that's all it takes for me to grab my stuff off of the counter, shove it all back into my backpack, and walk out the door.

My heart thumps painfully as I pass the sensors again, as I'm half afraid that Foster has managed to stuff something else in there, but thankfully nothing happens. I hit the glass doors hard, trying to soften my movement at the last second before leaving the store and taking off down the sidewalk with Bri behind me, calling my name and trying to get me to slow down.

But I don't want to slow down. I don't want to catch the bus back to campus, or a taxi. I want to just keep walking until I'm not crying and I don't feel like my insides are burning in the worst way possible.

This is too much. Everything up until today was bad, sure, but today? My backpack? *This*?

It's too fucking *much*.

"Mercy!" Foster's voice is still overly friendly, and unlike Bri, he doesn't just try to call out to me. He jogs to catch up on the deserted sidewalk that borders the park, reaching out and grabbing my arm to get me to stop.

For half of a second, I think he's going to apologize. The concern on his face is so real that I'm sure that's what's going to come out of his mouth.

Until he holds up *Nightmare on Elm Street*, and his smile turns less friendly. "I bought this for you," he says, holding it out for me to take. I just stare at it, sure this isn't fucking happening, and he isn't being this mean. "Since you wanted it so badly—"

"*What is wrong with you?!*" The words come out as a scream, and I shove the movie back into his chest. "Why would you *do that?!* What if she'd called the cops on me, you piece of shit? What if she'd had me arrested?!"

He just keeps smiling. "I'm sure she was just making empty threats." He tries to tuck the movie into my arm, but I snap and hit his arm away from me, the DVD clattering to the ground.

"I can't do this anymore! You guys just get worse and worse for no fucking reason! I'll *beg*, okay?" Bri catches up to us, skirting around Foster with wide eyes as she comes to stand next to me. "Whatever you want me to say, I'll say it. I just want you to leave me alone. That's all I've ever wanted, and if getting on my knees on your shitty dorm room carpet is what it takes, then I'll do it to get you out of my life permanently."

13

It isn't until the weekend that I find myself at the front of their dorm.

While I'm one hundred percent sure that Foster had told me to show up Saturday night at eleven pm, I'm still here waiting and I've been here for at least ten minutes. Is this another trick? It's definitely starting to feel like one, and I shiver in my lightweight hoodie that swamps my torso and falls halfway down my thighs. I'm still in shorts, because I'm clearly a savage who likes to be cold, but now I'm starting to regret that choice and wish I'd worn pants.

In my defense, though, I expected this to not take a lot of time. I show up, Foster lets me in, I do this stupid *begging* thing that Dorian wants, I cry a little, I go home. Perhaps this one time, the omega helplessness that I try to avoid will do me a favor and Dorian will have no choice to forgive me. That's how it goes in my mind, anyway. But I'm not so sure it's going to work out like that in person.

With the way things have been going for me lately, it probably won't.

"Hasn't anyone told you that it's cold here in Maine, little omega?" the purr from behind me that curls over my body isn't Foster, like I'd expected. It's August. His scent, that mix of lavender and rain, washes over me and I surreptitiously suck in a breath. He really is the most mild-scented alpha I've ever met, and it's a real shame that his personality sucks. Especially since he's incredibly intelligent as well.

I would like him in another life.

"Even in September?" he goes on, brushing past me to slide his keycard in the door of his dormitory. He opens the door and jerks his chin in invitation, holding it open as he watches me.

For my part, I don't want to go inside. Not whatsoever. I would much rather stay out here in the cold all night long than go inside and talk to Dorian and Foster, who's now competing with the top spot of being my most hated individual with Dorian. Though, I suppose it's not too late for August to take the lead if he trips me down an elevator shaft or something.

I rub my eyes and sigh, walking through the door and moving as far from him as I can when I do it. He notices, clearly, because when the door shuts behind him, he slings an arm over my shoulders and steers me towards the elevator, even though I haven't said a word to him.

"I don't like the other dorms," he says conversationally like I'm participating in this chat. His long finger taps the button twice, and when I look up at the lights above the elevator, I see that it's making its way down from the fourth floor. "I don't know, I couldn't live without Foster and Dorian, I guess. Maybe that's weird of me."

I just shrug, choosing not to reply verbally as I look anywhere but at him. I *hate* him, just like I hate the rest of his pack.

"So Dorian made sure we were already living together in a suite, even though Foster only got here this year. He's a freshman too, you know. Though he spent enough time here last year that he might as well have been enrolled already."

I don't know why he's telling me any of this, and I shake off his arm as I walk into the elevator, resting my back against the wall as August comes in after me and presses the button for the third floor.

"What about you? Do you like your roommate? It's random for freshmen, right? Unless you request someone, and I'm guessing you didn't." His smile is friendly, which only makes me grind my teeth, jaw clenching as I do it.

"She's great," I say finally, my voice flat. "Love it here." Part of me is ready to quit, go home, and beg for a scholarship to one of the other schools that had offered me one, but somehow, I'm pretty sure that's not how it works.

It's Winter Grove or nothing, and *nothing* isn't an option. It makes my stomach sink just thinking about it, and when I think about what my life would be like as an omega in Ohio without an education to back up my name, it takes all of my willpower to not start screaming at August for trying to fuck this up for me.

If I have to *beg* for Dorian to leave me alone so that none of this gets any worse and my time here is no longer in jeopardy, then that's what I'll have to do. Even though I'll probably throw up afterwards. On him.

The elevator doors open, making me jump, and I follow August out of the elevator and down the hallway, pretending to ignore the looks he throws me that seem too close to concern for me to want to see them.

There's no way he's *actually* concerned, obviously. He's part of the reason I'm here, and that it's come to this.

It's not until we're at his door that he speaks again, though I'm too busy noting how quiet it is here tonight to notice right away. Finally when I do look up, he's halfway through, and as if noticing that I'm not paying attention, says again, "Don't worry too much about *Video Valhalla*. The owner's cranky and everything, but she won't even remember in a few weeks. I promise."

I don't know what to say to that. Is he baiting me? Trying to et a reaction out of me?

I shrug one shoulder in response. "Whatever. I didn't need anything from there anyway." Though my heart twists at the memory of my excitement to get the vintage DVDs I'd wanted for my room. Sure, they aren't a big deal in the scheme of things. But that's not the point.

The point is that these vile boys are uncannily good at ruining everything in my life lately, and it has to stop, one way or another. And since I'm not capable of murder, probably, I'm going to have to beg.

August watches me for another few seconds, and I look up at him with raised brows only to see him look away and turn the handle of his door. He opens it wide, going in first, and I force myself to suck in a breath as I follow him with steps that drag on their surprisingly expensive carpet.

Letting the door close behind me, I look around the room and try to appear as though being here doesn't make me want to throw up, even though it obviously does. Foster sits on the couch, legs under him as he types away on his laptop, while Dorian takes up space on the floor in front of his legs, glasses on as he scrolls through something on his tablet.

It's amazing how domestic they look. And how it doesn't *seem* like they're the incarnation of evil on the mortal plane. But of course, looks have a tendency to be deceiving.

As the door closes, Dorian looks up and takes off his black frames, laying them down gently on the coffee table as he gets up and does the same with his tablet. He walks toward me, passing August as the latter goes to take up his position on the floor. Suddenly, Dorian is too close to me and I take a step back until my body is pressed up against the door behind me.

If anything, the look on his face proves how much he likes my reaction to his nearness.

"I didn't think that would be what did it," he admits, leaning on his arm that's pressed to the door above my head. I raise my brows at him, not wanting to answer, but his grin only widens. "Over a movie, really?"

"You wouldn't understand," I mutter, tucking my hair behind my ear.

"Try me."

I shake my head. I'm not about to spill my guts to Dorian Wakefield. Not about this, and not about anything.

"I don't know..." he sighs, almost like he's thinking about it. "I can be pretty understanding usually. And I'm empathetic."

I can't help it. I snort. His cruel grin curves back onto his face as he looks back down at me, and his dark eyes glitter. "But you don't really believe that, do you?"

Closing my eyes hard enough that it hurts, I let out a long breath and don't respond with the first thing that comes to mind. Instead I say, as mildly as I can, "I'll believe whatever it takes to get you to leave me alone."

"But how can I leave you alone when you're my astronomy partner, little omega?"

I want to correct him. I want to tell him that he's not welcome to call me that, but I just shrug, trying to seem bored. Maybe if I don't give him the reaction he's expecting, if I act like I'm just done and can't do this anymore, he'll see that it isn't fun for him and leave me alone.

It's my best shot, anyway. I try to remember every movie I've watched with a wounded omega and imitate the pose, my shoulders rising as I hug my arms around my body, making it look like he's the big bad evil thing that's trying to kill me. I'm sure my scent is tinged with fear as it is, and it's easy to gaze at him with wide doe-eyes. Or, at the very least, what I hope are doe-eyes. I've definitely never tried to do this before, and I'm a little old to start now.

However, I have no idea if it works. He just looks at me, his face unreadable as he scrutinizes my expression and my pose.

"You told me you wanted me to beg," I murmur, putting a small tremble into my voice. I'm not afraid of him like I'm pretending to be. I hate him, and I'm afraid of what he could do, I suppose.

But I do not fear Dorian Wakefield.

As he looks me over, hand comes up to rest on my chin and tilt my head up to his, a jolt goes up my spine. He doesn't believe me. There's no belief on his face, only scrutiny and something else that's harder to read.

Disappointment, maybe?

"You're going to beg for my forgiveness, little omega?" he purrs, mouth close to mine. I force my breath to stutter like he has some kind of romantic effect on me, though I think if I widen my eyes anymore, they're going to pop out of their sockets, so that's a no-go.

"Yes," I reply in a whisper. I hope it's a whisper, anyway. I have trouble judging my own volume sometimes.

"On your knees on my floor? We can do it right here if you want, right in front of my door. You'll look good on your knees, won't you?"

Oh. *Oh.* That has an unintended effect on my insides that I smack down with a proverbial stick. I know it's not him, it's just the way he talks, his scent, and the idea of doing things on my knees with anyone other than him.

God, I wish I was anywhere but here.

"I asked you a question," he repeats, his tone even.

I don't want to do it. I hesitate, even, to do it. But when he growls ever-so-softly in this throat, I know that it's time.

I whimper.

While I'm not proud of it, it has the intended effect. His gaze softens, if only slightly, and his hold on my chin loosens. All I have to do is stand here and look terrified, and Dorian will think he's won. Which is a-okay with me if he leaves me alone after this.

"If that's what you want," I say finally, cutting my gaze away from his like I'm a submissive omega not wanting to upset an alpha. "If that's what it takes so that you—"

I break off as Foster suddenly makes a sound like he's choking. I look around Dorian, only to see that Foster has his hand stuffed in his mouth, and he's not choking.

He's fucking *laughing*.

"I'm so sorry, Mercy," he says, finally getting ahold of himself. "It's just that you're probably the worst actor I've ever seen, and so is he." He nods his head at Dorian, who rolls his eyes. August reaches up to grip Foster's thigh, giving him a warning look, but Foster doesn't stop. "You're both acting like you're in some kind of fucked up romance novel, saying all the right things, and when you whimpered? *Jesus*?" he snorts. "I don't know, I guess if this is you performing a telenovella, you're perfect."

"What?" I try to keep my voice soft, like I'm stunned and taken aback by his words. I glance at Dorian, but he's still glancing at Foster as well. "I'm not acting, I'm—"

"No, he's right." Dorian drops his hand with a sigh. "You're really bad at this. I don't know who taught you how to make an alpha feel badly for you, Mercy...but this isn't it."

"I'm not trying to—"

"You're not much better," August comments from his spot on the floor, and Foster reaches up to tangle his fingers in

August's hair and tugs, looking at him fondly. "Was that a growl? I thought you were going to vomit on her."

Dorian rolls his eyes, but I refuse to break my act. They're bluffing, surely. And even if they aren't...

"Okay, well..." I try for a deep, shuddering breath again, and ignore Foster's snicker. "You want my apology, right?"

"I want you to *beg*," Dorian corrects me, stepping back. "On the floor. On your knees. Want a pillow?"

"Umm. No, that's okay." *Am I really going to do this?* Somehow, getting on my knees for them like this feels like a slap in the face to everything I've worked for. Not to mention it seems that my knees lock up whenever I consider it, not letting me move from my spot on the door.

But I *have* to do this. I *have* to get them off my case, or else I'm not going to make it through the semester.

"You need help?" Foster offers from the couch, lazily. "I can totally help."

"No, God, no," I assure him. "I'm working on it."

"Take your time. I've got all night," Dorian responds sweetly.

Of course he does.

I take a deep breath and will my knees to unlock, nausea rising with the bile in my throat as I look at the floor. I can't do this.

I have to do this.

My knees start to bend, and it's so difficult that I'm sure my joints are about to snap at how little my body wants to do this. *It'll be quick*, I tell myself, staring at the floor. It'll just take a moment. It'll be worth it in the end. My knees fold a little quicker, and I'm halfway to the floor when Dorian speaks again.

"Oh, crap. I forgot something, Mercy." His voice is sickly sweet, and I stand up straight as my eyes jerk upwards to find a wide, cruel grin on his lips. "I *just* remembered how nasty you were to me the other day when I returned your backpack in the gym complex. Remember that?"

"....No?" I ask hopefully.

His grin widens. "Well, I do. And I *think* I may have mentioned that begging isn't enough anymore, didn't I? If not, let me say it again. We're past begging, Mercy. That offer expired days ago. I think we should play a game."

"A game?" I repeat, like a mynah bird.

"Yeah. A really fun one. If you win, I'll forget your name. I'll move seats in astronomy. I'll go apologize to the owner of *Video Valhalla* for you." He stops, looking at me expectantly.

Taking a breath, I take a moment before asking the obvious question. "And what if you win?"

"Oh, nothing big," he assures me, in a tone I don't believe for a second. "Let's just say...if I win, then you belong to my pack."

"For how long?"

"For the rest of the semester."

14

His words give me pause. The rest of the year? Eyes darting up to his face once more, though I'm not sure when I looked away, I study Dorian. He doesn't seem to be joking. In fact, he seems incredibly serious. But even if he is, and he means to actually play some kind of game with me, how in the world do I know he'll keep his word?

"I wouldn't promise you something and go back on it," Dorian assures me, as if he'd heard my thoughts. He leans on his arms on the door above me, causing my eyes to dart up to his. "It would be bad business, and I wouldn't want people to think that's something I'm into." He's too close for me to get a breath of fresh air, but I have a feeling that's completely intentional. Not that he has any idea how much I adore his scent. In his eyes, I hate it so much I choked on it that first day.

God, if only that were the truth of it. Hating his scent would be so much easier than enjoying it as much as I do. I'd hoped to find a pack whose scent I loved before I even considered dating an alpha and his pack. But here are these three boys, shooting that dream in the foot with their amazing scents and shitty personalities.

"What kind of game?" I ask finally. Though by his words, I don't have a lot of choice here. Either I play and win, or I don't, and I'm assuming that constitutes a loss.

"What kind of games are you good at?"

"Probably not charades," Foster murmurs from the sofa with a snicker.

I think about it. Not just because I genuinely need a moment. Because I want to think of a game he *won't* be good at. A simple one, so that he won't be able to twist it into something else. But hopefully something that he won't know. Though since I don't know much about him, I'm not sure what kind of games he knows. Of any variety.

When I think of something, I internally cringe. I doubt slapjack is the game to pin my future on, but I have to think of something.

"What about...memory?" I murmur. "We can play with a deck of cards." I watch him as he thinks about it, my heart pounding in my throat. I love memory games, and I don't see how he'd be the one to beat me in this one. August, maybe. But not Dorian, surely.

Foster is up even before Dorian answers, and goes to grab a deck of cards out of a drawer by the television. He brandishes it as I watch, and finally Dorian sighs. "That's not the game I was expecting you to say," he tells me finally, a small smile on his face. His gaze gleams with curiosity, which makes me feel kind of weird, but I give into my own indulgence with a grimace.

"What kind of game did you think I was going to suggest? Solitaire?" I motion for him to let me off of the wall and he does, to my surprise. Then he walks to the coffee table in the middle of the living room where Foster is shuffling cards. He sits down, and plucks the cards from his betas hands to offer them to me.

I follow him, sitting gingerly at the far end of the table closest to the door, just in case I need to run. I feel weird just sitting here on the carpet, but what else am I going to do?

"Maybe Uno or Go Fish. Monopoly? You seem like a Monopoly person." I take the deck from his hands as he speaks, shuffling them through deft fingers with the ease of long practice. I've been playing memory since I was a kid, and the first thing I'd learned from my long-deceased grandmother was how to shuffle like a casino worker. The cards flutter between my fingers as I arch them, folding them in with each other loudly.

"I don't play Monopoly," I mutter. The other two options hadn't crossed my mind even once, and I'm certainly not about to tell him slapjack had.

"Solitaire's a single player game," adds August, leaning his elbows on the coffee table. "How were you going to play it with him?"

"I wasn't."

It takes him a minute, but he snorts and wordlessly watches me shuffle the deck in my hands as my heart speeds up and my stomach twists into an origami swan.

"I'd say they're shuffled," Dorian remarks, causing me to slow my movements almost nervously. He's right, and I jerkily lay the cards out on the table, face down, so they're interspaced as evenly and as cleanly as I can get them.

The red and black backs of the deck stare back at me, like they're judging me or willing me to fuck up. Either is an awful option, and I will myself to stop humanizing the cards.

I'm *good* at this game. I always have been. There's no reason to think that I'm not going to win and this is all going to be over–

Dorian claps his hands, startling me and causing me to flinch. "This is fun," he says, nodding at me. "You can go first. And the first one to fourteen pairs wins? Don't you think this is fun?"

I don't think this is fun at all, but I give him my most winning, sarcastic smile and say, "Yeah, I'm having the time of my life, actually." Reaching forward, I flip two cards at random, noting that they're a jack and a seven.

Dorian hums and flips as well, turning over another seven and an ace. On my turn I take the pair of sevens, then flip another couple of cards. This time, a king and a four.

On Dorian's turn, he unearths the other king, takes the pair, and flips two cards at random. For three turns neither of us find a pair, but I sigh in relief when I find first the fours, then the aces.

"Don't be so tense," Dorian hums, flipping over two cards that don't match. "We're playing a game, right? One that you're good at, too, since you picked it. Who taught you to play?"

"My grandmother," I reply, distracted, as I grab another pair. My heart lightens a little as I snag two pair, and when I glance over to see that Dorian is still at just one pair, I'm able to let out a breath and relax just slightly. "She, umm. She was a casino worker back in the day and loved card games. I loved memory things, so she taught me...this." I trail off as I miss my next match, and Dorian hums in reply.

"My dad taught me how to play," he says, flipping over a match instantly. He does it again, and again, and suddenly my heart is sinking in my chest. "He's really good at this too. Probably as good as you. And I was always looking for a way to beat him, so I had my nanny practice with me all the time." He finally misses, but by the time he does, he has seven matches to my five.

Crap.

I hadn't expected him to have any idea how to play this game, and when I flip over a card, a breath of air whooshes from my chest. I flip over another, and another, until I have ten matches at my side of the table, and we're running out of cards.

I need to not miss. As less cards are on the table, the game gets incredibly easy and if I miss, I'm going to be fucked.

I only need four more pairs to win.

I get another one, and after a minute, eleven pairs sit on my side of the table, and for the first time tonight I feel like I have the upper hand.

I go to flip another one, but my hand stills and I look up at Dorian. Quietly, I ask, "You really mean it? When I win, you're going to leave me alone for the rest of the year and not do...*this* anymore?"

He reaches out and taps my fingers with his playfully. "Yes, little omega." God, I wish he'd learn my name. "*If* you win, I'll leave you alone. I promise." I go to move, but his fingers wrap around mine. "But I want to tell you something." His voice is deeper, more dangerous, and his eyes glitter, so I give him my full attention.

"What?" I ask, more confused than anything.

"I know where the rest of the matches are." His hand doesn't leave mine, though my fingers twitch at his words. I try not to let it show on my face, and instead frown at him in disbelief.

"No you don't. You're bluffing."

"Do you want to take that chance? If you miss this, you're going to lose. So let's add to this wager. You can give up right now, and I'll only own you for, oh, let's say six weeks. That's fair, right?" Still feels like the rest of the semester to me, but I don't argue. In my head I count up the time between now and winter break, and find that we have a little under thirteen weeks before break. So they would 'own' me for a little less than half of that.

I still hate the idea of it.

"And if I don't take it and still win? What do I get?" I prod, wanting to know the incentive for me not taking his dumb deal.

"Then you get a public apology from me."

But I don't *want* that. He must see it on my face, because his head tilts to the side in surprise. "Unless...hmm. You're not interested in that offer, are you?"

I shake my head and say, slowly, "I just...want you guys to stop making my life hell. Things are hard enough here at Winter Grove, you know? All I want is for you to leave me alone."

They trade a look, and Dorian shrugs. "If you win, I'll make Foster go into *Video Valhalla* and admit what he did. And buy you whatever you want from there. Whole store included."

My brows shoot up, and Foster's do as well. He makes a noise of concern in his throat, trading a look with August. "*Will you?*" he asks, as if he's unsure of the response.

But Dorian doesn't answer.

Still, there's one incredibly important question that I don't know if I want the answer to. "What happens if I deny your deal, and I still lose?" It's worth knowing if he's going to murder me, or something, and I'm signing the agreement that says he can.

Dorian watches my face, unmoving, before finally pulling his hand away from mine and snagging his backpack from behind him. He drags it to him, undoing the zipper a second later, and finally sets an object down between us, just at the edge of the remaining cards.

It's a collar.

There's no getting around it, even though it looks inconspicuous enough to be a choker. The smooth leather is thinner than a pencil, and a delicate, silver 'o' ring hangs from the front, a small circular charm inside of it. I reach out to touch it, stopping only at the last minute when I remember I do not want anything to do with that.

"If you still go through with this, and you lose, then you belong to us *and* you get to wear this for the rest of the semester anytime you're in public. Or any other collar I give you."

Suddenly there's a tone to this game that I wasn't expecting. Everything seems to shift as I stare at the *collar* on the table, and I feel nausea trying to claw its way up from my stomach.

"I'm not wearing that," I say flatly. "Not on my life."

"Then forfeit so you won't have to," he agrees with a shrug. "It doesn't matter to me one way or the other."

But it *does*.

That's the real problem here. If It didn't, he wouldn't have offered.

If it didn't matter, there wouldn't be a fucking collar on the table between us. I taste bile in my throat as I sit back, staring at it and what it means. He won't just *own* me, though before I wasn't quite sure what that meant.

Now, I'm not sure I *want* to know.

But I'm good at this game, and I'm three matches away from winning. Am I really going to give up everything now, when he's definitely bluffing about knowing where the other cards are?

No. No, I'm not.

Though I'm scared he knows it too, and knew it before he even asked.

I sigh and raise my hand, shaking my head as I flip over another pair.

Eleven.

"I'm not afraid of you," I say flatly, not sure who I'm trying to convince. "I don't like what you do, but I'm not afraid."

I flip over another pair.

Twelve.

"And I don't believe that you know where every card is. You'd need a miracle to beat...me." I trail off, only a little less convinced when I *miss*. The card I needed was an ace.

But a jack stares up at me mockingly.

August whistles and sits back, and when I look up at Foster, he's staring at Dorian with rapt attention.

"Okay, so let's address that." Dorian's tone is polite, conversational, and confident. He flips the jack I'd just had, and flips another one to match it. "I don't lie, really. Not about things like this." Another pair joins the first, and I take a breath.

I just need him to miss *one.*

"Like I told you before, I've been playing this for a long time, and my memory is very good. Maybe I can't beat you on a biology quiz show, sure." He flips another match, and another.

I count, and realize suddenly that we're tied, and there are only two cards left on the table.

"But you got cocky, didn't you?" He flips over a card, but before he can grab the other one, my hand flies out and I grip his fingers, unsure of what I'm doing.

"Wait," I say, my tone pleading. My heart hammers against my ribs, looking for any kind of escape, and Dorian's smile turns sweet.

"No," he replies, and with my fingers wrapped around his hand, he turns over the last card and reveals the match. "I win, Mercy Noble. Fair and square."

15

"I'm not putting that on." The words are out of my mouth before I can even think, and I lurch to my feet at the end of the coffee table, nearly upending it. Cards scatter on the carpet as I look at Dorian, sure that the horror on my face is apparent now. There's no pretending, and no acting involved.

I can't believe I lost to him.

Dorian gets to his feet smoothly, without banging his knees on the table like I had. He picks up the collar as he does, coming around the table to stand in front of me. If I'd expected him to be mad, I see now that he isn't. If anything, he's just... interested. Maybe a little amused, but there's no irritation or anger on his face.

"That's okay," he assures me, reaching out and gripping the collar of my hoodie before I can stop him. "I'll put it on for you this time."

"No." He can't *make me* wear it. And even if he snaps it around my neck right now, I'll just throw it in the trash as soon as I'm out of his room. Or take it off and strangle him with it. "I don't get what you think you're doing, or if you think this is funny, or–"

"I don't think it's funny at all," he says, cutting me off. Gently he pulls me closer to him, and it takes me a moment to realize that August is up as well and standing right behind me, his arms suddenly encircling my waist.

Instantly, my heart kicks into overdrive, and I pull away from Dorian, leaning into August. "I don't want to–"

"But you lost, and you made a deal with me," Dorian reminds me. I've gone as far as I can, and August is warm and solid behind me as he keeps me in place.

"But–"

"I'm not going to *hurt you*, Mercy." It's so sweet that he's finally learned my name, but I don't think I like how he says it. My stomach twists in fear, and when I jerk back once more, I only end up with my head on August's shoulder.

"I'll just take it off and lose it," I threaten vehemently, hoping he can't tell how nervous I am. It isn't that the collar isn't cute. It's subtle, too, and I doubt anyone else on campus would know what it is.

It's just...everything else.

"No you won't." He sounds so sure that I want to vomit. One of his hands comes up to cup my cheek, and his eyes narrow as he watches me. "You need a minute. So let's talk this out."

I'm not sure what there is to talk out, but I'm willing to do anything to convince him *not* to put that around my neck. "O-okay," I agree, trying to pull away from August and failing. I flinch as Foster leans on my shoulder like its his personal headrest, then glare down at him and jerk my shoulder to get him to move.

He does not.

"So we made an initial deal. You win, you walk away and I

leave you alone. You lose, you're *ours*," Dorian reminds me, with too much emphasis on the last word. "You remember that?"

"No shit. It's been literally–" He reaches up to grab my chin, his thumb on my lower lip.

"Don't talk back," he advises. "Not when I'm trying to explain something to you." His thumb is heavy on my lip, and it's worse when he moves to stroke along my skin.

I don't reply, but it's mostly because I don't know what to say or whether or not I should bite him.

"You said yes. And then, when you were about to lose, I offered you a different deal. Kind of a double or nothing. And I think you should've considered something, Mercy." He leans in close, until I can feel his breath on my lips. "I never would've done that if you had any chance of winning. I didn't do it sooner, because you could've beaten me. But then you second-guessed yourself. I saw it in your face. You knew where that ace was, but then you decided that maybe it was the other card you were going to pull next."

It's...terrifying that he can read me so well when he doesn't know me. My breath hitches in my throat, and he pulls away, granting me some personal space.

"If you'd thought about it, you wouldn't have taken my deal," he adds. "But you did. Instead of taking the easy way out on an offer that really was the *sweetest* thing for you and would've guaranteed you'd only have to deal with us for six weeks, you were over-confident. So you said *yes*, again. To this, to me, to them. To *us*. And *we* includes *this*." He brandishes the collar, lifting it high enough for me to see it clearly. "There is no *not* wearing it. Not anymore. You don't have a choice. Cry or beg or bite me–yes, little omega, I know you're thinking about it–but it's going around that pretty throat. And since you wouldn't put it on yourself, I'm going to have to be the one to do it for you."

"What if I take it off?"

"Stop talking," August murmurs in my ear. "Stop trying to rile him up. You won't like the result."

I'm not trying to rile him up...exactly.

"Take it off all you want in your dorm room."

"We only have one class together. Jackets exist. You won't know–"

"I'll know. I'd say stop being so difficult but well..." He shrugs, his grin anything but friendly. "It makes things better for me when you think you're putting up a fight. Are you going to lift up your hair for me, or is Foster going to do it?"

"Wait," I say again, my mind racing as I try to think of something, *anything*, to get me out of this.

"No."

"But–" Foster reaches out and twines my hair around his fingers, picking it up off my neck.

"It definitely says something about you that it's taking three people to put this on you," Dorian remarks, unclasping the collar as my heart tries to bang its way out of my ribcage. When my hands come up between us to grip his wrists lightly, he just *looks* at me. "Do you want August to hold those too? He doesn't mind, but I would think you're going to get tired of this after awhile."

"What if it's too small? Too big? Maybe it'll choke me. Maybe I'm, uh. Allergic to whatever metal that is on the ring?" God, I have no idea what to do, and this is really starting to feel like a reality.

Maybe there's no way out of this for me after all.

Tears prick at the corners of my eyes, though I blink them away wordlessly.

"It's not, and you'll be fine. You can hold onto me if it

makes you feel better. But that's as nice as I'm going to be, and you're not going to try to *stop* me." He meets my eyes as he says it, his own dark and glittering. He doesn't ask if that's all right, but I guess we're past that.

Instead he reaches forward, my hands still on his wrists but just resting there, not stopping him. When August tugs on my arms I let go, sucking in a breath and holding it as the cool leather presses against my throat.

It takes a second, and it's really not the traumatic experience I'd thought it would be. Not physically, anyway. I can barely feel the collar on my throat when Dorian pulls away, though his gaze is fixed on the silver ring that hangs at the base of my throat.

Foster lets go of my hair and steps away, moving to prowl around Dorian's back, but August doesn't let me go, and I don't immediately try to pull away. I could, probably. He isn't holding onto me tightly.

Instead, I shake free of his grip on my wrists, reaching up a hand to touch the collar. Dorian tilts his head to the side, like a warning, but I'm not trying to take it off. I just touch it, running my fingers around the cool leather that's warming up to my skin and to the metal clasp at the back of my neck. I don't touch the silver ring. It's the most offensive part of the whole thing, to me, and I'm pretty sure I could pretend it's a choker without that.

"Are you *happy*?" I spit finally, shoving away from August at last. "You got what you wanted, I guess." When I start to leave, because I'm really not sure how much worse I can actually make this, Foster reaches out and grips my wrist, stopping me in my tracks.

I sigh, rolling my eyes up to the ceiling before whirling on him. "*What?*" I demand, though my voice comes out less certain than I'd expected or hoped.

"Why do you want to go?" he inquires, a smirk tugging at his lips. "There's nothing to be afraid of anymore, right? Our game is over, and you lost."

That doesn't make it any better, and the word *lost* twists my insides painfully. "Clearly I want to go because I'm a sore loser," I reply, perplexed at why he wants me to stay.

Foster opens his mouth again but Dorian reaches out and drags him over with an arm hooked over his shoulder and hand splayed on his stomach. "Not tonight," he purrs in the beta's ear, and Foster's eyes close when Dorian nips at his jaw. "You're being cruel."

I mean, in my opinion all of them are pretty awful, but I don't say that.

"I'm leaving then." I try to not let the question show in my voice, but I do turn to glare at them with my hand on the door. "Unless there's something else you want?"

"Not tonight," Dorian assures me, both hands on Foster and making the beta writhe under his touch with appreciation. Are they going to fuck? It's starting to feel like it.

"Want me to walk you out?" August offers, brows raised.

"Nah, August," I assure him. "Frankly, I'd rather die in any number of ways than–"

"Enough." Dorian's voice is still amused, but holds a tone of warning that I dislike. Already my insides don't know what to do with themselves, with their scents mingling in my nose and the echo of his growling tone in my ears.

I don't need an alpha, nor do I want one.

But God if they aren't the most gorgeous, best smelling ones I've ever met. Yet again, I lament that it's a real damn shame how awful they are.

"Cool. Great. *Bye.*" Without waiting for them I yank the door open and slam it behind me, wiping away the tears in my eyes that are finally pushing past my will for them to go away.

Self-consciously I pull up my hood, hoping it hides as much of the choker as possible as I all but run back to my dorm to get away from them.

Naturally, Bri is waiting up for me, the TV on and her phone is lighting up her hands from her place on her bed. She straightens when I close the door behind me, looking at me with concern. "You're good? It took longer than I thought, and I thought about texting you...but..." She trails off when I fall onto my bed and press my face to my hands, legs curled under me. "Is everything okay?" She gets up from her bed and comes to sit beside me, shoulder pressed comfortingly against mine. Her scent washes away anything lingering by the boys, though when she takes a deep breath to scent *me*, I have a feeling she knows that they've been touching me. "Mercy did they do something to you?"

I shake my head. "They offered me a deal," I say finally. "If I won a card game, they'd leave me alone."

"Oh, Mercy. You didn't do it, right? *Everyone* knows not to do shit like that with Dorian."

"Well I'm not everyone!" I lift my head to glare at her, and her eyes fall to the stupid collar around my throat. "Yeah, I fucking *lost*, Bri. And when Dorian doubled down, I fell for that too!"

"...Oh. Umm." She watches as I unclasp the collar and chuck it onto the nightstand. "But everything is...mostly okay?"

"If by mostly okay you mean that I'm 'theirs' for the semester, whatever that means, and I'm wearing a fucking collar to prove it? Yeah. Everything is great."

"I'm sorry." She puts an arm over my shoulders, taking the lead in comfort for the first time since we've met. "Look. We'll have breakfast with Zara tomorrow, okay? And, I don't know, we'll think of a way to get back at them. We'll...mess up their cars, or something."

"Or poison their water supply?" I murmur, face pressed to her tee.

"Okay, well. That's a bit extreme, don't you think?"

"No. It's not extreme *enough*, actually."

"I guess we'll see what we can do then."

16

Sunday does not yield any productive ideas on getting rid of Dorian and his pack, or how to get me out of this situation. In Zara's opinion, I should just take *it* off and get on with things. They can't do anything to me, in her eyes, other than embarrass me.

But I don't agree.

They can do a lot to me, and they know it. That's the problem.

She is, on the other hand, enthusiastically in agreement about murdering them, and the topic comes up again Monday morning as I stare at my food with mixed feelings.

I'm not very hungry, and I'm pretty sure it's from taking too many medicines earlier this morning that have my stomach twisting in despair and protest.

Would I feel better by eating? Most likely. Does that make it any more appealing?

No, it really doesn't.

"Poisoning their water supply is my bet," I mutter, rubbing my temples. I've avoided a migraine, sure, but I still feel just a little bit achey, though that's fading as well since I caught things early enough and luck is on my side today. With this, at least. Maybe I've used up all my good luck dodging migraines on really important days, and that's why I'm stuck with the rest of this mess.

"We could frame them for something?" Zara offers, always on board with doing *something* to piss them off. She doesn't like them, which is pretty clear, but when I asked her about it, she just shrugged and didn't give a real answer. That's fine, though. It's none of my business how she feels, as long as she's still going to help throw me a pity party.

Bri opens her mouth to say something, then pauses and looks over my shoulder with a frown. "That's weird," she murmurs, ducking down slightly. "Why are they here instead of at the Lakeside dining hall?"

I let out a breath, still staring at my food as I close my eyes hard. "It's them, isn't it?"

Both her and Zara 'umm hmm' to confirm my suspicions.

Surreptitiously I drag my hood over my head, ducking my shoulders as I try to be unseen in our booth. "Just. Umm. Look innocent. They don't know you guys that well, right? Like they have no reason to think I'm hanging out with you, and–"

"They're coming over here," Zara observes, watching them with an even expression. "Want me to be mean to them?"

I do, but I don't think that'll go well, so I shake my head. Instead of looking up at their approach, however, I stare at my food and continue to poke at my French toast with a fork, trying to look like it's the most interesting thing in the world.

Even when they stop at our table, clearly knowing it's me, I don't look up.

"It's dead, Mercy," Foster points out with a snicker. "You don't need to keep stabbing the bread."

Still, I don't look up. I only shrug one shoulder. "Come eat breakfast with us," Dorian invites, though I know it's not an 'invitation' at all. When I don't move, he leans down and yanks my hood off of my head to say against the shell of my ear, "*Now*, little omega."

"I have a name," I mutter, throwing my friends a plaintive look.

"Why don't you just leave her alone?" Zara is trapped against the wall by Briella, who's sitting at the outer edge of the booth, but she looks ready to jump *over* her girlfriend when she glares at Dorian. "She doesn't like you, Dorian."

"Shame," he says, looking at her with boredom. "I would leave her alone, if she hadn't agreed to–"

"Whatever," I interrupt, standing up so quickly I almost nail him in the face with mine. He jerks back just in time and I scoop my tray off the table along with my backpack from the bench. "I'll see you guys later, okay?"

Briella waves at me, making me feel momentarily bad for her. She's *afraid* of Dorian and August. That couldn't be any clearer. Zara just seems angry.

I follow the boys across the dining hall, trailing behind them like a lost puppy until they sit down at a booth in the opposite corner, out of sight of my friends. Foster slides against the wall, Dorian slotting in to sit beside him, and my stomach unclenches the tiniest bit when I see that I'm left to sit next to August.

"I'm getting a chair," I state, dropping my tray so hard on the table it clatters when it hits. Thankfully my drink is in my hand, or else it might've spilled on one of the boys. Which clearly would've been a tragedy indeed.

"Sit," Dorian orders, pointing at the booth across from him.

"I'm allergic."

He doesn't argue. Instead, the dark-haired alpha sighs and

gets to his feet, coming to stand in front of me as my insides twist in trepidation.

"I'm sure you didn't mean for this to happen," he adds casually, reaching out to my throat. "And you probably didn't notice. But your collar is twisted. I'm going to fix it for you." He takes his time in pulling it around, his fingers gentle when they brush against my skin. "And to think," Dorian murmurs, his hands on my shoulders when he finished. "I was going to praise you for being a *good girl* and keeping it on. But maybe not now." He sits and points at the booth seat.

Hesitantly, I sit. It most certainly wasn't an accident that the ring was skewed to the side, causing it to look just like a regular choker with my hair down. I may not be able to take it off while I'm awake and out of my room, but I'll be damned if I wear it like he wants me to. Just to piss him off, even though he won't be around to see it.

I'll just have to remember to keep it straight when they're around.

As their conversation picks up, I stab softly at my soggy French toast, considering cutting up the grapes on my plate just for something to do as I think. Do they take a long time to eat, or will they be out of here in fifteen minutes? I don't have class for another hour and a half, so I don't exactly have an excuse to go anywhere, and I'm sure they'll somehow know if I lie and say I do.

I blink, realizing August has said something to me, and look into his face expectantly. I didn't hear him, thanks to the conflicting sounds of the cafeteria, but that's not his fault. And I suppose that's something all of them should know so they don't think I'm purposefully ignoring them.

Even when I am.

"I didn't hear you," I say, looking at him. "But umm. If you tap me first, I'll be able to read your lips."

"You couldn't hear him?" Foster doesn't share my hesitancy about eating as he shovels another piece of French toast down his throat. His auburn hair is tousled and barely combed, though his light blue eyes are bright. "But isn't that what the hearing aids are for?"

"Conflicting sound. And you're quiet," I add, looking at August. "So talk louder or tap me on the shoulder."

"Sorry," he apologizes, and it's so surprising that I think I might have a heart attack. "I didn't even think about that, and it's my bad. I asked why you aren't eating."

"I'm not hungry?" I offer, tilting my head to the side. I'm not sure why he cares, or why he's pretending to.

"If you weren't hungry, then you wouldn't have gotten any food to begin with," Foster disagrees.

"You guys just turned my appetite is all. But I was trying to be polite. You want it?" I gesture at my food, eyes on Foster.

But Dorian doesn't give him a chance to answer.

"Oh my, little omega," he purrs, leaning his elbows on the table. "Are you trying to get out of eating breakfast? Don't you know it's the most important meal of the day?"

"What can I say? I'm just a heathen who doesn't know these things."

"That's all right. I'm sure I can help you turn your life choices around. Nice guy that I am, and all." He reaches out a finger and scoots the tray of plates closer towards me. "Eat your breakfast, Mercy."

"I'm not a *dog,* Dorian."

"No, but you do growl like one."

The insult catches me off guard. I hadn't expected the comeback, and I stare at him as my brain processes it. Finally I drop my eyes back to my food, pressing my fingers to my temples. "I don't feel well," I admit finally. "And that's not me setting up to insult Foster again. Though I probably could, if you want."

"Are you sick?" August rests his arm on the top of the booth behind my shoulders, brushing my hoodie as he does.

"No. I just took too much medicine this morning. I know I'm old enough to know better and..." I let out a sigh, closing my eyes hard. "And I don't know why I'm trying to explain any of that to you guys. I'm not eating. I don't feel like it. I'm an adult. End of discussion."

"*Well*." When I look up, Dorian's grin is wolfish. "That's pretty inaccurate."

"I hate it when you say things like that."

"Oh, don't worry kitten. I know."

Kitten?

Kitten?

I'm going to vomit.

"You know, my appetite was coming back," I remark mildly, laying my fork on the table to make a point. "Until you said that. Thanks for chasing it away completely. I really needed you to add to the nausea—"

"Eat at least half of what's on your tray or I'll clip a leash on that fucking collar and lead you around for the rest of the day." His tone doesn't change. It's still as mild mannered as it was before, but the words have me staring at him as he sips coffee out of a paper cup, glasses on as he scrolls through his phone.

When I don't make a move to do as he says, he lays down his phone and reaches for his backpack on the floor beside him.

He's bluffing. He absolutely has to be bluffing, but he pauses when his hand finds the zipper.

"If I open this, then it's going on," he says without looking at me.

"He's not joking," Foster tells me, voice over-sweet. "In case you think he is."

Unfortunately, I don't.

"Okay, *okay*. Down, Cujo," I mutter, my hands raised in surrender. I grab my fork and stab a grape, putting it in my mouth and chewing as he sits back up.

"You know, this would be so much easier if you just, I don't know, did what I said?" he offers, brows rising towards his short black bangs. "Instead of me having to threaten you, and them trying to warn you I'm serious? What'll happen when they aren't around to do that, kitten?"

"Stop calling me that," I say in-between bites.

"It bothers you. So I don't think I will."

"If you don't stop calling me that, I'm going to *meow* anytime you talk to me." I meet his eyes, stomach doing a little flip at the unconvinced, challenging look in them.

He leans forwards as I eat, resting his arms on the table as he smile turns sweeter. "If you fucking *meow* at me in any capacity, you're going to find yourself regretting it sometime in the near future. And that's the only warning you're getting about that."

Foster looks between us, excitement glittering in his eyes.

I open my mouth, intent on meowing, until Dorian's eyes narrow just enough for me to notice.

So I stuff a bite of French toast in my mouth instead, pretending I don't hear the approving purr that emanates from his chest as he goes back to conversation with August while I act as though I don't exist.

In my break before astronomy, I find myself seated in the courtyard, legs crossed under me, as I copy Zara's notes from the class that I missed. I hate that I've taken so long to get around to it. And I hate that, thanks to Dorian, I haven't started the project that's due in a couple of weeks to our professor.

I scrawl notes on my iPad as I flip through Zara's notes, sighing heavily even though no one is around to hear me. While I had eaten some of my food at breakfast, it wasn't enough to actually fill me up, and I'm *hungrier* now than I usually am. Unfortunately, since I'm finishing this, I won't be able to grab anything to eat until after astronomy. Which is... fine. I'll just suffer. Which I seem to be doing a lot of lately.

Blinking, I realize I'm no longer alone, and I jerk my face up to meet Cecily's eyes as she studies the notes on the low wall in front of my crossed legs.

"Umm..." I trail off, unsure of what to say. "I missed a day of class last week? I'm just–"

"He copied the collar from me." Her gaze moves from the notes to my throat, where the crooked collar sits, looking like just a black necklace. "I've known for awhile he wanted to collar someone. But Foster doesn't like it, and while August might tolerate it, he doesn't like it either."

"You...collar people?" I ask, wincing at my words. I don't need to know, and it's not my business what the red-haired alpha does.

"My omegas," she agrees, reaching up as if she's going to twist the collar back. I pull away, gaze searching her as I do, and she grins. "*Oh.* So it's not accidental. I was wondering... one of my omegas did that once."

"Yeah? Because they don't like collars?"

"Because she wanted to see what I would do. I gave her what she wanted, and now she wears it straight, just like a good girl should." The words cause heat to flutter through me, but Cecily isn't an alpha I would ever want to end up with. Not because she's a woman. She *is* actually my type, but...

I don't know. It's just not something I'd consider.

"Don't let him see," she remarks, crossing one leg over the other. "If he notices more than once, he's going to know you're doing it on purpose...and by that look on your face, he's already caught you with it turned around once, hasn't he?"

I grimace, nose scrunched up in distaste as I look away. "Whatever," I say, brushing off her words. "I don't like him the way your omegas like you, Cecily."

She just hums a noncommittal reply and gets to her feet. "It's kind of plain. Does he have another one for when you guys play..." Realization dawns on her face a second later as she trails off. "You don't play with him, do you?"

"God, no." I shudder, slipping the notebook and my iPad back into my backpack. "No, I really don't want anything to do with him, Cecily. The sooner this is over, the better."

"Are you sure?"

The question gives me pause, but I nod enthusiastically as I stand. "Yeah, I've never been *more* sure."

She shrugs, not arguing with my statement. "Just don't let him see," she reiterates, and gets up to walk in the other direction, toward the campus center.

"You have my notes?" Zara's voice surprises me, and pushes the conversation with Cecily out of my head as I fumble through my backpack and give them back.

"Thank you. I appreciate it," I tell her, falling into step with her as we head into the science center. My stomach clenches painfully as we pass the smoothie place, and I sigh wistfully towards the sustenance I won't get until later. Though it's only been a few weeks, I've fallen in love with their peanut butter-banana-chocolate smoothie.

But we walk right on past, going to the elevator and up to our floor.

"We're going to see a movie tonight," Zara tells me, leading the way down the hallway. "Do you want to come?"

I assume by 'we' she means her and Briella.

"What movie?"

"*Tooth.*"

"It's supposed to be scary, right?" I can't help feeling excited. I love horror movies, and it's been a while since I've gotten to see one in theaters.

"Hopefully, yeah." She pushes open the door to astronomy. "Is that a yes?"

"Absolutely," I agree, waiting as she sits down at her spot near the back of the room.

She grins in sympathy, eyes flicking down the rows toward my own seat. "Wish I could say he's sick today, but..." We can both see him, sitting at our table near the front of the room with his notebook out in front of him.

I sigh, the sound turning into a groan as I tilt my head back theatrically. "I hate him," I tell her, and she nods in agreement.

"He sucks. But..." She trails off with a shrug. "I'll see you later?"

With a nod I walk away from her, stomping down the stairs until I'm standing at our table and I can slam my backpack down with just enough force not to hurt my iPad, but enough for him to get the point.

Lazily, and unhurriedly, Dorian looks up at me, mouth open to say something....until his eyes fall on my throat.

Oh.

Oh *shit*.

Before I can reach up to fix it, he points at the chair in front of me. "Sit," he orders, and I'm glad the person who sits behind us isn't here. "Don't touch it. *Sit.*"

I sit.

"Is there something wrong with it?" I ask innocently, eyes wide.

"I wondered this morning if you were doing it on purpose," he admits, reaching out to run his fingers along the leather. I don't move, afraid it'll trigger some kind of predatory response. "You are."

"I am?"

His gaze is unamused when it finds mine.

"Don't touch it," he warns, as Professor Beckler walks down the stairs to the front of the room, huffing and puffing.

No matter how my fingers itch to fix it so that maybe he'll forget, I do as he says and I don't touch it.

Even with the way I *fly* out of astronomy, Dorian catches me outside the doors. His hand grips my wrist hard, fingers tight, and he *drags* me around to the other side of the building. Here there are fewer people and enough shrubs to block us off from everyone else before he shoves me against the wall so hard that I gasp.

Only then does he lean in, his arms pressed to the brick on either side of my face.

"I think we need to have a quick chat, don't you?" He reaches down to hook one finger in the collar, pulling it around until he can loop that finger in the 'o' shaped ring and pull outwards just enough for me to feel pressure at the back of my neck. "Maybe you were unclear about how all of this works. You lost. So you're *mine*, Mercy. I've been really fucking nice, don't you think?"

I realize it isn't a rhetorical question a second later, and press my lips together before saying, "Look, I don't think you want me to answer–" He twists his finger in the ring and I gasp, though the pressure is just this side of painful.

"I haven't asked you to do anything major. I don't even count wearing this as something major. I've been *nice*." It isn't a question this time. "And I get it, you're not used to this."

"I don't like packs or alphas very much," I whisper, hands coming up to press against his chest. He lets me, and doesn't remark on the touch.

"Kitten I'm not asking you to join my pack. I'm not courting you so that you can be my omega. If you were a beta, we'd still be right here and you'd still be collared. No, you lost our *game* so you are *mine*. I *won* you."

"You can't own me, Dorian—"

"You bet your ass I can. And I think I've done a really good job of restraining myself today with your mouth and *this*." He tugs on the collar once more. "I'm not humiliating you. I'm not letting Foster bully you or take your shit anymore. And we're not going back to that. You're going to do what my pack tells you to. I don't even mind the backtalk so much. But if I have to drag obedience out of you after today, then it's going to be at the end of a leash, and I don't think you'll like that."

"Maybe I'm into that." The words are instinctual, and spat back at him. I don't think I am into that, and the response was a defense mechanism more than anything, but when I say it, I freeze. "No, wait I'm not—"

Too late.

Dorian drops his backpack to the ground and reaches into it, and when he pulls out a black, leather leash, he puts to rest my ideas of not having one with him.

"No, no—" Despite my protests he clips it onto the collar at my throat, winding the free end around his hand.

"How does that feel, *kitten*?" he purrs, leaning in to crowd against me. A slight jerk on the leash has me gasping, and pulls my body against his for a second before I jerk back against the wall.

I want to meow at him, just like I'd threatened.

I blink, my eyes narrowing, but just as my mouth forms the 'm' he laughs and jerks the leash again before I can talk.

"You're such a self sabotager, aren't you? You're really going to do it. With a leash and a collar on your pretty throat, you're going to fucking meow in my face like I won't make you regret it."

"With what?" I snap. "Ears? A tail? *Paw mitts?*" My heart is pounding in my chest and when I take a deep breath, it's full of his scent that clouds my mind and makes logical thought harder.

"You know, I think we should revisit the idea of you begging," he replies, leash still wrapped around his hand and voice a half-growl.

My heart jumps erratically in my chest. "No. What? You said–"

"Get on your knees."

When I hesitate, he jerks downward on the leash, bending down and giving me no choice but to follow as he puts the leash on the ground and steps on it, giving me just enough slack to sit on my knees in front of him, my face at the level of his thighs.

His hand comes down and he grips my chin, pulling my face up to look at him as he towers above me.

"S-someone is going to see," I whisper, my hands clutching at the denim of his jeans. "Dorian, someone is going to see us–"

"Tell me you're sorry, then. You want to get up? Then tell me you won't twist the collar around again unless you really want me to make you regret it."

"I'm sorry." I bite the words out, tasting the bile along with them. "I'm fucking *sorry*."

"Keep going."

My hands tighten on the denim above his knees, and when I try to turn away, he grips my chin harder.

"I'm *sorry*! I'll wear this stupid fucking collar the right way and I won't meow at you. Is that what you want?" He moves his sneaker off of the leash so fast I nearly topple backward, but instead, he pulls me to my feet, hands gentle around my throat as he immediately unclips the leash and puts it back in his backpack.

"That's all I wanted," he assures me, touch light against my skin. "None of this hurts, right?" The switch between angry-Dorian and caring-Dorian is too fast for me to keep up with. I blink at him, before finally shaking my head.

"No...it doesn't hurt now that you aren't pulling on it."

His smile is charming. "Good. Get your phone out. I want to put my number in there, and take yours as well."

17

With my phone ringing in my pocket, I sigh and stare down at the biology homework that I'm not very close to completing. Worse, my part of the astronomy project sits untouched on my desk as well, and both of them are staring up at me with accusations in their inked scrawl notes I'v jotted down on the papers.

God, why is this so difficult today?

My phone stops ringing, and before I can decide whether or not to ignore it, it starts up again, right away.

I know that ringtone. It's my mother.

She hasn't called in weeks. Not after the dead body I hadn't told her about. Not when Dorian's pack decided they own me. And not in the two weeks since then that have been relatively quiet, thanks to exams in some of our classes that the boys have been too fixated on to really pay attention to me.

Save for the little things, like dragging me away for breakfast every once in awhile, or insults hurled from Foster. Still, I know their exams, like mine, are now over, and I worry that means starting today and going through this weekend into the second part of the semester, that they'll have more time to make my life hell.

I catch the phone before the ringtone ends, answering it and putting it to my ear. "Hello?" I ask, and I'm greeted to the sound of my mother's harsh, loud sigh. She's been practicing so that I can hear her disdain over the phone, and the loud whoosh of air is impressive.

"*Why haven't you called me?*" she snaps, not letting me say anything else or delivering a greeting of her own. "*Are you mad at me for something? For going to the lake?*"

"No, Mom. I've been really busy. Like, insanely busy. Do you know how much homework they give here?" It isn't only that, and the homework is relatively easy, if time consuming. But of course it isn't that. Not that I'm going to tell her the real issue, obviously.

"*Are you coming home for fall break?*"

I shake my head, realize I'm an idiot and she can't see it, then say, "No. Sorry. I know we kind of talked about it, but I have an astronomy project, a bio project, and–"

"*Fine. Your aunt was hoping to come see you. But I'll tell her you're too busy. I hope everything is going well, other than you being busy?*" Approval and affection enter her voice at the question, though I'm not sure how genuine they are. Despite her not wanting me to attend Winter Grove, I think she's sometimes-happy I got in here because she can tell everyone about it and what a good mom she is.

"Oh. Umm tell her I'm sorry. I like seeing her."

"*You aren't overeating, are you?*" Of course we're back to that. I press my lips together in a line as my stomach turns, threatening me with nausea.

"No, mom."

"Have you weighed yourself to see if you've gained anything? You're bad at noticing unless you keep track."

"I..." I swallow, and glance up at the door when there's a knock on it. "Hey, someone's here Mom. I'll talk to you later?" She says a quick goodbye and I go to the door, expecting Briella or Zara.

Or hell, maybe even one of Dorian's pack.

I don't expect a thin, blonde-haired police officer. Her scent hits me first, like cigarettes and flowers, and the alpha smiles tightly at me as her brown eyes wander my dorm room. "Can I come in?" she asks, sounding almost...friendly.

I nod once, then again, trying not to look suspicious since I've done nothing wrong. "Yes umm. Uhh, is everything okay?" I step back, pulling the door wider as I do, and the woman steps inside to look around more thoroughly. Her eyes fall on my desk, and the homework there, and she wanders over to look at it curiously.

"Everything isn't okay, I'm sorry to say," the officer says finally, gesturing for me to sit on my bed as she takes the chair. Her hair is drawn back remarkably tight, and I wonder if she's used hairpsray to get it so flat. Lord knows my own hair would have no chance in hell of doing that, even if I were to use every product available on the market.

"Is this about the body from a few weeks ago?"

"Sort of. But it's also about the body we found last night."

My eyes widen at the words, and I'm left not knowing what to say. "Holy *shit*. Was it? You know...bloody? Like a murder?"

"I can't disclose that kind of information about an ongoing investigation," the police officer dismisses. "I just came to ask you a couple of questions. Where were you last night?"

"You think *I* did it?!"

"No," she tells me quickly. "Not in the least. But I'd like to know anyway, if you please."

"I was here, with my roommate. We were waiting for her girlfriend to get out of class before we went to dinner. Then we came back here to watch a movie since all of our exams were over." There's nothing false about it, though it makes me nervous anyway to talk about it.

The officer nods, leaning back in my chair. "And you don't have any idea who the victim was that you found? Or who might be doing this?"

Doing this, implies that it's the same situation, and this body was murdered as well. Though I guess there wouldn't be an officer here if that weren't the case.

Slowly I shake my head, twisting the blanket between my fingers. "No."

"Where's your roommate now?"

"She's with her girlfriend," I reply, somewhat awkwardly. "In her girlfriend's room." My brows raise as I try to get across what I'm trying to say, and after a moment she snorts. "I get what you're saying, Miss Noble. And I'm really sorry to show up and disrupt your night. I hope I'm not interrupting any plans."

I gesture at my TV that's on mute, and the homework on the table. "Those are my plans."

"On a Friday?"

"I went to a party for the first time a few weeks ago." A rueful smile finds my lips as I speak. "And found a dead body on my way home. I'm not really excited to do it again. Besides, it's just not my thing, I guess."

She nods again, quiet for a few long seconds. "I have one last question for you if that's all right?"

"Yeah, of course. Anything."

From her pocket she removes a small plastic bag, holding it up for my inspection. "Do you know what this is?"

It looks like a *speck* from six feet away. Getting to my feet I pad forward in my socks, squinting to look at the small, red object in the bag.

It looks like a jewel. There's residue on one side that leads me to believe it was once attached to something, and it's the color of fresh blood, but I shake my head. I've definitely never seen this before.

"Is it expensive?"

"No. It's fake, like it came off of some cheap piece of jewelry. We found it with the body."

How strange.

"And it's not the, uh, victim's?"

"We don't think so. There was nothing on him that leads us to believe–"

There's another knock on my door and I jump, trading looks with the officer. She gestures for me to open the door, and when I do, August's grin turns questioning when he sees her there.

"Did you do something bad, Mercy?" he teases, brushing past me to come inside.

The officer stands up and offers her hand immediately. "I'm Officer Dennings," she introduces, and it makes me feel a little miffed that she'd never introduced herself to *me*.

"I'm August Frost," he replies, clasping her hand warmly. "But I guess you already knew that."

"I was just leaving, actually," she goes on, putting the bag with the little stone back into her pocket. "Have a good night, both of you." She nods towards me, then towards him, and takes her leave rather quickly.

I watch her go, bewildered. "...Huh," I say finally. "You're really good at that."

"Good at what?"

"Making people leave. That was weird how she just...got up and *went*."

"It's not weird," August assures me, looking at my homework. "You're taking a long time on this, aren't you?"

"Why isn't it weird? And I've been distracted."

"Bring it with you. It isn't weird because my dad basically funded their entire department. It was his…gift when I was accepted to the university."

"Like a bribe?"

"Whatever you want it to be, princess." This new, unexpected nickname makes my eye twitch, but I don't say anything. "Anyway, come on. And put your collar on. I'm not Dorian, but he will notice if you aren't wearing it when we get there. Unless you want him to put you on your knees again?"

"Don't call me weird shit, August." I'm not afraid of him. Especially without Foster or Dorian here. "And *where* are we going?"

"Back to my dorm."

"Why?"

He looks at me, his gaze direct and unimpressed.

I get the memo quite clearly that I'm supposed to just go. Distracted, I shovel my homework into my back with a sigh, but before I can go anywhere, he bars the way to my door and just stands there.

"It's October," he reminds me, glancing down at my bare legs. "In *Maine*."

"And I don't like wearing pants unless my legs are in danger of falling off. It's a ten minute walk at best? I'm really not worried about it." I do, however, slip my feet into my sneakers and grab my oversized, black and red hoodie from the chair to shrug on. It falls down almost as far as my shorts cover, and when I look up at August again, he's rolling his eyes.

"What if we're going on a field trip?"

"Then I guess I'll have to stay behind, because I'm going to freeze."

"You're such a child."

"*I'm* the child?" I take a step closer to him, wanting to prove just how little I'm afraid of him. He isn't Dorian or Foster. He's never done anything hurtful like they have. If anything, August is the closest any of them are to being my *friend*. Not that he is one, but if I had to pick one of the boys to hang out with, it would be him. "You're dragging me out of my dorm room while I'm doing homework just to prove a point, but *I'm* the child?"

He just watches me as I speak, emerald green eyes studying my face. "You don't treat me like Dorian. Or even Foster. I know you're worried about him ever since the *Video Valhalla* incident and when he walked away with your backpack."

I shrug one shoulder, pushing up the sleeves of my too-big hoodie. "That's probably a compliment or something that you aren't as bad as them."

"You really don't think so?"

I shake my head and straighten to face him again, only to find that the stupid collar is in his hand from where I'd left it on the desk.

"Come here."

I hold my hand out for it instead, shaking my head. "My floor is dirty. I'm not getting down on my knees on it."

"I'm not asking you to. Come here." There's a note of an alpha-growl in his voice, and it tugs at something in me to do what he says. That I *want* to do what he says. A part of me itches for his hands on my skin, around my throat, or wherever else he wants them.

But I let out a breath and gaze at him, bored, while shaking my head once more. "Give it to me, and I'll put it on. But I'm too tired for–"

He moves so fast that my brain doesn't have time to react.

August grabs me by the front of my hoodie, pushing my backpack down my shoulders and to the floor as he backs me up until I'm forced to sit on my bed.

"You should probably bite your tongue on whatever compliment you were trying to give me." He twists my hair up and away from my neck before dropping it, as if he's just doing it so that my scalps stings with the pressure. I reach up to grab for his wrists, but his movements are still so fast as he grabs my hands in his and looks at me with raised brows. "Hook your fingers in my belt loops. Now." It's certainly not a request, and when he lets go of me and I hesitate, his hand is back in my hair and twisting again, until I gasp. "I don't like to be *mean* like they do, I guess. Maybe they need some balancing out in that regard. But I'm not your white knight who's going to let you push me around, either."

"I wasn't trying to—"

"No. But you like to push boundaries." He waits, still holding my hair, until my middle fingers are hooked in the belt loops of his jeans as he stands between my thighs.

"Tilt your head back for me, princess."

"Why are you calling me that?" I'd meant to tell him to *stop* calling me that, but this makes me feel incredibly...vulnerable There's no other word for it. I don't know what it is, exactly. The way he grips my hair, or his scent that suddenly overwhelms me. The growl in his throat has me wanting to fall back and give him mine, but that's not right.

I'm not his omega.

"Because I can," he shrugs, hands gentle at my throat as he clasps the collar and then slowly spins it so the ring is at the front. Before I can move, August hooks one finger in the 'o' ring and drags me to my feet, still so close to me that our bodies are pressed close together and I can feel his breath on my lips when I look up at him. "I'm still not going to be *mean* to you," he assures me, like I'd asked or made some inclination of being worried. "But I am part of Dorian's pack. And that means you belong to me too. For the record, though? I thought you were going to win, and I was kind of looking forward to the idea of Foster apologizing to the lady who owns *Video Valhalla*."

18

I shiver, my legs *freezing* as we get closer to their dorm. August looks at me, one brow raised, but I look away from him. "I'm shivering at your presence. And I'm clearly just so *shook* by how mean you were to me," I drawl, the words a complete lie.

I'm *cold* as fuck.

August snorts and runs his card through the door. "Sure you are, Mercy. I absolutely believe I'm the thing that'll be in your nightmares tonight."

"Yeah, maybe you'll replace the donut pulling out my teeth," I sigh, trudging to the elevator behind him.

When we're inside it, he looks at me strangely, like he's just now digesting the words I'd said to him. "...What?" he asks after a moment, as the elevator dings on the third floor.

"You don't have teeth-losing dreams? I read in a dream book it's pretty common. Well, for people like me with my, you know, thought processes. Then again, in the last book I read, losing teeth in your dreams has to do with a deep, personal loss. And I can't think of any I've had since my dad—" I stop talking for a second, cutting myself off, then add. "But I have no idea why it's a donut that's pulling them out."

He pauses at the door to his room, drumming his fingers on the handle. "Your dad died?" he assumes, turning to look at me sidelong.

I gaze back at him, not answering for a few seconds. Finally, I snort, though my heart constricts in my chest as I try to push away the memories. "That's what you got out of that?" The door swings open, but I continue. "You're not going to question my teeth getting pulled out by a donut?"

Foster looks up from the counter beside the fridge, confusion apparent on his face. "...What?" he asks, looking between us. "I'm sorry, did you just say–"

"She's talking about her dreams," August interrupts, walking past him.

My eyes find Dorian, who's lying on his back on their huge, plush couch that clearly isn't standard dorm issue. Hell, I wonder how they even got it through the door. Still, my hand goes up to my neck, fingers brushing against the ring that still sits at the hollow of my throat.

At least he can't say anything about it this time. Or make any weird remarks about making me regret meowing.

God, I wish I'd meowed at him before. Though I suppose that's easy to think about now, when I'm not longer in the danger zone. But yesterday, just getting out of the situation was all I'd wanted. Today is a different story.

"So...why am I here?" I ask, my eyes flicking to Foster's as he puts butter on a bagel. He chomps down on it a few moments later, turning to lean against the counter.

"Did you have somewhere better to be?" he asks, once his mouth is no longer full.

"I did, actually," I reply, my tone matching his challenging one.

"Where?"

"*Anywhere.*"

He snorts at the word, shaking his head slightly before opening his mouth again. This time, however, it's Dorian who says, "Stop it. *Both* of you. If you're going to fight, you can go to Foster's room with him and do it there." He rubs his temples like he has a headache, and takes off his glasses to lay them on the table.

"Astronomy project," he reminds me, when I look at him questioningly. "That's why you're here. Have you started it yet?"

"Have I...started it yet?" I reply, confused at his question. "Are you being funny?"

"No, Mercy. I'm not being funny. Did you start it yet?"

I throw another sneering glare in Foster's direction as I walk further into the room, dropping my backpack onto the coffee table with a soft thud.

"You know how I am, right? Not in the 'has a lot of money' or 'dad owns a police department' way." August snorts at that, but doesn't respond as he lifts Dorian's feet an sits on the couch beside him.

For my part, I sit down at the end of the coffee table, legs curled up under me as I sort through the notebooks, iPad, and textbooks in my backpack.

"As in, 'I'm the scholarship student'." Opening two notebooks, I spread them to the pages that I've used to work on this project, and turn on my iPad to the moveable, interactive diagram I've created of our constellation. The notebook icons detail each and every little star in it or around it, and by tapping on them on the diagram, a box comes up. Though for now, those boxes are empty.

I brush my hair back behind my ears, shoving my bio textbook to the side, along with the packet I'd been working on, and the notebook I've been using for homework. A small, glittery notepad is on the table as well, and I open it to the pages that I've used to draw the constellations by hand from my digital diagram.

And then I look up at both Dorian and August expectantly, eyebrows raised.

But only August is still on the couch, and he looks impressed.

Dorian sinks down beside me, his arm brushing mine as he leans over the table. I pull it away from him, placing my head on my hand as he reads through my notes and taps the stars on my iPad, moving it around so he can see it in fake-3D.

"Mercy..." He frowns, and my heart twists in my chest.

"What? Is it...not what we were supposed to do? You told me I could pick the constellation, but if *Ursa Major* isn't okay, or it's too basic, I can do another one. You can do this, too." I tap one of the icons on the diagram, and white lines form on the dark blue background to show what the constellation is supposed to be. "I just thought that since it's so recognizable and has more stars–"

He loops a finger in the collar at my throat, still frowning, but it has the effect of making me shut up in surprise.

"Mercy, I wasn't trying to make you do this all on your own. I thought we'd do it *together*. What? Did you think I was going to force you to do all the work so I could take the grade?" He meets my eyes, and sighs. "Fine. Don't answer that. I see it on your face anyway." He plays with the diagram a little, unhooking his finger from the collar.

My insides twist, though I don't understand why. But it's almost like his disappointment hurts my *feelings*.

If anything, it's the last thing that should hurt my feelings.

"I just...thought that's what you wanted," I murmur, unsure of what to say.

"No. It isn't." My heart plummets. It feels like he's my *professor*, telling me that I did a bad job, and I don't like it one bit. "Because I do my own work, and I pull my own weight. I might be pretty awful to you sometimes, though it's well-deserved–"

"No it isn't–"

"But..." He snorts softly. "Look, no one in the class is going to be able to top this, that's for sure. This is *amazing*."

Suddenly my insides twist again, but in a different way. I have to remind myself that his opinion *does not matter*, and I should not let it matter to me. He's a dreadful piece of crap, and it's his fault that I'm here anyway.

That thought helps me clear my head, and I sigh. "I was going to do it all myself anyway," I point out. "It's not like you've made it worse or anything."

"What still needs to be done?"

"Umm. Transferring my notes and any other relevant facts to their stars, I guess? None of them are filled in, see?" I tap the stars, showing the blank boxes to him. "But there's some information I'm missing on them. I know that we're only supposed to list their distance, name, and type, but I've been trying to include anything I can find about them as well. Then I'll have to transfer this to my laptop, and put it in a format that's able to be opened on other devices."

"I'll do it," he replies, voice nonchalant.

I blink. "Do what?"

"All of that. It's not a lot, and nowhere near what you've done so far. But I'll do it."

"Why?" His words are absolutely bewildering to me. "Why do it, when I'm already planning to? Besides, you'd have to do it all on my iPad, and the information part would take me at least a couple hours."

"Yeah?" He drags my notes closer to him. "Do you have a pencil for this?"

"For my iPad? What do I look like I am? *Rich*?" I brandish a generic stylus from my backpack. "We middle classers use these." I know an Apple pencil isn't expensive, exactly. But there have always been better things to get, and my stylus works fine. Mostly.

Dorian snorts and gets to his feet, disappearing in his room before coming back with a white Apple pencil in his hand. Because of course he has one.

"This works a lot better than a stylus," he informs me, snapping it to the magnetic charging side of the iPad. It syncs instantly as I watch, and I'm impressed to see that the pen is fully charged. If it were mine, it would be dead anytime I need it. "Don't you have something else to do?"

"Maybe, but I'm not letting you keep my iPad, Dorian." There's a not of unsureness in my voice as I shake my head. "No way. I need it—"

"I'm not *keeping* it. Just do some other homework. I don't need you hovering while I work on this. And it's my turn to do stuff on it."

My nose scrunches at his words, and I grimace. "I'm, umm. Done with all my other work," I lie, feeling uncomfortable with all of this. I don't *mind* finishing my project. It's what I'd planned to do in the first place, and it's weird to have him working on it like he actually cares. "That was the only thing—"

"You are such a little liar." August slides to the floor, and I grab for my biology book and the packet we'd been assigned.

But I'm too late. He opens it up to the page I'd stopped working on, showing it to me like I'd forgotten. "Pretty sure you still have quite a bit of this to go before Monday."

"Well, okay. But I just meant..." I look between him and Dorian. "Well that I'm done for *now*. I've been working all night, you know?" I give a fake yawn. "I was going to sleep when August barged in. The officer basically woke me up."

"Officer?" Foster plops down on the sofa, looking interested. "Did you do something bad, Mercy?"

"She was getting questioned about the body she found."

"They found another one," I say automatically.

Dorian pauses, brows raised. "They did?"

"Yeah, but I don't know where or anything. The officer just wanted to ask me a couple of questions is all." I think about telling them about the little red gem, discard the idea, then think about it again. Might as well, I guess. "They found this little red jewel? Looks like it's from a necklace or something. They asked if I knew what it was, but I've never seen it in my life."

"God, Mercy." I gaze up at Foster as he murmurs the words, concern on his face. "That really sucks and all...but you're really the absolute worst liar I've ever seen."

Ouch.

Fucking *ouch*.

"Going to sleep? Please. If you're going to say shit that isn't true, stop stammering when you do it. Cut out the 'uhhh' or the 'umm.' You're so predictable and easy to read that it's unreal."

"Maybe you're just so used to *lying* that you spot it so easily in others," I snap. He brings out the worst in me, that's for sure.

Dorian sighs. "Don't make me ground you," he states, though I'm not sure who he's talking to. "I'll send you to your rooms."

"I don't live here," I remind him, my tone sickly sweet. "But *please*, send me to my fucking room. I'd love to go back to my dorm."

When he pauses in his transcribing, I tense. I know what comes next. This is where he throws me to the ground, humiliates me a little, and makes me apologize before letting me up. It's getting predictable by now.

But then he just...doesn't. He looks plaintively at me, glasses back on his face. I've never seen him with them up close, and the heavy black frames suit him incredibly well. "Do your homework, Mercy," he says finally, tapping the pencil on my bio work. "You could get it done faster with August here."

I don't know what to say. It's such a weirdly even response, that I turn my backpack upside down again so that my pens and pencils rattle out. Along with the empty box for my injection, my migraine tablets, and my emergency ibuprofen.

Unfortunately for me, Foster is like a magpie. He's on the ground and snatches the box of tablets and the injector box before I can put them back up. "Migraines, huh?" he remarks, looking them over. "You get them a lot?"

"Yeah. Or I wouldn't be jamming an injector in my leg like I'm the greatest zombie-action movie hero that ever lived who's trying to fight off the impending injection," I say, the explanation as long-winded as it always is. He blinks, eyes finding my face.

To my left, August snorts on a laugh.

"If I don't say it like that, it sounds more serious than it is." I pluck the empty box from his hands, and my tablets as well. "I don't like giving myself shots, so I have to amp my brain up for them. Otherwise I'll just sit there all day and whine about it."

"I'll do it?" Foster offers.

"Uh, no. You'll probably jam the needle in my neck and kill me."

He scoffs. "No I wouldn't, you drama queen. Let me do it for you next time."

"No."

"Why?"

"What the *fuck*–Because I don't know you that well, you psychopath."

"He'd do it right," Dorian assures me, not looking up. "I promise."

"Yeah? And why's that?"

"Because he wouldn't want to miss seeing how much it hurts you."

I start to reply, but then his words do another circuit in my head and I stop. My eyes narrow, and I look down at my hands. I don't know what to say to that. What *is* there to say to that, even?

So I just look at Foster, who meets my eyes and smiles. "Guilty," he agrees. "I don't know if anyone's told you this yet, Mercy?" He leans in close, like he's telling me a secret. "But I'm a bit of a sadist, myself."

"...Oh yeah? I never would've guessed–"

"And a masochist too," August interrupts. "So don't sell yourself short, Foster."

I've definitely never met anyone who admits they're a sadomasochist. But Foster doesn't look put out about it.

"We could probably finish this tonight," August points out, gesturing to our biology homework. "Then you can just, I don't know, go back to your dorm and sleep the weekend away?"

That sounds great. Frankly, having him to help me with bio, and Dorian doing the rest of my astronomy work would be...amazing. And probably the nicest thing they've ever done for me. Though, the bar is so low that it doesn't take much.

And at the rate Dorian's going, I'll be back in my dorm in three hours, max.

. . .

The television is the first thing I notice when consciousness rolls back into my skull. My eyes don't open immediately, but I'm...confused?

The pillow under my cheek doesn't feel like mine. It's smoother than mine, and fluffier. Not to mention, the blanket over my body is fleece, instead of the cheap comforter I bought at the store. I own a fleece blanket, but it's still in my closet. I won't pull it out for another few weeks, at least.

So when did I get it out of the bag?

My eyes open, and that doesn't help my confusion at all. I'm staring at a TV up high on the wall, and the volume is low as Michael Myers chases someone through a house. Had I put on *Halloween*? It's October, so there's a high chance that it's just *on*, and whatever I was watching before just turned into this.

But I can't remember what I was watching before.

And this isn't the angle of my dorm room's television.

I bolt up, the blanket falling off of me, and Dorian glances up at me from the floor, one knee up while the other leg is stretched out against the carpet.

"Holy shit," I murmur, blinking as I look around their suite. He's the only one still in the room, and all of my stuff is off of the coffee table. "What the hell?"

"You fell asleep, Mercy," Dorian replies, a purr tinging his tone like he's trying to calm me down.

I'm absolutely ashamed that it works.

I gaze at him, the low light from the TV and from a room down the hallway the only things illuminating his face.

"How did I fall asleep?" I demand, rubbing my hand against my eyes. "I wouldn't have...I don't trust you guys enough to *sleep* here." My heart is pounding in my chest as I work myself up, and a moment later Dorian's hands are on my wrists, tugging them down.

"You were tired, kitten," he chuckles. "What's the big deal? Nothing happened, except that we gave you a blanket and let you sleep for awhile."

I stare at him, nonplussed. Finally, I ask, "What time is it?" Because I don't know what else to say.

"Around three in the morning."

"*Shit.*"

"But it's Saturday. You could just go back to sleep."

"I'd rather sleep in an ocean. With sharks. And no scuba tank," I reply automatically, pulling my hands out of his grip. "I need my stuff."

He gestures to my backpack and I get to my feet, stumbling a little as I get my bearings.

"Here." He holds up the *stupid collar* that's going to haunt me for the rest of my life, and I just stare at it.

Had I taken it off?

"You were tossing and turning a lot, so I took it off. Put it back on."

"No, that's okay. You seem really attached to it, so you can keep it."

"Mercy..." There's a warning in his voice, but I'm too sleepy and bleary-eyed to really care.

"No, really. Consider it my gift to you, Dorian. I wouldn't want it to get lost, or stolen, or something."

He gets to his feet much more smoothly than I had, the flickers from the TV reflecting in his glasses as he meets my eyes. "Why do you do this?" he asks, backing me up until I'm against the wall next to the window.

"Why do I do what?"

"You know this is going around your neck, kitten. You know it *so well*. We do this all the time, and *every time* we do it, you make it difficult. I'm really starting to think you want me to make you sorry."

"Nah," I assure him, pulling away so I'm flush against the wall. His hands come up to my throat, sliding the leather around my neck.

"Really?"

"Really," I assure him. "I promise."

"How can you be so sure of that?"

I don't mean to do it.

Really, I don't.

But I'm *so tired*, and he confuses me so much with his moods and his actions, that I'm at the end of my rope.

I clear my throat, then open my mouth to say, in a high-pitched tone, "*Meow*."

He stops. Dorian goes dead still in front of me, his eyes on mine. He's surprised. I see that clearly, and he doesn't even bother trying to hide it.

"...Excuse me?" he says finally, voice carefully empty.

"*Meow*," I say again. It's not like he hadn't heard me the first time, so why the fuck not?

He looks thoughtful, not angry like I'd expected. His fingers clasp the collar and he hooks one in it, dragging me upward so I have to stand on the balls of my feet. "Okay," he says at last. "Alright, kitten. If you say so."

What?

"Aren't you mad?" I demand, reaching up to grip his wrist. He doesn't stop me, or mention stopping me.

It's so weird.

"No," Dorian replies, and *smiles*. "I'm not mad at all. How can I be mad, when you clearly can't help yourself?"

"So you're not going to do anything?"

He shrugs. "If you were worried about that, you wouldn't have done it."

Clarity is coming back to me in cold waves of trepidation.

There's no way he isn't mad. No way in hell. I take a deep breath, his sweet and musky scent clouding my nose.

God, I wish anyone else on the planet had that scent. I could wrap myself up in it and go to sleep as easily as...well, okay. So that's sort of what I'd just done, isn't it?

But still. Dorian Wakefield is *not* my alpha. He doesn't even want to be, as he's pretty much told me before.

"I want to go back to my dorm," I tell him, my eyes on his. "Are you going to let me?"

The finger in my collar pulls away. I drop down to rock back on my heels.

"Of course I am, kitten," he promises. "I packed your stuff up for you, too."

"...Okay." This is *so weird*. I slip around him, grabbing my backpack to slide it over my shoulders as I stride to the door before he can stop me.

Once there, however, I pause with my hand on the handle. "You *really* aren't mad at me? You're not going to tackle me at the door or anything?"

"Of course not." He grabs the blanket and pillow from the bed, tossing the pillow onto a shelf and folding the blanket. I'm halfway out the door before he adds. "Because we've learned that just doesn't work for you."

19

As I stare at the article, the low conversation behind me fades in and out of my ears. Zara and Bri aren't quiet, exactly. But I'm not focused on what they're saying. Nor do I care enough to be. Our movie doesn't start for another thirty minutes, so we have five or so before we need to leave, since the theater is only a few miles off of campus and into town.

In fact, I think they're talking about the theater. How it's old, vintage, and a classic building that's been in the newspaper a few times or something. Hell, according to Zara, it might even be haunted. But as interesting as that is, it isn't as interesting as the newspaper article I'm reading.

"This is so weird," I murmur, flipping the page to finish reading. "Have you read this, Zara?" I brandish the paper that she'd snagged on our way up to her dorm room from the front desk at her, and she looks over it with a quick shake of her head.

"No. It only came out today, and I just grabbed it," she

reminds me, which makes sense. "I thought I'd look at it after we go see *Tooth*."

My stomach twists in excitement at the idea of seeing a horror movie. I *love* them, after all. And I can't think of anything I'd rather do on a Saturday. Especially since it'll chase away any lingering thoughts about the night before.

And the scent of Dorian that won't leave my nose. My brain keeps tripping over it, reminding me how much we love his scent. How much I love *all* of their scents. It really is a damn shame that it's, well, *them*.

I put the newspaper down, still staring at the picture of the dead boy they'd found in town, but my eyes flick to the other side of the desk, where a metal object shines in the light. A few metal objects, actually.

"Oh, Zara. Is this the pin you had on your backpack?" I pick up the part of it with the sharp point still attached, looking at what remains of the broken off, little knife. The handle is in the small plastic bowl as well, along with the back of the pin. "What happened?"

Zara comes to stand beside me and sighs, picking up the pieces to hold them in her hand. "These are so cheap. I shouldn't get attached to them, but I really like them. I dropped my backpack the other day and it hit a tile floor. The pin broke. I need to throw it away," she admits, going over the small pieces and then dropping them back into the bowl.

"Can you glue it back together? Find another one?" It had been a cute pin, and now it's just bits of shattered black and grey metal in the bowl.

She shakes her head. "No. But I'm keeping it for sentimental value. Maybe I'll give it a burial, huh?" she grins at me, then adds, "Or you can take the sharp end and stab Dorian with it? I'm not sure it'll kill him, but maybe you'll give him tetanus?"

I cackle, surprised at the words. "God, if only." She leads the way back out of her dorm, and down to her SUV that sits in the parking lot outside. Between the three of us, she's not only the oldest, but also the only one with a car. A nice car, at that. The SUV has heated seats and a sunroof, and while I've always been more of a fan of cars, I can't complain.

Especially since I get to stretch out along the back seat and stare up into the sky as she drives, the interior dark around me. As per usual, Bri shares the front with her, and I know that if I look to the side, I'll see them holding hands.

Admittedly, it makes me a touch jealous. Zara isn't my type, but their relationship is sweet. Sure, it's only been a few weeks, but I see a difference in Bri.

Would there be a difference in me, too, if I had someone?

"You have an archery competition on Tuesday, right?" Bri asks, turning to look over the seat at me.

"Wednesday," I respond automatically, my eyes closed. "It's not here, though. It's down in Royalwood." Not that I've ever been there. It's apparently a slightly bigger town than Winter Grove, and the students there are less-than competition for any of our teams. In theory, the competition will go smoothly, though butterflies take flight in my stomach when I think about it. Is it too soon? Will I be good enough? "Why?" I murmur, my eyes closing. "Are you still planning on going?"

The silence speaks for itself. My heart twists. I'd thought she was going, and while I don't need a ride or anything from Zara, it would've been nice to have the support.

"No," Bri says, with a sigh. "I thought it was Tuesday, I'm sorry. Mom asked me to come home—there's a family thing, and..."

"It's fine," I promise before she can launch into a huge explanation. I open my eyes again, expecting to see stars above me through the sunroof. Instead, I just see blackness. "It's cloudy tonight," I remark, trying to push my mind away from the thought of the archery competition. Maybe it's better Briella isn't going. Of course I know Zara isn't going. She has night classes on Wednesday, though she'd already told me she would if she could.

Maybe it's better that I go and see how things are on my own the first time. I'll have the team, Eden included. While we aren't friends, we aren't on awful terms. Especially when Cecily isn't around. And hopefully, Cecily *won't* be around. She's not into archery as far as I know, and has never acted that interested, even though Eden is supposedly her best friend and all.

My phone vibrates against my chest, one of my hands lying gently on top of it. I ignore it, wondering how long the cloud cover will last and if it means it's going to storm. As I've recently learned about living on the lake, we get lake-effect *everything*. My friends have assured me that not only means wind and rain, but it'll also mean snow.

Zara turns off of the main road and into the back parking lot, behind the bright lights of the retro cinema, and finally I glance at my phone, expecting my mother to want *something* this late at night.

Instead, I see a message from Dorian there.

I forgot to pack your bio packet in your backpack last night. August took it by accident, so it's here.

My heart leaps in my chest, then twists painfully. God, this means I can't ignore them for the rest of the weekend like I'd hoped to do. I need it on Monday, and while I'm sure August could bring it to me, that feels too much like a favor. Not only that, but I'd like to check it one last time tomorrow before turning it in.

I'm not home, I reply, hoping to get the message across that I can't be there right now.

Where are you? The text is immediate, as if he has nothing better to do other than message me in this group chat. I roll my eyes. My personal life is none of their business. Especially his.

At the movies, I say finally. Who cares if they know? They can't come fuck up my night once I'm in the theater, and I'll pretend they don't exist if they *are* here.

What are you seeing? The new text is from Foster, but even if I'd wanted to answer, he follows it up with another before I can. *Are you seeing Dandelion Lovers? It looks stupid.*

I still don't reply, because it's really none of his business. Slowly I sit up, opening the door, and walking to the side of the building where retro movie posters are framed behind glass and little lights that twinkle around the old artwork.

My phone vibrates again, but I ignore it for a moment to gaze at a poster for *The Thing* with a small smile tugging at my lips. It's been a while since I've seen the original artwork for the old movie, and it's nostalgic.

God, I wish I could've gotten the movies I wanted from *Video Valhalla.*

My phone reminds me I have an unanswered message and I sigh, closing my eyes for a moment while Bri and Zara talk against the side of her SUV. That, or they're making out. Knowing them, it's probably that.

Really, I am happy for them. But I'm also getting tired of her smelling like Zara and sex all the time.

I'm not jealous though. Not really. Not of her specifically, I guess. But the more that I'm around them, the more that I itch to know what any of that feels like. Rather than being stuck with some stupid pack of assholes that think they can make me do whatever they want.

Absently I look at my phone, unsurprised the message is from Dorian.

Come get your stuff, Mercy.

I take a deep breath and let it out slowly, cramming my eyes shut. The collar almost feels like it tightens around my throat, though I know it's all mental. *Fine,* I say back, sending the message. *Tomorrow.*

Tonight. After your movie.

Fuck them. I really can't just have this night to myself? Seriously?

Whatever. You could just hang it on the door or something for me so I don't have to go in.

And miss your company? August asks, his text the only small surprise. *When we haven't seen you in so long?* I hate his messages. I hate him, but I hate them all, and it's just so hard to pick favorites among Dorian's pack, since they're all so dreadful.

"You good?" Zara's voice is questioning, and I jump when I realize they're near the doors and waiting for me. I smile, trying to look excited, even though I don't feel it. "Yeah, of course. Sorry." I send one last text, lying and saying my movie is starting, and tell them that I'll let them know when I'm back on campus, but not to wait up for me.

Maybe they'll fall asleep and I'll be good for the night.

Enjoy your movie, is the last thing I get, and it's from August.

The movie sucks, which isn't a big deal, but the theater itself is *gorgeous*. The bathrooms, with their gilded mirrors and retro style, are as luxurious as the red-curtained, vintage lobby itself. Stairs lead up to the balcony of one of the two theaters, and with the way the employees are dressed, it feels like being back in time for a little while. The red and white popcorn boxes are a nice bonus, and it's so surprising to see everything but the candy looking so classic.

"I want to come here again," I tell my friends, as we get into the car. "I don't care what we see, or how bad it sucks. This is so cool."

"Too bad we didn't see the ghost, huh?" Briella teases, buckling her seatbelt. "If there really is such a thing."

"I don't think there is," Zara replies, her tone cool. "Do you want to come back to my room? We could watch something else, or even just go get a snack in the dining hall?"

My stomach twists at the invite. "Oh, umm..." I'm sitting up this time, watching the shops along the main street of Winter Grove march on by. A few of them are bars. There's a tattoo and piercing shop, with another shop one beside it, and from what I've heard there are a few nicer restaurants further back, overlooking the lake. A candy shop catches my eye, but it passes by as well as I sigh. "I can't. I have some stuff to do."

"Stuff?" Briella inquires, her voice already holding the edge of pity.

I don't want her pity, so I grin ruefully. "I have homework to do, and I'd like to use the twenty-four hour room at the library so I know I'll get it done," I laugh, the words a lie. "Seems like I'm always doing homework these days, huh?"

They agree, with Briella telling me I should learn to lighten up, and by the time Zara pulls up to the curb in front of our dorm, the wind is fierce but they've forgotten their misgivings on how I'm actually going to spend the rest of my night.

Good on me for not being as bad of a liar as Foster told me I was. Maybe I've improved with the criticism.

"I didn't know it was supposed to storm," I remark, as the wind whips my hair into a frenzy. There's thunder in the distance, and I hate that I'll have to go to the boys' dorm in this. One way or another, whether it's now or on my way back, I'm going to get rained on, I'm sure.

"All night," Zara tells me, as Briella waves from the open

window. "Call us if you change your mind. I'll come rescue you from the library." I agree, and by the time we've said our goodbyes, I'm starting to see lightning out of the corner of my eye.

I hesitate, glancing up at the sky when I'm alone again in front of the dorm. Do I run now? I want a hoodie, instead of the light jacket I wear, and I'd like to change out of my jeans if I'm going to be *sprinting* to the lakeside dorms.

Yeah, that feels like the better option.

It only takes me a couple of minutes to get into my room, and once I'm there I strip out of my jeans, boots, and jacket. After a brief hesitation, I chuck my shirt onto my bed as well and go to the drawer to yank out a long, red and black t-shirt that looks like tie-dyed blood, leggings, sneakers, and a zip-up hoodie that hangs halfway down my thighs and over my hands. At least if it rains now, I'll have some protection from it. I also don't bring my backpack with me, since I figure I can just stuff my bio-packet in my hoodie if I need to.

It could be worse, probably. At least when I get back I'll be able to ride out the storm with a movie or something, and they *really* won't have any cause to mess with me until Monday. Or at least, if they do, I'll be able to pretend they don't exist since I won't need anything from them. All I have to do is make it through this and pretend, for a few minutes, that they don't bother me.

Which is, admittedly, easier said than done.

20

Somehow, I luck out and there's a student leaving the boys' dorm when I get there. I jog to catch the door, glad I haven't been rained on yet, and walk toward the elevator with all the purpose of a hunting hyena. I want to be *done* so I can be *home*. The guys suck, but I don't want to get rained on tonight, since I know I'll be cold for the rest of the night if I do.

The elevator is blessedly empty as well, and I wonder just how many people are even here on a Saturday night. There's a lot more partying at Winter Grove than I would have expected, though when I'd mentioned that to Bri and Zara, they'd told me that just because it was a school for super-rich kids didn't mean they would all take it seriously.

When I'm in front of their door, however, I hesitate. My stomach flips and twists, trying to turn into an origami animal of some kind. I'm glad that I haven't eaten much tonight because this way I'm not too nauseous. One day, maybe they won't make me so nervous.

And one day maybe my ears will fix themselves and I'll be able to hear again without my hearing aids.

Hesitantly I raise my hand, knuckles finding the wood of the door but not making any noise as I lean in to press my ear against it.

Of course I can't hear anything. I don't even know if I could if they were talking, but to my ears, there's nothing going on.

Maybe they're all asleep. Unfortunately, my bio packet isn't hanging on the door, so I raise my hand again and knock tentatively on the wood, wondering if they'll be able to hear it.

Before I can pull my face back from the door completely, it opens, and I'm left staring straight into Dorian's face.

Or rather, his collarbones. Dressed in a loose, red tee with a worn-out neck, I can see the 'v' of where they meet quite clearly, and taking a deep breath is a *huge* mistake has me nearly choking like the day I met him.

"Oh yeah?" he murmurs, as I take gulps of air scented with *him* to try and not cough in his face. "Every time I see you it's like you've found a new way to try to upset me, Mercy. Is it a hobby?"

I shake my head, because it's decidedly not, and glare at him balefully. "Bio packet," I say finally, clearing my throat and holding my hand out to him.

He steps back and gestures for me to come inside, though I hesitate.

Do I *really* have to?

"Come on, Mercy," he teases, his voice wickedly amused. "You really didn't think this was going to be that easy, did you? That I'd just hand it to you so you could be on your way?"

"What can I say? I guess I'm just devoutly hopeful. Come on, Dorian, please? It hasn't started raining yet and I would like to not get soaked on my walk back."

If he cares, which he doesn't, he doesn't act like it, he flicks his fingers at me again to come in, and I roll my eyes before stepping inside so he can close the door. Just like always, my ribs take that time to contract, and my heart picks up its pace as I wonder what he's going to do to hurt me this time.

"Are you mad?" I ask, trying for passive and unworried. Instead my voice is high and unsure, like I really am nervous.

Which, I am, to be fair.

"And...where are August and Foster?"

"Out," he replies, skipping my first question. He walks to the coffee table with me trailing behind him and scoops a black plastic bag off of the surface, before turning and handing it to me.

My eyes narrow, confusion rising in my chest as I stare down at the unmarked bag. "Is this...my bio packet?" I ask, head tilting to the side. The contents make the black plastic bulge, and unless he's wadded it up, I can't imagine how it would be.

"No. This is how you're going to *get* your bio packet," he replies, his voice just as level as it had been.

Suddenly, I don't want to know what's in the bag.

In the dim light, it's easy to see the flicker of lightning outside the window, and my eyes slide to gaze out of the large panes of glass to the blackness over the lake that makes everything look almost surreal.

For some reason, Dorian lets me. I can feel him watching me, though he doesn't say anything as I sigh and gaze down at the black plastic again.

"I'm not going to like it, am I?" I ask flatly, still unwilling to open it.

"I don't know." His tone is still passive, but there's something there that sounds like amusement. "You told me leashes were actually your thing, not that you acted like it when I was so nice as to put one on you, but maybe you'll enjoy this one."

God, I'm really not going to like it.

"So I open the bag, and then what? A poisonous animal bites me? I die? You resurrect me?" It's impossible for me to hide the anxiousness I feel, and I shift my weight from foot to foot on the carpet.

"Open the bag and see. It's pretty self-explanatory," he assures me blandly, shoving his hands in the pockets of his black sweatpants. I gaze at him, until finally he looks down at the black bag as well, clearly wanting me to open it.

That can't be good at all.

"God, this had better be my bio packet," I mumble, and pull open the bag to see what's inside.

Except...I have no idea what it is. In the dim light I can see brown fur, the same color as my hair, but that's about it. "Umm..." I trail off, reaching one hand inside. My fingers brush against the soft fur, and finally I pull out one of the objects from the bag so I can gaze at it more clearly.

When I do, my heart nearly stops, and I kind of wish it would.

It's a cat ear.

There's a clip lying flat against the bottom, and the fur along the inside of the ear is long, plush, and white. It blends in seamlessly with the darker, outer fur, and if I wasn't horrified, it would be adorable.

Instead, I'm pretty horrified.

"It goes in your hair. They both do. And the tail—"

"Is going to get *shoved up your fucking ass—*"

Dorian reaches out and hooks his finger in the o-ring of the collar, drawing my gaze up to his.

"Careful, Mercy. You're almost making me wish I didn't get the clip on version of this tail for you."

I hate it here.

"I'm not wearing these," I snap, jamming the ear back into

the bag with whatever else is there. "No fucking way. I'm not into this, and I don't know why—"

"You don't?" he slides his finger free of the ring. "You really don't? Well, you don't have to wear them, but I wonder what'll happen on Monday when you don't have your homework for your class. Will you maintain your A in there without it?"

I blink up at him, my heart in my throat. "You can't," I whisper. "Dorian, I need these professors to think I'm a good student—"

"And you're such a good student, aren't you Mercy?" There's a note of a purr in his voice that I can't deny, no matter how much I want to. "And if you want everyone to know that, then you're going to be a good *kitten* for me."

Oh.

Oh, *God*.

"I'm not leaving this room," I snap after a few seconds, trying to hide the fact that my hands are trembling.

"I don't want you to. Why would I want to parade you around the dorm, when I'm the one that wants to see you with those on?"

Somehow, his words don't make it better.

I let out the breath I'm holding, wondering if I'm going to pass out from lack of oxygen as I set the bag down and draw out the ear again, glaring at it with the anger of a thousand suns.

"Let me help you." It's not a suggestion. Dorian pulls the cat ear gently from my fingers, sliding the clip along my scalp until he can fix it on my head. A soft pull makes sure it's sturdy, and within a minute I have an ear on the other side of my head as well.

He's the one who pulls the tail out of the bag, because of course there's a two-foot long tail that's covered with brown fur except at the tip. The top of it has a loop that comes away from the fur, and I can't help but raise my brows.

"Sorry, seems I can't wear it," I tell him, my words flat. "I'm not wearing a belt. Or anything with belt loops."

"Yeah, that's a shame." He reaches into one pocket and holds a safety pin up to the light. "As if I don't know you normally wear leggings. Turn around."

I don't want to. My legs don't want to move, but when he grips my hoodie and tows me forward, I can't do anything else.

"I can do it—"

"No you can't." It takes him only a couple of seconds to pin it to my leggings, and when he pulls on my hoodie, I'm too stunned to do anything other than let him drag it off my arms and toss it onto the sofa.

"There," I say, unable to keep the tremble out of my voice. "You got what you wanted, so—"

"Almost," he interrupts, and reaches up to drag me forward by the collar again. He reaches his hand back into his pocket, and when he shows me what's in it, I raise my own like I might hit him.

"Oh please. It's not that big of a deal," Dorian scoffs, also unable to keep the grin off of his face as he attaches the silver bell with a little pink bow to the collar's ring. Before I can react, he has a leash from somewhere that goes on the o-ring as well, and when he gives a little pull, it causes the bell to jingle.

I've never been more mortified in my life. I stare at him, feeling heat rush to my face as I look up at him with wide-eyes and fingers that feel clammy. *I don't want to be here* is an understatement, and for the first time in awhile, I don't know what to say.

"Dorian—" I finally manage, but he gives a little tug on the leash and grins.

"That's not what cute little kittens say," he growls, and the warmth of his alpha-purr rolls through me unexpectedly.

"There's no way I'm—"

"You are if you want your fucking homework back, *kitten*."

I stare at him a moment longer, incredibly aware of the ears, the tail, the leash, and the bell. What other choice do I have, when he holds all the cards and the *leash*?

"Come on," he goads, when I don't make a sound. He pulls forward on the leash a little, and I take a step toward him begrudgingly. "What did you want to say to me?"

When I still don't make a sound, the grip on his leash becomes tighter, and he pulls up until I have to go up on the balls of my feet.

"Meow," I whisper, but he shakes his head.

"That's not how you said it the other night."

I suddenly regret the other night more than any other moment in my life.

"*Meow*," I snap, my voice higher than I'd like it to be.

Dorian visibly thinks about it, then shrugs. "Good enough for now," he says finally. "Are you hungry?"

"No," I snap, but he just looks at me, waiting.

I roll my eyes, linking my hands behind my back so he can't see them shake. "How the fuck do I meow a *no*, Dorian?"

"Try."

"I..." I bite my lip, frustrated and humiliated at his patience and the way he's just standing there, waiting. "Meow?" I try finally, the sound soft.

"Yeah, you're hungry for a snack, aren't you kitten?" He walks away from me suddenly, the leash still in his hand as he goes toward the kitchenette. I'm too dumbfounded to move, until the pressure pulls me forward, but almost immediately Dorian turns, his dark eyes glittering. "Silly kitty," he chides, reaching out to flick the bell. "Cats can't walk on two feet, can they? And they don't wear shoes, either."

As he watches, I drop to my knees. I don't know what else to do, and kicking my sneakers off to leave me in my pink socks is an afterthought. I hope he continues to forget that cats don't really wear clothes either.

He tugs on the leash again, and my face burns as I follow him on all fours until he stops at the fridge and opens it so he can reach inside.

If he pulls out milk, I'm going to lose it completely. I'll strangle him with the pink leash he's holding so thoroughly that not even the devil will be able to send him back.

Instead, he pulls out a bottle of water, presumably for himself, and then reaches into the cabinet to pull out something else that I don't get to see before he's striding back toward the sofa, barely giving me time to crawl before the leash is pulling at my throat again.

When he sits, the bottle goes to the coffee table and I'm finally able to see what's in his hands. It does nothing other than make me want to curl up in a ball and die, but I doubt even that would get me my bio homework back.

He's holding a small carton of goldfish. While I watch, he shakes it, and I can hear the crackers inside rattle against the sides of the carton.

"Here kitty, kitty," he murmurs, pulling one out and setting the box on the sofa between him and the arm. He holds up the goldfish, waving it a little like that's going to make me crawl over there.

I don't.

I sit there, on my knees, and stare at him instead with narrowed eyes. I'm not going over there, and I'm not eating a stupid goldfish.

"Kitten..." He smiles as he says it, though the words are

anything but nice. "It's not that I don't love it when you're difficult. Isn't that what got us here? But I swear on my life that if you don't *crawl* over and sit in front of me that I'm going to go get your homework and tear it up. Do you understand me?"

My stomach plummets at the threat, and meeting his dark eyes doesn't convince me he's joking or that it's an empty threat. If anything, it's just the opposite.

He'd really do it.

Slowly I get to my hands and knees, eyes firmly on his as I crawl over to him on all fours. I hesitate in front of his knees, but he pulls on the leash lightly until finally, I'm sitting between his thighs, right in front of the couch itself.

This time, he lifts the goldfish up so it's higher than my face and I have to look up at it.

"I bet my kitten is so hungry, isn't she?" he teases in a honey-sweet voice. "Have you been playing with your toys? Your cheeks are so red...surely you can't be embarrassed?" He knows damn well I am embarrassed. "What do you say, kitten?"

It doesn't take a tug on the leash for me to know what he wants. I meow again, the sound pathetic to my own ears. I wonder if he'd notice if I removed my hearing aids and just read his lips. At least then I wouldn't have to hear his voice, and that would make this somewhat better, probably.

"You can take it, kitten. I got them just for you."

I fix him with a hard glare again, but he only reaches forward with the hand that has the leash and flicks the bell at the hollow of my throat to make it jingle once more. "I know you heard me."

Tentatively I sit up some, opening my mouth and using my teeth to take the goldfish as quickly as I can before sitting back down, chewing it, and swallowing it quickly even though it feels and tastes like sawdust in my mouth.

Goldfish are going to be ruined for me from now on, I just know it.

"Good kitty." He pulls out another goldfish and feeds it to me, then one more. "Why don't you clean my fingers off for me? Pretty sure that's what *cats* do." There's that note of a growl in his voice again that has me shivering in front of him. And it's not all from dread or humiliation.

"I'm not licking your fingers," I say quickly before he can stop me.

"Yeah, you are," he replies smoothly, holding them out in front of me. "And if you say anything other than *meow* from here on out, you're not getting your homework back. Last warning, Mercy." There's definitely a threat in his words I can't ignore, and even though I'm watching his face and trying to simultaneously glare at him and silently plead, I can still see his hand in front of my face, fingers outstretched towards me expectantly.

It looks like I really am doing this. My ribs seem to constrict harder as I dip my head so that I can lick his fingers, running my tongue over the pad of his index finger first. I don't look at him while I do it, though I'm sure he can see the embarrassment in every line of my body as my tongue swipes over his skin until I don't taste the goldfish dust anymore. He moves his hand, but before I can lick his thumb, he slips it into my mouth to rest against my tongue.

"Get it all off, kitten," Dorian murmurs, and for a moment I'm sure that I can hear his words falter. At the very least, it's the quietest he's spoken all night. But I'm too busy trying not to focus on the taste of his skin to really notice.

My heart thunders in my chest when he strokes my tongue, and when I'm sure there can't be anything else on his hand, I jerk backward and look down, curling my fingers into the carpet I'm sitting on. My cheeks are hot, but they aren't the only thing, and a full body shudder ripples down my spine as the taste of his skin lingers in my mouth.

"...Meow?" I say finally, hoping he can somehow translate that into *is that good enough, you asshole?*

"You must be thirsty, right?" He grabs the bottle of water off of the table and starts to hand it to me, but just before my fingers make contact with the bottle, he pulls it away again. "I almost forgot. Kittens can't drink out of a bottle."

Yeah, I have a hard time believing he 'almost forgot.' Especially with the wicked amusement on his face as he uncaps the bottle.

"And unfortunately, I don't have any bowls here." I don't believe that for a second either, but just fix him with a disbelieving look. "But that's okay. My mom would always just pour water into her hand for our dogs when we were out hiking. I'm sure that'll work for you, won't it? Since you'll just lap it up?"

I want to tell him where he can shove that water bottle, but instead I just *meow* at him in a way I hope gets it across. His smile widens, and Dorian sits forward on the couch until there's barely any room between his body and mine. My heart takes up its pounding drumbeat in my chest again, and as I watch, he pours some water into his hand, uncaring that at least half of it splashes onto the carpet below, and the rest slowly streams from his fingers.

"Drink it fast, kitten," he tells me, the purr in his chest louder and more overwhelming than before.

I don't mean to just *go for it*. Especially without giving him a piece of my mind through a meow or body language. But before I can think about it, I'm leaning down toward his hand, my tongue out, and finding his skin as I lap up the remains of the water he'd poured out.

Do it for the homework, I think, as my tongue laps against his smooth palm.

Do it for the homework, I tell myself again, as his other hand reaches up and smooths down my hair. He repeats the process, the water in his palm harder to clean up than I'd expected which gives him ample time to run his fingers through my hair again and again. He moves his fingers around the base of the ears, tickling the shell of *my* ear when he does so and causing me to suck in a surprised breath.

"Are you ticklish?" he breathes, doing it again. I squirm on the floor, trying to pull away from him, but he has more range of movement than I do right now, and easily does it again.

"Don't–" I whisper, before the sound falls off into a *mew* of protest instead.

Do it for the homework.

"Make that sound again." His voice is rougher than it has any right to be, and the hand that had held the water reaches up to grip my jaw lightly, the leash forgotten on the sofa beside him. I hesitate, but when he touches my ear again, I comply.

And immediately I'm privy to the shudder that goes through *him*.

"One more thing, kitten," Dorian says, his voice gentle in the dimness of his suite. Somehow it still isn't storming, but when he says that, I close my eyes hard and dread what he's going to say next. "You can take one more goldfish from me, can't you?"

Yeah, sure. I can do that. That wasn't as bad as the water, after all.

I open my eyes, watching as he shakes another goldfish free of the carton. Only, instead of holding it in front of my face, he sits back on the sofa and reaches up to take it lightly between his teeth, brows raising in an obvious challenge as I stare at him in what's hopefully horror and disbelief, and not something else entirely.

Do it for the homework, I tell myself, and take a deep breath.

21

I have to take another deep breath before I can move, but the goading on his face is what gets me going. He's not doing this because he likes me, or anything so sweet. He's doing this because he knows I'm humiliated. It's pretty obvious by now that it's his *thing*, but if doing this will get me out of here faster, with my bio homework intact, then I'm willing to climb his stupid body like a ladder, take the goldfish, and get out of here.

Besides, the longer I hesitate and stare at him like he's kicked my puppy, the more enjoyment he gets out of this.

I get to my knees, floundering a little because there's no way around the fact that with him leaning back, I'm going to have to get up close and personal with his everything

Don't give him the satisfaction of winning, I repeat, over and over like it's a mantra in my brain. Though when I go to stand, he yanks on the leash once more and shakes his head, though his mouth isn't exactly free to talk, which might be the only good thing about this situation.

When I drop back down, my knees are on the edge of the

sofa. He doesn't protest when I hesitate, so apparently, that was an acceptable way to get up here, even though he's making it harder to straddle his thighs without touching them since they're still somewhat spread.

Fuck it.

I lean forward, hands going to his chest as I press myself against him until I can finally grab the stupid goldfish from between his perfect teeth. I drag it into my own mouth, barely noticing that he crunches off the tail end of it before I'm chewing it as quickly as I can and pulling away.

Or I would, if his finger through the ring of my collar wasn't stopping me.

"You know how this works," he murmurs. "Clean up what you missed."

What I *missed*? There's nothing there. Any goldfish crumbs still remaining aren't on his lips. If anything, they're–oh.

They're in his mouth.

Fuck.

I press my lips together, still only inches from his face as I meet his dark eyes. The look there isn't what I expect. There's amusement, sure. And something that's probably arrogance. But that's not all, and I look away before I'm able to identify what the rest of that *look* is that he's giving me. Instead I stare at his slightly-parted lips, and take another deep breath as my heart beats harshly against my ribs.

Before I can reason with myself that maybe I can find another way to do the bio packet, I press forward. My mouth finds his, and I lick over his lower lip a couple of times, just in case there's any remains of goldfish there. He doesn't do anything, which I'm grateful for, and I move to the seam of his mouth to do the same thing there.

Then, finally, I coax his mouth open with a nip to his lower lip and let my tongue find his, searching his mouth for any hint of goldfish while I try to ignore every single shiver that's making its way down my spine.

At least after this, there's really nothing else he can make me do that'll be worse. After this, he'll have to give me my homework back.

I pull away, confident in the fact that there's no way he can say I didn't do what he'd told me to, only for an arm to slip around my waist and pull me back to him.

This time it's his lips that find mine, and his teeth that worry at my bottom lip until I open my mouth with soft gasp so that his tongue can slide against mine. He explores every inch of the space between my lips like he wants to memorize it, his arm that's locked around my waist keeping me there while his other hand tugs lightly on the leash, as if to remind me of its presence.

"I can't believe you really did it," he purrs, pulling back just enough to breathe the words against my swollen lips. He nips at them again, drawing a soft whine from me, before going on, "Fuck, Mercy. You got into my fucking *lap*. Look at where you are. What the fuck are you even doing?"

I try to pull away, to stand up, anything, but he holds me on his lap, still straddling his thighs as my body is pressed to his.

When I open my mouth, he kisses me again and growls against my lips, "That had better be a cat noise that's about to leave your lips, *kitten*."

It was not going to be, that's for sure.

He kisses me again before I can think about it, his mouth more demanding this time as he lifts his hand to grip my hair. His fingers scratch against my scalp, and with him holding me here like this, there really is nowhere for me to go unless he decides to release me.

A sudden nip to my lower lip draws a whine from my

mouth that disappear into his, and his answering purr makes it clear he is *not* about to do something like let go of me.

At last, however, the need for oxygen wins out. He lets go of my hair and pulls away, breathing slightly heavier as I gasp for air, my hands still pressed to his chest. It takes me a minute to register that I *could* move if I wanted to. His hand isn't holding the leash anymore, and the one around my waist is at his side.

But I can't bring myself to, damn it. Not when I'm so transfixed on the heady edge that's come into his scent, and the way that his eyes watch my face with pleasure and surprise. Would it be too much to demand for *him* to be the one to purr? Not that I'd know how to, without saying it.

It's hard to ignore the heat in my own body, and the excitement that runs through me every time one of us shifts enough that he rubs against me in the best way possible. I want him to ignore it, though. At least until I know how I feel about it.

Then, his eyes darken. He sits up straighter, putting just a slight bit of distance between our bodies. "This isn't...for your homework," he says, reaching out and tucking my hair behind my ear. "You can get up now. I'll give it to you, and I'll help you take those off. You did everything I asked, and more. I wouldn't push this further when you don't want–"

I have no idea what I'm doing, only that I'm moving. Before he's finished speaking I kiss him again, letting out a soft sound against his mouth that has him growling in response. The moment his chest rumbles with the sound, his arm is back, locking around my waist as he relaxes against the back of the couch. His mouth is warm, and I can't get enough of the taste of him as I sink down against his body once again and any concern about him pushing me away evaporates almost instantly.

If anything, he won't stop pulling me closer. His hips arch

up into mine, grinding against me as he devours my mouth until both of us need air again.

"If I'd known you tasted so good, I would've made you eat goldfish out of my mouth a week ago," Dorian laughs ruefully. "But God, Mercy. I'm going to do so much more than just kiss you. After all, there's so much more of you to taste, isn't there?"

If I wasn't speechless and dumbfounded and more than slightly horny already, I would be now.

"Dorian–"

"Do you want me to take these off? We can keep going without them. I'm not going to make you wear them if you don't want to, kitten. Though, the collar and bell stay of course." He watches my face, reaching out towards my hair like he really is going to take the ears off.

Options run through my brain, and for a moment I'm content with him doing that.

Except...I *like* this. More than I ever thought I would.

Before he can remove the cat ear, I turn and lightly nip his hand, my eyes finding his as I narrow them so he gets the point. Dorian sucks in a breath, his eyes darkening once more.

"So *mouthy*, kitten," he tells me, turning his hand so that he can grip my jaw. He slips his thumb between my lips, stroking it suggestively along my tongue. I can't help closing my eyes and tilting my head back as he does it, wishing I had the nerve to slide my fingers under the waistband of my leggings and touch myself where I want it most. "Do you need something to fill that mouth of yours?" Without waiting for an answer, he adds, "And if you're biting me, I'm not sure you belong on the couch." The wicked amusement is back in his voice, and gently he pushes me back down to the floor, until I'm on my knees between his thighs again.

When his thumb leaves my mouth, I nip at the tip of it, giving him a soft *meow* of protest.

"Just wait a moment," Dorian chuckles, leaning back on the sofa again as his hand slips past the line of his sweatpants.

It hits me, as I watch him pull his cock free from his pants and it's obvious he's into this just as much as I am, that I'm really about to do this with *him*. Yet, I can't find it in myself to regret my choices or want to back away, even though it's clear he'd let me.

"Here kitty, kitty," Dorian purrs, crooking the index finger of his hand that holds my leash again. "This is all for you." My stomach flips at the words as I lean forward, my mouth open as I take a breath and press my hands lightly against his thighs.

He's bigger than I ever would've thought. If I'd ever stopped to consider it. He's an alpha, sure, so some of that goes with the territory, but looking at his length, I can't help but imagine how that would feel inside of me, and just how well he'd fill me up.

I lick a line up the underside of his shaft, lapping my tongue over the top only to do it two more times. I know it's not enough. I'd know even without the soft sounds he makes when I pull away to do it again.

"Mercy..." There's a warning in his voice, and the collar pulls at my throat. "I want your mouth on my cock right–"

"Meow?" I interrupt, grinning at my own stupid joke. His mouth twitches upward with amusement, but he pulls on the leash until I get the memo, and I lick at his tip once more before opening my mouth and taking as much of him as I comfortably can.

It isn't as much as I'd thought it would be. There's still enough of him left that it's a little intimidating, especially when his hand leaves his cock to curl in my hair encouragingly.

"Shhh," he murmurs when I make a soft sound of surprise. "You can do it. I know you can take me in your pretty mouth, kitten." He lets me take my time, my tongue pressed against him as I slowly work to take all of him or as much as him as I can.

Though, when my nose finally presses against his skin, my eyes are watering from the effort. He really is big, and my brain just cannot stop imagining how he'd feel inside me for real.

"Good girl." Dorian's voice is rough, and his eyes are bright when I look up at him. "Aren't you just so fucking perfect? Maybe I'd be lying if I told you that I hadn't thought about this before." He smirks darkly when my eyes widen in question, and the hand in my hair guides me up his length, before pushing me back down. "Is that better? Would you like me to fuck your face just how I like it while you look at me like that?" His hips rock upward, pushing more of him into my throat as if to emphasize his words, and I whine around him.

"Or are you just surprised about what I said?" His hand tightens in my hair, and this time he pushes me back down faster, in time with the movement of his hips. "Yeah, you like it when I do that, don't you? I knew you'd look good like this when I put you on your knees the first time. You liked it then. I could see it on your fucking *face*, kitten."

He's totally not right.

Except, he is. Maybe just a little, and my cheeks burn when I realize it.

"Tap my leg if you need me to let go," Dorian instructs, at the same time he grips my hair more firmly. "At any time. It's your choice, Mercy." When he talks like that, it's like he's a completely different person. One who gives a damn about how I feel, and what I want or need.

It's confusing, quite frankly.

His movements get faster and more intent. He rocks his hips continually into my mouth, making good on his word of fucking my face and using me just how he likes. It's hotter than it has any right to be, especially when my fingers tighten on his thigh and he hisses and jerks upward hard, filling my throat and causing my eyes to water.

Not that I'm about to tap out. He gives me a moment, but I just fix him with a look that draws a chuckle from him and he continues, murmuring praise and promises that my brain barely recognizes as real words when every movement builds an ache and heat between my thighs. Finally, when I'm sure I'm going to die if I don't get some kind of relief, I pull one of my hands off of his thigh, but he growls and says, "Don't you fucking dare touch yourself kitten. You put your hand back up here unless I say otherwise."

Another sound leaves me, this one closer to a whimper of protest, but it only drives him onward, his cock sliding down my throat and leaving me grateful I don't have a gag reflex.

"Your mouth is fucking perfect. Maybe this is what we'll do from now on, hmm? You mouth off to me like you just love to do, and we come back here so I can clip a leash on that collar and I'll fuck your *mouth* like you deserve. You're never taking that collar off, you hear me? Not when I'm going to be using it so often. Yeah. *Often*." He laughs, almost breathlessly. "Because I can't get enough of you looking like that, or how you feel–" The door opens suddenly and I try to pull away, but his hand on my hair stops me.

"It's just August and Foster," he laughs, almost sweetly. "What's wrong, kitten? Don't you want them to see you putting your mouth to good use, finally? Don't you want to make them jealous?" A groan leaves his mouth, almost cutting off his words. "August, get her homework out of my room. It's–"

"I know," August replies, and his footsteps recede down the hallway behind me. I can't look at August or Foster, but I can feel the embarrassment rising to my face once more, and I consider tapping his leg. And I would, really...if I wasn't in so deep now.

If I didn't enjoy this so much.

"I didn't think you were going to do *this*." Foster's voice is carefully neutral, and I finally eye him reproachfully when he moves to stand over Dorian's shoulder, looking just a tad worried. "Dorian–"

"Mercy, tap my leg if you're enjoying every second of this," Dorian interrupts, breathless and irritated.

I tap his leg.

"Tap my leg if you want me to stop, *or* if this is in any way related to getting your homework back." I clutch his sweatpants but don't move to tap.

"Now shut up, Foster. Can't you see I'm a little bit busy?" There's more of a growl there than I'm expecting, and when I think Foster is going to walk away or look taken aback, he only raises a brow and looks at me.

"Can I play with her?" he asks finally, and Dorian's movements lessen.

"You can't hurt her."

"I don't want to."

Both of their eyes find mine, but I look at Dorian for an answer. He shakes his head. "It's up to you, not me. Tap now, and he goes somewhere else. And even if you let him touch you, we'll stop this anytime you want to."

Yeah, there's no way in hell I trust Foster enough to do anything like this with me.

But my fingers don't move. My eyes narrow at Foster, but the grin on his face is just as dark as the one Dorian's worn on and off tonight. He circles the couch and shoves the coffee table back, sliding to the floor behind me and bracketing me with his body.

"He tastes good, doesn't he?" Foster purrs in my ear,

tucking my hair behind it. "And he has you all dressed up like a cat for this, huh? Guess you guys were a little more into it than you thought." He nips the shell of my ear, causing me to gasp and swallow Dorian down deeper.

"*Fuck*," the black-haired sophomore snarls. His grip tightens again. "I'm going to come if you do that," he promises, and Foster chuckles just as August slides onto the couch beside Dorian.

"A shame you can't talk back to me with your mouth full of his cock, but that's all right." He nips my ear again, and it draws the same reaction from me as one of his hands travels up my side, under my shirt.

"Shit, I'm serious, Foster. If you make her do that—"

This time Foster traces the shell of my ear with his teeth, causing me to shudder, before biting down harder than before. I yelp, my fingers tightening on Dorian's sweatpants, and he hisses.

"I'm going to come." His grip loosens. "You don't have to— tap if you don't want to—"

"She wants to," Foster promises him, and runs his free hand up Dorian's thigh. It doesn't take anything more. He grips my hair hard, drawing my face down as his hips arch up and he buries himself as deeply in my throat as he can as he comes. I close my eyes, focusing on not choking on him and breathing through my nose. Dimly, I'm aware that August has captured Dorian's mouth in a kiss, but it's all I can do to think about what *I* have going on.

Finally his grip loosens, and he lets go entirely before I sit back on my heels and gasp for breath. Reaching up, I wipe my mouth on the back of my hand, staring up at him with something I can't name, and an emotion churning around inside of me that I can't quite place.

It feels like something it shouldn't, that's for sure.

"Come here, Mercy." Dorian reaches out for me when he has his breath back, and once August has sat back up.

"Why?" I ask, a little less sure now that the others are here.

Dorian's brows climb towards his bangs. "So I can return the favor."

When I hesitate, he looks at Foster. "Hands off so she can think." Foster raises his hands innocently, to prove he's not doing anything to sway my opinion.

"You don't have to," I say. I don't want to *owe* him for it, or something equally as stupid. Though I do ache for it, and it wouldn't take much.

"I *want to*, little omega." The nickname is back, and it sends a shudder through me. "It would only take a few minutes, wouldn't it? I bet you could just ride my thigh and get off, but I won't make you. Not after that."

He reaches out, coaxing me up to sit on his lap so my back is pressed against his chest before he kisses me again, long and deep. "You want to let them touch you?" he asks, nodding at Foster and August.

"If they want to," I reply, trying to sound like it doesn't make a difference to me.

Foster moves first, and when he touches me, it's to hook his fingers in the waist of my leggings and *jerk* them off along with my underwear. It only takes him a few seconds, but before I can press my thighs together, August's hand is on my left leg, holding me open as Foster slides between them, running his hands up my inner thighs.

"You're so wet," he says, almost appreciatively. Dorian's hand wanders down the front of my body, the other keeping me held against him while Foster teases me with his fingers, refusing to touch me where I want it most.

"Bet she tastes good," August murmurs, and when I turn to look at him, mouth open to say *something*, he catches my mouth with his, fingers under my chin. "Yeah," he says a second later, moving closer so he can kiss me again. "You taste so good."

"Yeah? I bet she tastes better here." I can't see him, but I can feel Foster's breath against my wetness and I shudder seconds before he runs his tongue up my slit, until he can lick my clit. I can't help it. I gasp into August's mouth, my hands going up to find *some* kind of purchase before Dorian guides them up over his shoulders to twine in his hair.

When Foster's nails dig into my inner thighs, however, I flinch, and Dorian growls a warning above me before saying, "*Don't* hurt her. Not this time, Foster."

"I didn't," Foster promises with a chuckle, and swipes his tongue up against me again. "Not really. She's just so pretty, Dorian. She tastes so good. I bet she'd taste better with your cum leaking out of her. Both of you." He licks me as he talks, one of his hands moving to tease my clit. "You'd let me do it, right Mercy?" His tone is teasing, and by the way August is trying to suck my soul out through my mouth, I can assume he isn't looking for an answer. "You'll let them fuck your pussy so I can taste you after?"

It's probably a good thing I *can't* answer because I don't know how anyone would say no to that. Though to be honest, I still feel like I'm just *here*, and I don't know how to respond to any of this. Their scents are thick when they're this close, and when they're together, they smell even more wonderful than they do when it's just one or two of them.

It feels like I'm drowning in Dorian's pack, and at this rate, I don't know how I'm ever going to pull myself back to the surface of this ocean.

Foster's tongue dives into me, going deeper and deeper as he tastes every inch of me he can reach. "You want to play with her clit? She's so close, Dorian, I can tell. Help me make her cum so I can taste it. *Fuck*, I'm not letting you go until I've tasted every inch of you, Mercy."

Is that a threat? It feels more like a promise.

Dorian chuckles and his hand skims down my body, pausing to rest just below my navel before his fingers find my slit and he teases along it, close to Foster's face.

"Please," I gasp, trying to pull away from August's mouth so I can tell them what I want.

Instead he *growls*, the sound louder than Dorian's growl, and yanks my face back to his before telling me, "I'm not done yet, Mercy. You're not going anywhere." I start to reply, to say *something*, but he kisses me hard again, his tongue diving between my lips again as his hand in my hair keeps me just how he wants me.

It's only a second later that Foster starts licking me again, tongue diving deep as he spreads me with his fingers and Dorian's touch finds my clit. I whine into August's mouth, for more or for something else I can't name, though I'm not sure which.

"Come for us," Dorian urges, his voice in my ear the thing I zero in on. "You heard Foster, didn't you?"

I did hear him, but I can't exactly say that. Not with how intent August is on my mouth and everything between my lips.

But there's no denying any of them when I'm this close. I rock into Foster's mouth, my hands tight in Dorian's hair as his fingers on my clit become more intense. I try to pull away from August again, just to tell them how close I am, but he reaches out to grip my throat and pins me back against Dorian's shoulder, mouth back on mine to absolutely devour it.

Unable to do more than cry out into August's mouth and rock my hips against Foster's tongue with my fingers scraping Dorians' scalp, I come. There's a groan from Foster when I do, and his hands grip my thighs hard as he buries his face between them. His tongue feels like he's trying to taste every bit of my release, and Dorian keeps up his movements as well.

I want to tell them to stop. It's becoming too much, and I need them to give me a break, to let me come down from this so that I can catch my breath. If only August would let me, anyway.

"She's still fucking coming," Foster laughs, sinking three fingers into me and fucking me with them. "I bet it's too much, isn't it Mercy? You need us to stop, right? You need us to let you take a break?" Contrary to his words, he keeps up with what he's doing, until I'm coming *again*, fiercely this time, and finally August pulls away to let me whimper my protests into the side of Dorian's neck as Foster dives in one last time to taste my release with his tongue.

"That's enough. She's had enough." Dorian pulls his hand away from my clit and almost absently slides them into my mouth. Not that I mind, obviously, since I automatically clean them off as though he's *asked*.

Foster climbs onto the sofa beside me, and as I watch, he kisses August hard, shoving his fingers into his mouth when he pulls away.

"She tastes so fucking good," he purrs, and August growls in what seems to be agreement.

Finally, somehow, I stumble to my feet and grab my leggings off the floor, dragging them and my underwear on as I look at the three of them with wide eyes and a heart that's racing.

Dorian looks back at me, though Foster and August are clearly too busy to pay me any notice.

"I gotta go," I mumble, sure that there's a fierce blush on my cheeks. "I need to...leave."

Dorian opens his mouth, as if he might protest, but instead gets to his feet. He reaches out, carefully removing the ears from my hair and drops them on the table as Foster reaches out and does the same with the tail.

"All right," the alpha of their little pack agrees. "You can leave whenever you want, Mercy." I open my mouth to argue, to say something, but I don't know what to say. Instead I accept my jacket wordlessly from August, unable to look him in the eye as I jam my sneakers on.

"Homework," I manage to squeak at last, and when Dorian points at it on the counter, I snatch it up and shove it into my hoodie that I zip up.

"Come back soon," Foster calls lazily, when I'm already halfway out the door and trying to flee before they can see the war of emotions on my face. "I'm sure we could find something else to hold ransom."

22

Four days later, the events of Saturday night still won't stop replaying over and over in my head. Through classes with Dorian and August, and when I'd bumped into Foster on campus and stammered my way out of it, even. At least they hadn't brought it up, and honestly, the three of them hadn't bothered to talk to me very much.

Which shouldn't hurt as much as it tries to. I should be *happy* they've cut out most of their bullying, aside from some snide remarks from Foster.

I should be *thrilled* to be out from under them for the most part.

Except, a big part of me wants to be back under them, in a much different way. God, maybe I really am getting fucked up by Bri and Zara's relationship. Could it be affecting me so much that I'm craving something I shouldn't? Or maybe there's something in the food that would explain why I haven't washed the tee that I was wearing that night, and why sometimes I drag it to my face to catch their combined scent in my nose before I go to bed.

That isn't normal. Not one bit.

With a sigh, I drag my eyes up to the lockers in front of me. In my hands, my bow weighs heavily, and my gloves feel almost strange on my fingers today. My bow release, a small device that I'll use to fire more precisely than drawing back with my fingers, swings from the strap on my wrist as I run my fingers along the fiberglass of the compound bow.

In my chest, my heart flutters. It's been months since I've shot competitively, though I practice multiple times a week. I know how these go, of course. And I don't want to let my team down. Not that anyone other than my team is here to watch me fail, at least. My mother isn't about to drag her ass up here. Not when it was never her thing in the first place. It was my dad who got me into the sport, and my dad who'd come to my competitions as a kid to cheer me on.

Here, on Winter Grove's team, it's only me.

"Are you okay?" I flinch when one of my teammates, Kiara Red-something, catches my attention with her worried tone. She stands by the door, her gloves on and in place, a bow release on her wrist as well. Like me, she's dressed in a navy blue polo with her last name embroidered on the chest, and a large symbol for Winter Grove University on the back. Hers looks ironed, or pressed, and fits her a little more loosely than mine does on me. Both of us are wearing black pants as well, and where she has on new red sneakers, mine are black and white and worn in.

"Yeah, I'm good," I reply, getting to my feet smoothly. "Sorry, I was just thinking."

"About winning, right?" She gives me a half-smile, concern still heavy on the beta's face. "You're really good, and Abby's shooting first." I don't react, but internally I wince. Abby is... not as reliable as I'd like in a teammate, and all of us know it. "Maybe you can uh, fix things if they're unfortunate."

"So no pressure, right?"

Kiara's smile widens. "Yeah, absolutely no pressure to do well in your first Winter Grove competition. Do you want me to hold your bow while you finish getting ready?" She pushes her light brown hair back over her eyes, and her blue eyes are wide as I hesitate. The only thing I have left to do is put my hair up.

"Thanks," I say finally, handing the black compound bow with its mounted scope over to her. I've never loved a bow more than this one, except maybe the one my dad got me as a kid so many years ago. I'm comfortable with it in my hands, and nothing about the weapon intimidates me anymore. It's a stark contrast to the way I'd fumble and second-guess myself until halfway through high school.

Quickly I gather the wavy mass of brown hair into my hands, dragging it up into a high ponytail that pricks painfully at my scalp. It goes away by the time I have my bow back, however, and I follow Kiara out of the locker room and to the field where an awning is set up for both teams and chairs placed under it. Our coach, an older woman with a severe face and high cheekbones, smiles when she sees me, and waves me over to sit in the chair nearest her.

"Don't get nervous," she instructs, and I wish I could follow the advice. How can I *not* be nervous, when this is everything to me? How can I be anything but anxious?

"I'm not nervous," I lie, testing the pull of my bow without lifting it properly. It moves just as it should, with no catches or stops. "It's the same as practice, right?" Except, with all that added pressure of winning.

She agrees and walks down the line, stopping to speak to every girl as I turn to let my eyes wander over the stands. Have many people from Winter Grove actually shown up? Archery isn't exactly the most popular sport in the world, and while it's held in higher regard at Winter Grove than other places I've seen, that doesn't make it well-loved. And since this isn't a home competition–

Auburn hair catches my eyes, and my thoughts ground to a halt. My eyes drop to the face under that hair, heart catching in my throat when *Foster* grins back at me.

What in the world is he doing here?

As I stare at him, he tilts his head to the side, grin growing as he does, and I drag my gaze in the direction he gestures to see first August, then Dorian, who pulls off his sunglasses to meet my eyes over the twenty-five foot distance.

What are *they* doing here? Memories flicker through my mind again, of Dorian's mouth on mine, of August's, of Foster, with his tongue–

"Are you all right?" Beside me, Kiara doesn't sound too sure. "You smell, umm..." She's always been so polite that it's no surprise she's doing it now. "Worried."

"Yeah, umm. Hmm. I'm nervous," I say, and the words aren't quite the lie I wish they were. Are they here for Eden? I know Cecily is here as well, and since she's a friend or something to Dorian, maybe they're here together.

Absently, my hand reaches up to touch my throat, though I know there's nothing there. We aren't allowed jewelry during the competition. Will Dorian be upset with me?

Worse, why do I *care* if he is?

"You'll be fine. You're good at this, just in case no one's ever told you," Kiara says, nudging me lightly. She follows me gaze, a small frown on her face. "I don't know why they're here either," she admits. "I guess we should feel lucky? With Dorian Wakefield's pack and *Cecily* here, it's like God's telling us we have to win."

I respond to her grin with a rueful, humorless one of my

own. "I guess if we don't, then we just don't go home. The disgrace will be too much for us."

"Yeah," Kiara agrees. "So let's hope Abby's hands aren't sweating too badly today."

Unfortunately for us, Abby's hands betray her. She shakes like a leaf when she goes to shoot, and barely scores us twenty points. It's not a winnable score, especially with us being tied before that, and I cringe as she comes back to sit in her spot and Royalwood's archer, a tall blonde with eyes like stone and a scowl that could melt nations, takes her spot behind the line.

By the time she's done, we're behind twenty-eight points, and I'm the only one left to shoot. The announcer says it as well, his voice dry over the intercom as my heart takes that moment to go into overdrive.

I don't know if I can do this.

"I feel sick," I mumble, though I can't deny the thrill of excitement alongside the panic. "I think I'm allergic."

Kiara glances at me in surprise. "To what?"

"Archery."

She can't stop the snort of amusement, but covers her mouth before she can grin. "Look, you've got this. All you have to do is, umm. Be perfect. Almost perfect. Two perfect shots and one near-perfect shot. That's not so bad."

"That would be better than *Eden's* score," I point out softly. I need twenty-eight points to tie, and she'd scored that. To win, I'd need twenty nine.

"Okay, so, do better than Eden's score." Kiara sits back as our coach comes back, and when she stops to kneel down beside me, I take a deep breath to try and get a hold over my nerves.

"It's winnable," she tells me, a hand on my shoulder. "More than winnable, Mercedes." After all this time, I still haven't managed to get her to call me by *Mercy* instead of Mercedes, but I brush it off.

"It's barely winnable," I squeak, getting to my feet. I bounce on the balls of my feet a few times, unsure how I'm unlucky enough that I'm the last one to shoot and our win depends on me being amazing. Suddenly, I don't feel so amazing.

"Then you do your best, and we work with that. It's not the end of the world here, okay?" She watches me as I flex my fingers, following me to the line after I adjust the black quiver of orange and black arrows on my hip.

It's not the end of the world here, okay? I repeat those words in my head and turn to look at the stands, wondering if Dorian and his pack are still there.

They are.

Foster gives me a little wave, though I'm sure he can't see the smile I throw back his way. While they aren't here for me, maybe there's something a little comforting about having someone I know in the stands, other than Cecily.

The field feels quiet as I draw an arrow and nock it, my hands steadier than I feel as I clip the bow release onto the bright pink string. The targets have been changed out, though from this distance all I can see are the colored circles that represent scoring. To win, I'll need two bullseyes and one almost bullseye.

Sighting down the arrow and through the scope, I loose. Immediately my heart sinks because I know it won't be one of the two bullseyes I need. Sure enough, it lands just outside of the ten-point range and in the nine instead.

If I don't get it on this next one, the best we can do is tie. I smoothly draw back my bow once more, exhaling before sighting again. This time, I take an extra second before I pull the trigger on the release, the arrow flying forward toward the target and giving me a satisfaction I can feel in my bones.

Sure enough, even from seventy feet away, I can tell that it lands dead in the center of the target.

I can at *least* tie up this game, right? My coach says something behind me, but I'm not paying attention. I can barely hear her, and I can't hear anything else as I draw my last arrow to fit it to the string. The bow release goes on, the bow goes up, and I pull the string back smoothly with a motion so practiced it feels more natural than running.

Again I sight down the scope, along the arrow, and let out a breath as my whole world becomes the arrow and the target at the end of the field. There's nothing else that matters in this moment, and when everything just clicks, I loose.

The arrow buries itself near the middle of the target, and my heart leaps into my throat. It's a nine at least, but I don't know if it's a ten. It's too close to the line. Too close to my other arrow for me to reasonably say, but I'm pretty sure it's a nine.

The judge goes jogging down the field, observing the spread of arrows before he says something into his walkie-talkie and the field's speaker system crackles to life.

"Well folks that wraps up the competition for today. And with a round of remarkable shooting, Mercedes Noble has scored–" My breath catches in my throat. I think I'm going to be sick, and my coach's hand on my shoulder feels like a lead weight–"Twenty-*nine* points. She's secured the victory for Winter Grove, so–" I don't hear anything after that. My coach pats me on the back, telling me she knew I could do it, and when I get back to the awning, Kiara jumps up and grabs me in a hug.

"Holy shit, Mercy," she laughs, her words the one thing I *do* hone in on. "You won. You scored twenty-*nine*. Look, she's so mad—" I look over at Royalwood's team, my eyes landing on the blonde.

Only, she doesn't look *mad*, exactly.

She's staring at me, her face calculating and maybe just a little bit impressed. She tilts her head to the side and turns back to talk to her coach, who frowns and nods at whatever she says.

Not that she has any reason to be upset, since she'd scored a perfect thirty. Even though I've won us the competition, she's still better than me in that regard.

I'm the last one to leave the locker rooms, my hoodie and leggings back on and with my brain feeling much more at ease. In my hand I carry my soft-sided case that holds my bow and other archery equipment, though admittedly I hadn't put everything back in its proper case so much as chucked everything in and zipped it up.

Though, that thought leaves my brain the moment I see Dorian's pack hanging out on this side of the fence that leads to the stands. They're talking to Cecily until the redhead gives me a knowing look and excuses herself as I get there.

"So you came to watch Eden?" I ask, watching Cecily go. A blonde boy waits for her at the end of the stands, and even this far away I'm able to see the collar around his throat.

"You're missing something," Dorian says in reply, reaching out to run his finger over my throat.

I turn to look at him, eyes on his sunglasses, and try to gauge his reaction by his tone. But I can't. Is he mad? Is he disappointed? *That* option turns my stomach, and I let out a breath.

"We're not allowed to wear jewelry, and I thought I'd lose it," I admit, telling them the truth before I can think to lie. I'm still a little worked up from the competition, truth be told, and I can barely think of anything other than a truthful reply.

"We're not here to see *Eden*," Foster drawls, hands shoved in his pockets. "Why the hell would we be? She has Cecily."

"So why are you here?"

They just stare at me plaintively, though August's lips quirk up into a small grin.

Then it clicks.

"What?" I all but gasp, nearly dropping my things. "Why? We're not–how did you even know about this competition, when–"

"It's a shame that you're on Winter Grove's team instead of ours." The voice is unfamiliar, though Dorian's mouth curves into a smirk at the words.

I turn, looking over my shoulder to see the blonde from Royalwood striding towards us. She's dressed more casually now, in black jeans and a tank-top that shows off the muscles of her biceps and a tattoo that rings her left upper-arm. "I bet your coach is thanking God every night for you, huh? Especially with *Abby* on the team." She holds out a hand to me that I just stare at. "I'm Amelia," she says, and I finally take her hand just as Dorian honest-to-god *growls*.

Both of us turn to look at him, Amelia's lips curving into an unfriendly grin as her fingers tighten on my hand. "Are you jealous, Dorian? Even though I don't scent you on her, so she can't belong to you." She doesn't wait for an answer before she finds me with her gaze again. "Maybe we'll shoot together sometime. You're not so far from me, and I don't mind making the drive for you."

"I'm Mercy," I respond, feeling a little unsure. She's an *alpha*, and her scent is overwhelmingly strong, but not unpleasant. In fact, it's almost as good as the way Dorian and his pack smell, and seems like a mix of spices, vanilla, and something earthy.

Unique, but certainly not unpleasant.

"See you around, Mercy." She gives Dorian one last grin that's more a snarling flash of teeth than anything, and turns to walk toward her team, not once looking over her shoulder.

"Huh," I murmur, watching her go. "Why would she want to shoot with me? She did *better* than me."

"By one point," August points out, drawing my attention back to them. "You were both the best archers of the day."

I just shrug. "So, back to what we were talking about. You did *not* come here for me."

"Why didn't we?" Dorian steps closer, his hand reaching out to grab the same one that Amelia shook. "I notice your roommate and Zara didn't show up." He runs his fingers along the back of my hand, and I have to fight back a shiver at the touch.

"Yeah, so? They were busy," I reply, feeling a little defensive over my friends. "It wasn't even that big of a deal, anyway. It's just an archery competition."

"That you were the star of," Foster points out. "Maybe they're waiting at the van to carry you back on a throne or something. You did win for your team."

"I don't think so. Besides, there's just as much of a chance that next time, I'll be like Abby and—*What are you doing?*" I demand sharply, when Dorian drags my hand to his face and runs the back of my hand along his jaw.

"Getting rid of *Amelia*," he mutters unhappily. "She fucking stinks, Mercy. How do you not want that gone?"

"...Does she?" I ask after a moment, and I shouldn't be surprised when it results in all of their gazes fixed sharply on my face. "Okay, sure, whatever. She stinks. Can I have my hand back?"

Dorian releases it, and I fight not to pull my hand to my mouth and inhale deeply, knowing what I would scent and how it would affect me.

"I'm leaving," I tell them firmly. "The bus is leaving, and I'm leaving on it."

"Well, not exactly," Foster says, when all I get is a smirk from Dorian.

"...What?" I ask, bewildered, as I turn to him.

"We told your coach you'd come back with us instead. Though she said you have to drop your stuff off at the archery shed, of course. But–"

"What do you mean 'with you?' is this another–"

"It's us driving you back to Winter Grove, Mercy," Dorian replies too sweetly. He reaches out and pets my head, like I'm a child instead of an eighteen-year-old adult. "And if you're good, we'll get you ice cream too. Won't that be nice?"

They *do* get me ice cream, though it's weird, rather than nice. Sure, the ice cream is better than anything I'd ever had in Ohio, but when I'm back in my dorm room finally and away from the boys, all I can do is stare at the little cup.

Why had they been so nice to me? Is there something to it, some aspect of cruelty I'm just not seeing? There has to be, right? And worse, why am I so blind to it?

The door opens, admitting Bri, and when I grin up at her, she looks down at my ice cream and sighs. "Man, now I'm jealous. Your team stopped for *ice cream* on the way home?"

I hesitate, then say, "Yeah, it's pretty great. Perks of being on the archery team, huh?"

23

God, when did my blankets get so heavy?

I throw them off of me aggressively, kicking them down to the bottom of my bed as I sit up with a sigh and press my palms to my eyes. Another sound leaves me, irritation is heavy in my brain and in my noises as I grope around on the bedside table for my hearing aids. First one, then I fumble looping the other over my right ear as sound leeches into my brain from the television on the other side of the room.

"-Found by the Winter River, just south of the main square in Winter Grove. Police are enforcing a curfew, and their investigative efforts are all being put toward figuring out who in our small town could murder four people like this. Sources also say that this body showed more signs of violence than the others, and was unnecessarily harmed post-mortem—"

"He was an asshole." Briella's voice is soft, and I almost don't hear her over the television. When I do, I glance over at my roommate to see that she's sitting up in bed, the covers drawn up over her legs as she stares at the TV. "He was a student here, actually. And he was so mean. He once asked me to join his pack, before I met Zara. But he didn't like hearing no. He..." She trails off, looking over at me with surprise, as if she wasn't talking to me at all. "You're awake," she adds, surveying my features. "I thought you'd sleep awhile longer."

"I'm hot," I tell her, shrugging my shoulders. "I don't know why. I just feel...*hot*. And I need to get up." I stand, grabbing my shower caddy off my desk with fingers that itch to do something productive like work on my homework or something. Even though there *is* no homework, since we have a three day weekend for Halloween and professors had decided to take it easy on us. In fact, the last bit of work I have, the astronomy project, will be turned in today. Once that's done, the only thing I'll need to worry about is what's coming up in November so I can start preparing for my finals.

But knowing that doesn't help ease my brain, and I snag a towel from my side of the closet before jamming my feet into my shower flip-flops. "I'll be back," I mutter, running my fingers through my hair. Briella turns to look my way, the blankets falling down from her body to pool in her lap, and I realize that even now she looks dressed, like she's about to leave, so I hesitate. "Are you going somewhere?"

She looks down, as if she's shocked. "What? No?"

"You're dressed."

"Yeah, I know. I'm not feeling the greatest, and I couldn't get warm, *or* comfortable. I took a walk while you were snoring." She smiles amicably, and her words are clearly a joke. Really, they shouldn't make my skin prickle like this, or make me want to sneer some stupid reply back to her that she doesn't deserve.

Not wanting to hurt her feelings or say something I don't mean, I just shrug and walk out of the room to go shower. Maybe some cold water, or scalding hot, will get me out of this weird mood I'm in so that I can just move on with my day and celebrate being done with astronomy shit. Not that I haven't enjoyed the class so far, exactly. But I've put a lot of work into the project, and even though Dorian assures me it's more than good enough, I still can't help going back once a week or so to put a few more details into it.

God, what if it's not good enough?

It takes ten minutes of standing under freezing water with my thighs pressed together and irritation building into a growl in my chest for me to realize that water isn't the answer here. Just like always, my stomach plummets when it finally goes through my head, and I gasp into the shower like this is something new, when it's not. It's just, maybe, not that welcome.

But thank God I have heat suppressants back in my room, and they'll work well enough that the only thing anyone will be able to scent on me is the chemical smell of them. Sure, I won't be the happiest, friendliest person for the next few days, but who cares?

Finishing my shower quickly, I grab my clothes and yank on my sleep tee and shorts, making my way back to the room with hair that's sopping wet and dripping onto the hallway carpet. But I don't care. The sooner I take my suppressants, the sooner that I won't have to deal with more and more symptoms of my heat that'll have me rolling over for any alpha with a knot who looks at me for even half a second.

Or Dorian and August. Yeah, that would definitely be worse. They might not bully me so much anymore. And maybe I've made a few questionable decisions with both alphas. But that's no excuse to fantasize over not taking my suppressants and strolling up to their dorm to knock on their door and wait for one of them to answer.

What would they do if I did? The thought won't stop sliding around my brain as I slam the drawer of my nightstand open, grab the tablet pack, and pop the first two pills in my mouth while Briella looks at me with concern.

Only when I turn to look at her, the pack in my hand, does her mouth form an 'o' of understanding. "I was wondering," she admitted. "You haven't had one yet, so I figured you were close."

"I'm a little late," I admit. "Not that it matters or anything. Especially when suppressants make everything a little wonky. Do you take them?"

She shakes her head, a small smile gracing her full lips as she tucks some of her silky black hair behind her ear. "Not anymore."

Oh. *Right*. Still, I can't help the curiosity in my voice when I say, "Really? Is it...enough? With Zara? She's not an alpha, I mean. I would've thought–"

"It's more than enough," Briella assures me, cutting me off smoothly and with a gentle tone. "I don't need an *alpha* like Aaron Gaines to make me feel better." Her voice turns bitter at the name, but when I search my brain, I find that I can't place it.

"...Who?" I ask, wondering if I've missed something important over the last couple of months. Is he someone I *should* know? Am I just a bad roommate for not listening better?

"Him." She flicks her fingers toward the television, though by now the news story has turned to something completely different and not nearly so violent. "That's whose body they found."

"Oh." I don't know what else to say, though when I catch her eyes again, it occurs to me she's no longer wearing her jacket and jeans, but a tank top and leggings instead, like she normally sleeps in. "Are you going back to sleep?"

"Yeah," Briella says, lying down. "I'm really tired, finally.

But if you start to feel like shit and you need a pep talk or anything, wake me up, okay?"

I snort and go back to my own bed, not caring how cold my pillow is going to be when all of the water in my hair sinks into it. "I don't need a pep talk. I'm not going to do anything about it, or anything. I just want to go back to sleep for a little while, get through the day, then we have a three day weekend starting tomorrow. Happy day before Halloween?"

She returns the sentiment, her voice drowsy, before fading back to sleep.

"You're going to have to get another pin." I keep my voice light, but as I catch up to Zara, the sophomore turns to look at me with her brows raised.

"Oh yeah?" she asks, mashing the button for the elevator doors to close. "Is it that bad of an empty spot where the knife was?"

"Yeah," I assure her, though I'm mostly joking and I'm sure my voice sounds a little strained. "I mean, I miss that little knife you know? Maybe you could find another one. What did it look like, again? I'll look on Etsy for you." God, I feel hot and heavy and it's not exactly pleasant. But her backpack does look empty without the knife pin.

"It was just a knife," Zara sighs, sounding a little over dramatic like she's fully getting on board with my sentiments. "Just a knife with its cool little silver blade and..." she trails off, squinting. "Shit. Was there glitter in the hilt?"

"I don't remember. Oh! There was a drop of blood hanging off the end, right? And it was really bright and glittering? Maybe that's what you're thinking of?"

She gazes at me again, thoughtful. "Maybe," Zara says finally. "I didn't think you'd liked it that much."

"I like anything that keeps my mind off of how crappy I feel today," I admit, following her out of the elevator and down the light-colored hallway that leads to our classroom. "At least we're turning in our astronomy shit today, yeah? No more project. No more Beckler droning about it."

"It wasn't so bad," Zara replies. "I like stars. I mean, I would hope so, in any case. Since I'm taking this class and all. But I guess you have other reasons to be happy, huh?"

My brain scrapes through what *other* reason I should be happy, but I draw a blank. "Do I?" I ask finally.

"Yeah. This means Dorian can fuck right off."

"Oh. Shit, yeah." I hadn't thought of that, and there's no relief in me. No uncurling of my guts or anything else at the idea of it. Maybe it's not the *relief* it should be.

More likely, my body is just all kinds of fucked up today, thanks to my heat and the pills that I don't particularly enjoy the side effects of. Like feeling foggy and the hot flashes. Still, anything to avoid my heat, since there's no one to help me chase it away any faster than normal.

"You're right," I say, just trying to sound like I'm not going crazy. "Anyway, I'll see you later." She never goes further than her table in the back, but I have the whole room to walk through before I finally find my table and sit down next to Dorian with a heavy sigh, collapsing into my seat more than sitting in it.

When I open my eyes and drop my backpack to the floor, I'm more than a little surprised to find Dorian's eyes on me, surveying my face and his brows furrowed.

"I suddenly feel like the nicest person ever," he drawls, sucking on the straw of a smoothie from downstairs.

"Why? Because you're *not* going to comment on how shitty I look? Or my subpar astronomy performance?" I mutter dryly, trying for a joking tone and failing. At least this is my last class of the day, and I'll have all weekend to work off this heat of mine. Sure, I might miss getting to celebrate Halloween in any meaningful way, but what was I going to do anyway other than watch a few movies?

Without a word, Dorian slides a plastic cup to me, a straw already stuck in the lid while condensation beads on the outside.

I just stare at it, dimly realizing that it's a smoothie, like Dorian's. Except, this one is a peanut butter, chocolate, banana smoothie.

My favorite kind.

"Wow. Umm. This is really nice of you. *Thank* you," I say, reaching out and snagging the cup to pull it to me. "What's the occasion?"

"Turning in our project, originally," Dorian remarks mildly, leaning his elbows onto the table. He casts a surreptitious glance in my direction, catching my gaze and holding it. "But now maybe it's more like moral support for you. You stink, by the way."

"Wow. You know, that was almost friendly of you, until that last part. I didn't know my scent offended you so much, Dorian."

He blinks once, looking down at the cup then back at me. His hand comes toward me, but before he can think to snatch the cup back, I slide it to the other side of the table.

But his fingers keep coming. He snags one in the collar, a rueful grin on his lips. "You don't normally stink, kitten," Dorian informs me in a low purr that's just loud enough for my hearing aids to pick up. "But with your suppressants? Yeah, it's not very pleasant."

"It's not supposed to be."

He lets go, and I hate that my movements mirror his,

following him until I'm leaning into his space and our thighs are almost touching.

Shit. *Shit.* The touch is electric, even through our clothes, and I sit back with a jolt, like I've been shocked. Dorian, however, just watches me with that fathomless expression that I'll never learn to read.

Thankfully, Professor Beckler takes that moment to breeze to the bottom of the classroom, though when he gets there it's just to press the button to lower the large screen from the wall. "If I don't have your projects in my email by now, I should," he states. "If they're physical, pass them down." He holds out his hands in a 'give them here' gesture, and the rustle of papers precedes a few people passing notebooks down to the front for him to stack on his desk. "I'm not feeling the greatest today, so we're watching a documentary. No need to take notes. Maybe just look interested. Just don't break anything, and if you're going to sleep, don't snore." He presses a few buttons on his laptop, and the screen lights up against the wall, showing the menu for a National Geographic documentary.

"I didn't know he'd ever let us watch anything like this," I admit quietly. "Didn't he say during the first week how against it he is?"

"Yeah, until he doesn't feel well," Dorian replies, leaning toward me to be heard over the murmur of voices in the room. Within another minute or so, Beckler has the documentary playing and stomps up the stairs, going to sit at the very back with his own tablet in front of him, the light reflecting off his glasses like he has absolutely no intention of watching the documentary either.

"Guess it *would* be a nice time to take a nap," I mutter, though i know I'm much too irritated to do so. Not only that, but I'd be too afraid to. With my luck, I really would snore.

"Yeah?" Dorian laughs quietly. "Never took you for a

student who sleeps in class, Mercy." I grimace at that, squirming in my seat uncomfortably. Everything is uncomfortable right now, and no amount of readjusting is going to make it better, though that doesn't stop me when the lights dim and my frustration grows. Why is Dorian's scent so *loud* today? It fills my nose more than it ever has, and every time I inhale, it's like it buries itself deeper into my lungs, making a home in my body so that I'll never stop scenting him.

God, I need help.

A hand rests on my leg, jolting me out of my thoughts, and when I turn to look at Dorian, there's concern in his dark eyes, and something darker that I can't read.

"Calm down," he murmurs, gripping my thigh loosely. "Your scent is getting stronger."

"So?" I mutter, feeling petulant as my thigh continues to shake under his hand. Then he squeezes harder, giving me a meaningful look, and slowly my movements come to a halt. "It doesn't really matter. All they'll scent is the suppressants and my normal smell, Dorian." I still don't know why he cares, but it's irritating nonetheless.

"It matters because I say it does." His fingers dig lightly into my thigh, but before I can say anything, they drag upwards towards my body and I choke on my words.

"You gotta stop that," I hiss, my hands flying down to grip his. "Seriously, Dorian. I can't handle–"

"Shhh," he murmurs, running his fingers back down toward my knee. "Just focus on that for me, kitten. Don't think about whatever else is bothering you. I know it must be difficult."

He's not making it any *less* difficult. My insides practically flutter at his touch, and while I keep one hand on his, I don't grip or try to make him stop. With the other one I pick up my smoothie, toying with it as I sip at my favorite drink in the world and try to focus on anything other than how my body feels right now.

It's too much. I can't deal with everything. Not his touch, the heat, the itching for more–

"Shhh." I don't know if I've made a sound, but Dorian urges me to lean against him, prompting me to do so.

Until I sit right back up, staring at him in abject horror. "People are going to *see*!" I hiss, loud enough for only him to hear. "There are other students here, Dorian!"

His answering smirk makes me want to punch him. "Yeah, Mercy. I can see that. And I'm just making sure none of them think *they* get to come down here and comfort you." Somehow, I don't think we have the same idea of what comfort means. "You don't want that either. That's what got you into this mess, so I'm just making sure you get your way." God, why does it sound so goading when he says shit like that?

"You'll be fine," he adds, when I cant find any words. "You have your smoothie. No one's going to notice. Just lean into me, all right? As much as you want." Tentatively I do so, like he might pull out a knife and *shank me* for it.

Instead, his chest rumbles with a purr and he continues to run his hand up and down my thigh with agonizing slowness.

"Don't be confused, all right?" he says, his lips moving against my hair. "I'm not trying to win you over, Mercy. But I'd really hate it if anyone else here decided they could move in before I'm done making your life miserable for this semester."

I let out a breath, my sigh audible as my eyes close, though I don't grace him with an answer as my body' excitement dulls with grim resignation. I'm such an idiot, at the end of the day.

Hasn't Dorian made it abundantly clear he doesn't want anything to do with me when all of this is over? Clearly, I need to learn how to take a hint.

24

It's just in and out, and at least this time it's not like they're trying to make my life hard. In fact, it isn't Dorian's pack's fault in the least that I'm at their door, my hand raised to knock.

It's my own. I'm the one that kept Dorian's Apple pencil, and that means I get to be the one to return it. I hadn't even realized it, truth be told. But when I'd gotten Dorian's text a little while ago asking about it, I'd sorted through the contents of my backpack until the white, gleaming pencil was in my hand and mocking me.

So really, it's my fault that I'm here.

Letting out a sigh, I knock on the door three times, the pencil in my hand. I need to launch it at someone's face and then leave. It'll be an easy enough thing to do and won't give any of them a reason to make this *worse*.

Though in reality, they're good at making anything worse.

The door opens, but when I see that it's Foster instead of Dorian, I can't help but be just a little surprised.

"You aren't who I expected," I tell him, my voice flat. Still, I hold my other hand up, the pencil poised like I might stab him with it. Not that Foster looks particularly worried about that fact, as he just stares back at me, unimpressed.

"I'm sure. Come on." He takes a step back and I reluctantly step into the suite, my stomach doing small somersaults and wrecking my insides. I'm still only a day into my heat, and even with my suppressants, I'm *uncomfortable*.

Not to mention that the combined scents of Dorian and August aren't making it better whatsoever. They pull at my urges, almost overwhelming the suppressants until I want to go find either of them and curl up against them, purring and begging for a knot.

Which is precisely what I'm not going to do.

"Can you give this to Dorian?" I turn to look at Foster, holding the pencil out toward him, but he shakes his head and leans on the counter to snatch a water bottle off of the surface.

"Nah, I don't like you that," he tells me with a voice full of mock-sweetness. "Just go give it to him, you chicken. He's in his room." He flicks a hand toward the left-side hallway, and I can't help but roll my eyes at him in irritation.

"You're such a jerk."

"Oh, I *know*," Foster assures me, still not making a move to go to Dorian's room.

So I sigh and walk in the direction he's pointed me to, dragging my feet on the hardwood floor until I can shove open the partially open door and get this over with.

Well, that's the plan anyway.

Until Dorian's scent *slams* into me and I can't breathe. I can't look anywhere but at him, and even that is doing things to my insides that it shouldn't.

Dorian looks...frustrated. Standing over his desk with his

hands pressed flat against it, I'm pretty sure that I can see a muscle ticking in his jaw and he looks like he isn't having such a great day with whatever is going on. My mouth opens, and I think about asking just what's wrong with him, but then I close it with a sigh.

It's none of my business what's crawled up his ass, died, and *rotted*. Besides, he's never exactly friendly, and I doubt he'd like the concern now.

"I brought you your pencil," I sigh instead, brandishing up the white stick. "And Foster wouldn't take it, so I guess here I am. Giving it to you."

He doesn't move, nor does he reply. In fact, Dorian closes his eyes and exhales sharply, though I still can't figure out what I've done to get the silent, and clearly unhappy, treatment.

Whatever. He's not my problem.

When I say his name and he still doesn't answer, I know that I'm going to have to actually make a point of giving it to him if I want to get out of here in the next century. My legs move before I've finished the thought, and it's a testament to how much I'd rather be in bed that I stomp across the room and gently set the pencil down by his hand.

Then, like an idiot, I take a deep breath so I can sigh my frustrations towards him.

It's a mistake because I catch his scent in my nose and choke, much like the first time I'd met him.

It isn't because I hate his scent. It never was. Back then, it was because of how overwhelming his scent had been. How *good* it had been. But this time it's for a completely different reason.

"Dorian–" I choke on his name, my fingers curling against the wood of his desk as his own fingers tighten, causing the wood to literally creak.

Dorian Wakefield is in *rut*.

His scent is strong, and more than a little bit overwhelming to my senses. Everything about it feels and seems magnified, and I'm pretty sure I could come right here, just from breathing it in. There's an edge to it that I've scented before on other men, though that's not the real issue, exactly.

The problem is that he's in rut, and I'm in heat. We're a perfect, terrible match to set the world on fire.

"I didn't know until after I texted you," he tells me, his voice a quiet growl. "It's—sudden. I think it was *you*." He spits the words like an accusation, and shocked indignation lets me draw away from him, toward the corner of his room.

"*Me?*" I spit, bristling. "I'm on suppressants, so fuck off with that."

"Then they aren't working. You need to get that checked out, Mercy."

"Yes, they are! No one else has this problem, and they've worked for years. Don't blame your time of the month on me."

My nasty tone draws his attention and he turns on me, teeth bared as he crowds me back against the corner I shouldn't be in. "I'm early. It is absolutely *you*," he spits, his hands *slamming* into the walls on either side of my face. I flinch, but it's not because I'm afraid.

I'm surprised, and I just can't stop scenting him. My body aches to press forward so I can climb him like a jungle gym to shove my nose in his neck and take a deep breath.

As if he can read my mind, Dorian growls, leaning forward just a little bit as his nostrils flare. "God *damn it*, Mercy," he hisses, and yet again irritation cuts through my clouded brain.

"No, you are not going to blame me!" I reach up and shove his shoulders, though he barely takes one step back, and it's not enough to grant me breathing room. "I'm not responsible for your body, Dorian. Or whatever alpha-shit that's going on. Maybe it's karma–"

He catches my hand in his when I go to shove him again, and yanks my wrist to his face to press it against his skin as he inhales deeply. Fuck, that's hotter than it has any right to be, and if I'm not practically dripping right now, I'll be surprised.

"Karma?" His voice is a soft, rolling purr as he eyes me with his dark, heavy gaze. "For who, Mercy? Because I don't think I'm the only one who's just a little bit fucked." I curl my fingers against his face, nails scratching against his skin.

"I'm doing a lot better than you are."

He raises a brow and turns his face against my hand, teeth skimming my skin as a growl vibrates against my palm. I shudder, but I mean what I say. Thanks to my suppressants, I can hang onto myself a lot better than him, clearly.

"Do you want me to get Foster? Or August?" I'm not quite sure who he fucks during his rut, but I can see it being Foster. "They could help with–"

"I don't want their help." His words are sharp, and his eyes burn into mine as he nips at my palm again. "Do you know why?"

Slowly I shake my head, even as I feel my self-control crumbling in my chest. He's really not the only one about go feral here. I feel like my insides are a furnace, and every touch just serves to heat me up more.

God, I want his fucking knot in me so badly it's unreal. I can literally imagine it, and I'm aching for more than just his touch, more than just Foster's mouth, and more than just some little game.

"Because I want to breed you so fucking bad that it hurts."

I should tell him to fuck off. I know he will. Hasn't he made it clear that he'd never force something like this onto me? That

I always have a choice with him? I'll walk out of here, go home, and get myself off until I pass out while thinking about the tone of his voice and his words.

That's what I need to do because it's safe. He has Foster and August. I have my pride.

"Okay," I breathe, eyes wide as I stare up at him.

He doesn't move, but he blinks, eyes narrowing at me. "Okay?" he repeats. "What does that mean?"

"In Merriam-Webster terms, I *think* it means that I'm giving you the go-ahead to fuck me however you want." Dorian still just stands there, teeth scraping against my palm almost like he's thinking about it.

"I can't," he says at last, but I can feel the disappointment in every line of his body. "I *can't.*"

"Because you don't like me like that?" I ask flatly, as though the words don't hurt. Like rejection isn't burning into my bones as he–

"Because I'm not going to *fuck* you. If you don't get out of my room, I'm going to pin you down to my bed and breed you until the sun comes up. And then I'll do it again. And you know what? If I'm feeling really nice about it, I'm going to let the others help me, just so we can make sure you stay nice and wet and open until I'm ready to do it again."

Oh.

Wow.

The words definitely aren't what I'm expecting, though that's the biggest understatement of my life.

"...Okay," I whisper again, though I can't deny that along with the thrill of anticipation and excitement that tingle along my nerves, there's definitely some nervousness there as well. Is he being serious? Is that really what he wants?

"Last chance, *kitten.*" He's still just standing there, unmoving. "You came in here at the worst time possible. But you can still leave. You can leave anytime you want, but it's going to be really hard to pry me off of you with my knot in your pussy." A small, rueful smirk colors his features. "Just in case you were thinking about it."

His words short-circuit something in my brain. I feel like I can barely think straight, barely *see* straight with him so close but not touching me how I want. Silently I grip his tee, pulling him closer to me so I can breathe in his strong, musky scent.

Wait—when did my face get pressed against his neck? His hand is at my waist, but it feels just right there, with my arms thrown over his shoulders and my face in his throat. My teeth scrape at his skin, and a low growl rumbles through his body.

"Mercy..." he breathes. "I mean it. I need you to know—"

"Fucking shut up, Dorian," I mumble. "And just let me scent you. God, it's..." I really can't get enough of him. Is this normal? Why aren't my suppressants working?

And why do I *care*?

He's walking backward, I think. For a moment I think that he's about to throw me out the door, since I can't see anything with my eyes closed and my face pressed to his neck. I don't want to move. I don't want to go anywhere but right here, especially when his thigh slots so perfectly between mine and pulls a soft keen from my throat.

"I'll stop if you say stop."

"But you're not even doing anything yet."

He chuckles. I can feel it in my chest when he does it, and his hand tightens on my waist. "Yeah," he agrees. "I'm not, am I?"

The world goes sideways. Before I can register what's going on, I'm on my back on his bed and Dorian's fingers are hooked in my sweatpants, which he yanks off my legs along with my underwear and shoes. In seconds I'm left only in my hoodie, but he doesn't seem to care about that.

Not with his eyes glued to the apex of my thighs, and his fingers digging into them to hold me open for him. I writhe on his bed, and that finally drags his gaze up to mine. "Kitten," he coos, leaning over the side of his bed for a second. "God, I'm going to make you regret coming in here." When he sits back up, he's holding that damn leash in his hands that he seems to have everywhere he goes, and he clips it to my collar before I can think to protest.

"I want to play with you. I want to take you apart until you don't even know who you are anymore, but *fuck*." His eyes go right back down to my slit, and my body burns under his gaze. "Tell me you want this."

"I want this so fucking bad. Dorian, I need your knot." I hadn't realized how true the words would be until they spill from my lips. When they do, it's like all of my reservations just evaporate. I hook my leg around his back and drag him forward, until he has to catch himself on his arm.

"Needy," he remarks, looping the leash over the head of the bed. "My needy little omega. Aren't you?" He *jerks* on it, and I gasp as he forces me onto my knees.

"Shit–Dorian. Are you *kidding me*?" With the leash like this, I can't do much other than pull or maybe turn onto my back again.

"Gotta keep you right there, don't I?" he chuckles. "And if you aren't good, I'm going to handcuff you. Is that what you want?" His nails drag up my thighs, causing me to gasp. "Want me to handcuff you here too, so you're on display for me and August to breed your cunt like the good little omega you are?"

The words do something to me that has me whining and burying my face into the pillow, my hips still high in the air for him.

"Good girl. Good kitten, presenting yourself for me like this." He slides two fingers into me, but I don't need him to. I'm so wet, and so ready for his cock that I *really* don't need him to make sure of it. "I'll be the best heat partner you've ever had."

"You'll be the only one I've ever had," I remark offhandedly, but my brain stutters with concern when he stops. He pulls his fingers free, hands on my hips, and my heart flutters. Did I say something wrong?

"Mercy..." His voice sounds strangled, but I can't figure out why. "You are not telling me that I'm the first alpha to fuck you during your heat."

I turn to look at him, my face still pressed to his soft, smooth pillow, and nod. "Is that...not okay?" I ask, my words uncertain. "If you're upset, we don't have to—"

"Upset?" His laugh sounds strangled, and when his cock slides against my slit, a shiver goes up my spine. "You think I'm *upset*?" He shoves himself inside without another word, and the surprise of it makes me gasp, back arching. He really is so fucking huge. He fills me perfectly, though without me being in heat, I'm sure it would be almost too much.

God, who am I kidding? It would be perfect no matter what.

"How dare you come in here like this?" He grips my hair with one hand, the other braced on the bed beside me. "Who gave you the right to walk in here with your perfect body, and whine at me like you do, huh?" He pulls out, only to thrust back in hard. "You pushed me into my rut early, and you thought I wouldn't take what you clearly were trying to give me?"

"I wasn't—"

"I guess it's no wonder you look so good on your knees; you're so good at begging for it, huh?" he chuckles, then bites my ear, and I gasp as my body jerks up to press against his.

"You look so good under me. You feel so fucking amazing. But you're going to look even better when you take my knot like a good girl." I shudder, not expecting the lick to the shell of my ear. "My good, perfect omega. I suppose I'll forgive you for pushing me into rut. Maybe this once." He picks up his pace, and *fuck*, he shouldn't be this perfect.

It shouldn't feel this good. Especially when he sits back and grips my hips, concentrating on how deep and how thoroughly he can fuck me.

It's so good, that I don't notice the leash being untied from the bed. I don't notice until August slides onto the bed under my upper body, pulling me onto his lap. "Oh, Mercy," he teases, with a light chuckle. "I could've told you that Foster only sent you in here so he could see what Dorian would do."

I glare up at him, but what am I supposed to say? It's not like I'm unhappy with how this feels.

Dorian growls, but August just grins. "C'mon, Dorian," he purrs. "She's in heat. There's room here for me too, isn't there princess?" He combs his fingers through my hair, and I whimper at his light touch. My face turns against his lap, my mouth open over his cock that's still hidden under his sweats.

Now it's August's turn to shudder. "You want my cock too, greedy princess? Want to suck on it while Dorian fucks that sweet cunt?" He reaches into his sweatpants and pulls it free, and I see that he's already hard.

"Depends," I say, meeting his eyes. "Are you going to knot me?" *Did I really just say that?*

His grin grows. "Yeah, princess," he promises, guiding my face to his shaft. "You use that perfect little mouth on me, and I'll make sure your pussy is full all night, okay?" I don't get to respond, however. He pulls me hard by my hair, jerking my face forward until I'm forced to swallow him down, all the way down, with my nose pressed against his pelvis and his strong scent mingling with Dorian's.

"You take me so well," Dorian compliments, hands still on my hips as he thrusts in and out of me in a fierce rhythm that helps August stay as deep as he can in my throat. The alpha in front of me works with Dorian's movement, arching his hips to fuck my mouth. He's not as big as August, but it doesn't matter. He's just as perfect as the alpha behind me is.

I whimper around him, fingers curling against his thighs, and find my hips rocking back against Dorian's. I want to come. I want his knot, I want *everything* and I feel so greedy right now that it's unreal.

"Come for me, kitten," Dorian coaxes, fingers digging into my hips hard enough to bruise. "You can do that, right? Fucking come for me so I can knot this perfect pussy of yours. C'mon, Mercy. I'm not going to ask you again."

He doesn't *need* to ask me again. Even before he's finished talking, I'm coming. I gasp around August's cock, tears streaming down my face as my orgasm slams into me harder than anything I've ever felt before. Behind me, Dorian buries himself in me one more time then leans over me to yank the hair up off my neck and sinks his teeth into my shoulder.

The combined pleasure and pain of him and August still fucking my throat is almost enough to make me pass out. Instead, I just keep coming, aware of a swelling pressure inside me that has me whimpering around August in question.

"Just like that," Dorian purrs. "Take my knot, just like that. Let me fill you up, kitten."

I don't exactly have much of a choice.

"*Fuck*," August moans, arching his hips off the bed. "Dorian, your *scent* and hers...Yeah, Mercy. Just like that. You can take it, just let me come in your mouth, princess. Just like *that*." He grips my hair hard, yanking me down as he thrusts his hips up one last time. Then he's coming as well, just like Dorian, and all I can do is lay there and take it.

Not that it's a hardship in any way.

August pulls away, tucking himself back into his sweats as he runs his fingers through my hair with Dorian still draped over my back. "You're perfect," he tells me, running the pad of a thumb over my cheek. "What a perfect little omega you are for us. Do you like his knot in your cunt, Mercy?"

"I think she likes it," Dorian chuckles like I'm not capable of answering. He pulls his hips back just a little, but before he's gone more than an inch, I'm whining at the feeling of his knot catching at my entrance. "I couldn't pull free even if I wanted to. She wants my knot so bad, I think she'd fight me to stay."

"Oh, yeah," I drawl, wishing I could drag August down for a kiss. "*I'm* the desperate one. *I'm* the one demanding it, and totally not you or anything."

Dorian growls and nips my shoulder. "If you're not careful, I'm going to make good on my threat. You want August back here next? You want his knot in you? His is bigger than mine. You'll be so sore that you won't be able to walk out of here until tomorrow."

Yeah, that definitely doesn't feel like a hardship.

"Like he isn't going to be too busy or tired or fucking Foster," I grumble, after a couple of minutes.

It's...the wrong thing to say. Or maybe the perfect thing. Minutes later Dorian is finally able to drag himself free, but the moment he does, I'm flipped onto my back and he exchanges positions with August, his arms wrapped around my body as August grabs my thighs and shoves one over his shoulder. Dorian grabs the other, and when I'm sure August is going to do something, he instead just reaches between us and plunges his fingers into my wet body.

"You came so much in her, huh?" he chuckles, leaning over

me to kiss Dorian. It's filthy, and in no way chaste. "She's staining your sheets, thanks to you."

"Make it worse," Dorian invites. "I want to have to throw them away." Naturally, the leash is wrapped around his fingers, and he jerks up on it to pull my attention up to his. "What do you think, Mercy? How many times will we have to breed your cunt until you've drenched my sheets?"

"That seems kind of unreasonable," I reply flatly. "Seems like something that only happens in porn."

Dorian's grin isn't friendly. "Hey Foster!" he calls, the door opening a second later. Foster's eyes go to mine almost instantly, and he takes a deep, almost shuddering breath. "Mercy here just said that the two of us aren't enough. That she wants you to fuck her too."

"Oh yeah?" he wanders closer to the bed, but before I can say something snappy, suddenly August is inside me.

He's not gentle, nor does he start off with a reasonable pace. Instead, I'm half sure my eyes are about to roll back into my skull at how hard he's fucking me. And it's not like I can go anywhere, with Dorian holding me against him.

"You're probably right," Foster agrees, sitting down on the bed beside us. He runs a hand up under my hoodie, his pupils blown wide just like his alphas. His fingers find my nipples, teasing me, and I whimper when he pinches them, drawing them to hardness. "She *does* look like she needs to be fucked way harder than this. Maybe you two are slacking."

His fingers wander back down my body, tracing my slit where August is fucking me. "Maybe she needs a little more, huh?"

Out of the corner of my eye, I see Dorian shake his head, and I can't help but wonder what Foster had in mind.

Not that I get much of a chance to focus on it, however. Because yet again I'm coming without nearly as much stimulation as what I'd normally need. My fingers twist in Dorian's hair, and a loud sound almost like a scream leaves me when August's knot swells and presses against my walls.

"I told you," the black-haired alpha purrs against my ear, as August just keeps *going* as much as he can. "Didn't I? Now take it all for us, kitten. Be a good little omega for us. I'll hold you just like this, right here. No point in closing your thighs when he's done since Foster needs to get a chance to play with you too."

"Oh yeah?" I ask, finally able to say something after nearly dying and resurrecting on the spot thanks to my orgasm. "Is that so? Maybe Foster doesn't deserve to fuck me. Maybe he's too *mean*."

Foster chuckles and grips my face, jerking it towards him so he can find my lips in a kiss hard enough to make it feel like he's trying to suck my soul out of my body. He leans into me, his mouth coaxing mine as August just continues with those infuriating little movements even though he can't really go anywhere.

"Yeah, maybe I don't have a knot," Foster agrees, his eyes dancing. "But I'm going to make you regret those words, I promise. I really hope you didn't want to *walk anywhere* tomorrow, darling girl."

I don't make it back to my dorm until almost dawn, and when I'm there I collapse on my bed with a groan, my body a whole, solid ache. To my credit, I had walked out, trying to *waltz* out to prove a point, only for my body to inform me that was not an option.

But I've never been so satisfied in my life. Nor so confused, since I never knew sex could be that good.

Dragging my blankets up over my body, I sigh and squeeze

my eyes shut hard. *It was just sex*, I tell myself, as my brain wanders back to everything that we'd done. *It's just sex*, I remind myself, as the smile on Dorian's face and the way he'd called me a perfect omega echoes in my ears. *It's just sex,* I sigh, resigned, as I drift off with the scent of their pack in my nose, and an ache in my chest that I can't place.

25

"You could spend the break with me if you wanted." The offer from Briella has been repeated at least twice, but I just smile at her and shake my head while she packs.

"And miss the chance to *finally* spend some alone time in Winter Grove? I've been dying to go to the tea shop. And maybe *Video Valhalla* will let me back in now," I laugh, though my heart twists at the possibility it *won't*. "No. I'm great here, actually." I know for a fact that Dorian has gone home, since I overheard him say it to August when we'd been working on our bio homework together. And since August had mentioned joining him, I'm going to be free from them.

Finally. Even though it's only for about four days, and I'm sure they'll be back with a vengeance since they're running out of 'own me' time. All in all, it's been less awful than it was when they were still trying to make my life hell. Though I suppose this is a different kind of hell that's hotter than it has any right to be.

Don't think about it, I remind myself, dragging my mind back from Halloween when I'd been in heat. All three of them had been...mind-blowing to say the least. But it was a one time thing, and only because of Dorian's rut that had hit at the same time.

It isn't going to happen again.

"Have a good Thanksgiving," I tell Briella as she heads out, happy that she's going home to see her parents, since her relationship with her mother is stronger than mine has ever been, or ever will be. I'm only a little of jealous of that, but it's easy enough to shrug off most of the time.

God, I miss my dad.

Once she's gone, I find that it's hard for me to sit still. Even with a movie on, I just keep getting up and doing small things like emptying the trash, sweeping the floor, and folding my blanket. Which is incredibly unlike me, and I know that I need to do something else.

Might as well go into town, right? I was going to save the tea shop and *Video Valhalla* for Saturday, but if I do it now then maybe I can go again in two days or so. Though, when I think about waltzing back into the video store, my heart does little flips in my chest and I have to take a deep breath to ground myself.

It's going to be okay. Probably. I guess I could always go beg Dorian to get Foster to apologize, or something. Though, the thought of that makes me cringe and I have a feeling I could land myself back into this *problem* I've spent the whole semester in.

Though...would that really be so bad?

Am I going to *miss* this? My fingers play with the collar around my throat as I slide my sneakers onto my feet and put my phone in the pocket of my tight jeans. It's officially jacket weather now, so I shrug into an oversized, long black hoodie with red bands on the sleeves that goes further than my fingers and makes me feel like I'm a child swamped in grownup clothes. My hair stays down, as it's still damp and I'd like to not twist it up into a ponytail right now.

It's not until my hand's on the door that I hear a soft knock, but by then I'm already opening it.

Foster stands on the other side, staring at me and looking less than impressed.

"Why would you ever want to live in Maliseet?" he asks flatly, crossing his arms over his chest. He cranes his head forward, looking at my dorm, and his nose pinches in disapproval. "God this is so small. What do you do for privacy? What if you want to fuck in here? Not that any of us *would* fuck you here," he adds quickly, as if I'd *asked*.

"I'm not going to suggest you do," I assure him, leaning against my doorframe nonchalantly, like I wasn't about to leave. "It's a dorm, Foster. Sorry it doesn't meet your expectations." It's nicer than the ones I'd toured back home, and roomier. I have no reason to complain, and I bristle a little when he suggests it's subpar.

I guess I should just be able to afford a *suite* like him and the others.

"What are you doing?" he demands, shoving his hands in his pockets.

"Standing here. What are *you* doing? Why aren't you with Dorian and August?"

His stare isn't that friendly. But then again, unless he wants something, it never is. Or unless I'm naked, but I chase that thought out of my head as quickly as I can.

"We aren't attached at the hip, you know."

"Could've fooled me."

His eye roll is dramatic, slow, and I worry he's going to hurt himself or get stuck like that if he ever does it again. "You're going somewhere, right? Where are you going?"

"Out, Foster. Why do you want to know?" It's so easy to snap at him, especially when the others aren't around. "Or are you going to ruin this for me too, just like you ruined swimming, the video store, and walking down the sidewalk?"

He starts to reply, but then pauses. The words sink in and he looks at me, eyes narrowed with confusion. "Ruined them for you? How?"

Is he really this dense? Or just this much of an asshole?

"If I go swimming, you'll probably sprint in and take my stuff again," I point out, though my heart beats wildly in my chest at the words.

"No, I won't. Dorian wouldn't let me, for one. And I didn't know what you had in your backpack. I wouldn't have taken it if I realized."

I don't know how to respond to that, so I just ignore the words. "I'm being facetious with the sidewalk part, I guess. But you know you ruined the video store for me. That's obvious."

"She won't care if you go back in. I paid for the movie, so what's the big deal?" He frowns, hands leaving his pockets as he fidgets. "Are those really so big of a deal? No harm no foul, right?"

"Not right."

"But you're fine. I didn't *hurt* you."

"Foster, there are a lot more ways to hurt me other than hitting me." I don't mean for the words to come out so frantic, so worked up, but I can't help myself. It's incredibly *frustrating* that he can't see what he's done, and it just makes me want to throw a bucket at him. A full bucket, filled to the brim with concrete.

"All right, then I'm sorry."

The words seem so strange between us, especially with his sweet, tropical scent in my nose with its heady edge. I don't expect them, that's for sure. But more than that, I don't believe him.

"No you aren't," I say at last, leaning harder on the doorframe.

I expect him to reply. To tell me I'm wrong, or maybe cackle and tell me that of course he doesn't mean them. Instead he tips his head to the side, and stares at me like he isn't sure what to say.

"You sound like Dorian when you talk to me like that," he admits, shrugging one shoulder. "He does the same thing when I apologize."

"So he just accepts you aren't sorry?"

A rueful smirk appears on Foster's lips, and his eyes glitter. "No, not at all. He makes me prove how sorry I am, *if* I even am." I don't need him to explain, when his meaning is incredibly clear.

"I don't think that's in the cards here, Foster. I'm not going to *make you* show me you're sorry."

"I think you could if you wanted to." Is that a compliment? It feels like one. "But hey, I'm not suggesting it, exactly. You're going somewhere." We're back to that again, and his transition back to his question is so fast I feel like I have whiplash. "Where are you going?"

Letting out a breath, I close my eyes and resign myself to the fact that he isn't going anywhere. "Tea shop and umm..." The second part of my day's plan makes me hesitate. I don't know if I want *him* to know what I'm doing. Would he do something again? "I'm going to see if I can get back into the video store. I really wanted some stuff from there, okay?" My tone is soft, and when I open my eyes to look at the blue-eyed brunette, I'm sure they're pleading. I just don't want him to mess this up for me.

"You haven't been back? It's been two months, Mercy. She would've been over that in a week." Slowly, I shake my head, and Foster frowns. "Oh."

He doesn't say anything else, just...*oh*. I can't figure out what that even means, exactly, so I just watch him as he thinks it through.

"Let's go then. I stole August's car, so we'll just drive."

"We?"

"Yeah, you and me makes *we*." He catches my gaze with his. "Let me show you I'm sorry, Mercy."

I'm going to refuse. I swear I am. Until he reaches out and twines his fingers with mine, barely giving me a chance to grab my key off of the hook as he drags me down the hallway to the elevator.

Am I really doing this?

"You can't actually want to go to a teahouse," I protest, again being pulled around by Foster as he drags me down the sidewalk away from *Video Valhalla*. My heart still pounds nervously in my chest, and a big part of me can't believe that the woman hadn't even remembered what 'I' had done.

And Foster had just strolled in, taking me back to the horror section where he'd found me before and talking my ear off about his favorite movies. Then, when I'd paid for what I wanted and he'd stood beside me at the counter while I cringed and flinched every time the woman looked at me, he'd just smiled and complimented the owner.

"Why not?" He turns, going up the concrete steps to the

front of the vintage building that looks like it was once a house. "You think I'm too manly?"

"You? Never." He lets go and opens the door, waiting for me to walk inside before stepping in after me. "But this can't be your idea of fun." My words are distant and I barely pay attention to what I'm saying as I walk inside the cafe-style building. There's only one other person inside, and they're sitting at a small table in the far corner drinking something that looks like iced coffee. The tile floor is decorated with flowers, and decorations hang on the walls along with fake greenery and little plastic hummingbirds. Taking a deep breath, I smell all kinds of spices, fresh bread, and of course *Foster*.

It's impossible to get him out of my nose today, especially being with him in August's car.

"Doesn't matter," Foster says, going to a table against the window and collapsing in one of the chairs. "We can just seat ourselves. They'll come take our order in a bit."

I follow him, bewildered, and sink into the chair opposite him as I survey his face that's lit by the sunlight filtering through the stained glass panes. He's so gorgeous like this, in a way that Dorian and August aren't. He doesn't have the arrogance, or the alpha-sureness that both of them possess. But the light that flickers in his eyes and the way he always seems amused is attractive. It's eye-catching, and this is one of the first times I've been able to just *look* at him.

At least, until he looks back at me. "I'm pretty," he tells me, and it's not a question. "You can keep staring at me. I just wanted to point out that I'm incredibly gorgeous, and that you shouldn't feel bad if you can't look away."

"You're also an asshole," I tell him quietly.

"Yeah, but the looks make up for it."

I shake my head in disagreement as the waitress walks over, reciting the daily special of a chicken salad sandwich on fresh-made rye bread with house fries. I order it, and tea, but Foster has to stare at the menu and analyze it for a good twenty seconds before he announces that he wants the BLT on sourdough.

"You're so picky," I scoff, when the waitress walks away to put our order in.

"Maybe you're just not picky enough." God, I wish he didn't look so good like this. "Maybe you should ask for what you want more often."

"Yeah? Like what? *Pretty sure* I was clear as a fucking bell when I asked for you guys to leave me alone," I point out, though both of us pause when the waitress puts down glasses of water in front of us.

"Well, I don't mean that. Besides, aren't you glad we didn't?" Foster slides his arms across the table until he's leaning halfway across it and his eyes are fixed on mine. "Aren't you happy we're here now?"

The 'no' is ready on my lips, but I don't say it. I stare at him, meeting those gorgeous eyes as he waits for my answer with his hands only six inches or so from my fingers. What would it be like if I twined my fingers with his, the same way I had during my heat?

What would it be like, if I admitted that I may not hate them as much as I once had, or as much as I should?

"I don't know," I say finally, sitting back as he does the same. "Things are really confusing, Foster. *You're* really confusing. Besides, the semester is ending. You're going to forget about me once our whole deal is off. Dorian's made that incredibly clear, you know?"

"Has he made that clear?" Foster's brows arch dramatically. "How? When? With his words? Tell me, did it feel that way when he was fucking you and knotting you, and–"

Heat rises to my cheeks, and I shake my head, cutting him off with a quick, "*Shut up, Foster.*"

But his answering grin is more than enough, and he doesn't need to say anything else as the waitress drops off our food and recedes behind the counter again, letting us know that she'll get us anything we might need while we're here, and that all we have to do is ask.

26

Dorian and August don't come back until Monday morning, so the rest of my weekend really *is* free. While Foster had refused to tell me why he hadn't gone with them, he stops by to eat dinner with me every night before classes start again, and I can't deny the obvious.

It's *weird*.

He talks about weird shit with me, like surface details of his life, and pries a few details out of *me* as well, until finally his pack gets back and our little dinner dates end.

Just like all of this is going to end.

I sigh, staring down at my table in the library as Dorian drops our astronomy homework down on the table in front of me. I have my choice of academic torture today, with both a bio study guide that I could be doing with August, and our astronomy study guide I could be doing with him. Of course coming here to do them wasn't by invitation. It was a 'request,' as Dorian likes to say.

"What's wrong?" August falls into the seat on my left, draping his arm over the back of his chair. He's close enough that his hand brushes my shoulder, and I glance up at him with a frown. I could tell him. I could tell *them*. They'd probably laugh at me for it, and remind me I should be grateful that this is ending.

Instead, I can't get my dinners with Foster or them showing up for my archery competition out of my mind. It's almost like we're dating, but we're not. It's almost like this is the start of something that could last.

But, it's not.

"Nothing," I sigh, opening my bio textbook. "Have you started this yet?" I barely notice when Dorian leans in close to me, but shivers run up my spine when his fingers graze the ring of my collar and the skin under it.

"Liar," he purrs in my ear, tugging on the ring lightly. "How has lying to us ever worked out for you, *kitten*?"

Pretty well, in my secret opinion. But I roll my eyes at him and shoo his fingers off my throat, only for them to be caught in his hand as he growls softly in disapproval.

"Study guide," I tell him, a pleading note in my voice. "I've *really* got to get this done. I need to study."

"God forbid you miss even one question, right?" August chuckles as Dorian lets go of my hand, thankfully not pushing it.

At least, not until he leans close and says just loud enough that I can hear him, "I'll make you tell me later. You're not off the hook, you know." I shiver again, my breath catching in my chest as his lips trail over the shell of my ear and I can feel the smallest brush of teeth.

"Whatever," I say, trying to ignore him.

It works, at least for a little while. With how nervous I am about finals, I dive into studying and filling out the study guides, so even if Dorian *is* trying to distract me, there's a chance I'm not going to really notice.

Sitting back after finishing the astronomy work, I blink my dry eyes a few times and sigh. "Are you–" I turn to look at him, wanting to know if he's finished as well, only to see that he's not there.

"He went to get something to eat. He asked if you wanted anything." There's a chuckle in August's voice, and I wince. Had I looked like an idiot, sitting here and drooling over homework while my eyes dry out?

"Wow. So, I get really focused sometimes," I admit, not willing to say that the level of noise in the library and the way things echo in here aren't helping the way that I hear, or not as the case may be. "But at least I'm done with astronomy?" If Dorian needs my answers to the study guide when he gets back, he's more than welcome to have them.

"Are you done with these?" He picks up a few of the books scattered on the table's surface, getting up as he does.

"I'll help you," I offer, not wanting him to drag the books I'd needed back even though I hadn't really used them in the first place. It's nice of him, which is always weird, but also it's my responsibility.

"You don't have to," he says, already walking away from me and toward the large rows of wooden shelves. There aren't many of them on the third floor of the library, and besides another table of students studying quietly, there's no one else on this floor. All of the noise comes from the floor below us, which is almost packed with people in the study rooms.

"How long as Dorian been gone?" I add, following August like a lost puppy. He really doesn't need my help, and since he won't let me carry anything as he takes them back to their shelves, I'm relegated to just following at his heels.

"About thirty minutes. I was expecting him back like five minutes ago, since he was just going for bagels and smoothies. But there was probably a line or something." He says the words smoothly, and when I calculate the distance between here and there, I have to agree with him. But really, there are lines there at the *weirdest* times, so I'm not super surprised.

"Oh. Well, do you want to do our bio work? You're about half done like I am, right?" I lean against the shelves as he slides the last book into place, waiting for him to get done. "We could, I don't know, just be done with everything so that—"

He moves faster than I can think to dodge, and almost instantly I'm shoved back up against the shelves, his knee pressed between my thighs and his lips slanting against mine.

"August—" I protest, the growl from his mouth sinking into me. I shudder, his hands at my waist are hot against my body. "We're supposed to be studying—"

"We're taking a break," he purrs, sliding his hands up my sides until he can cup my jaw in one and press his other forearm against the shelves beside my head. "Fuck, Mercy. I can't believe I'm going to have to go a whole month over break without *this*."

The words are slow to register in my brain, and when they do, I don't know how to respond. I'm suddenly so grateful for his mouth that's back on me, teeth digging into my lower lip hard enough that all of my attention is fixed on the hot, bright pain that feels like something else entirely.

His thigh rubs at my center, pulling a whine from my throat, and at the sound his lips crush against mine in earnest once more.

"What if I fucked you right here, huh?" he chuckles, his hand going from my jaw to my waist. "We'll have to get you to start wearing skirts next semester. If you were, I'd already be inside your pussy. Don't act like you wouldn't want me to be."

He's not wrong, honestly. Even just this has me wet for

him, something he'd realize pretty quickly if he wanted to check.

"You deserve a study break. A longer one," he goes on, words like silk coaxing against my ears. "More importantly, *I* deserve one. I'd be a lot more efficient if I could fuck you right now and get some of this boredom and frustration out of my system. I'll make you love every second of it."

"I know you will," I breathe, surprising myself at the words. And him too, judging by the look on his face. Before I can add anything, however, he's kissing me again. His hand on my waist moves to grab my ass, and he shifts so that he can grind against me, the front of his jeans providing not nearly enough friction against my leggings.

"Want me to breed that cunt, Mercy?" he asks, his voice a hiss. "Want me to pin you against that shelf behind you with your hands spread and fuck you right here?"

"Someone could see," I reply in a whine, though I'm not exactly protesting. Especially when he grips my thighs tighter and rocks his hips against mine in such a perfect way that I'm close to begging for it.

"Who? Dorian? Princess, we both know he would do more than just *watch*. He deserves a break too though, doesn't he? Should we let him fuck your ass while I take your pussy? Too bad Foster isn't here. We all know how much you like your mouth full of cock. So come on Princess. Tell me how much you'd like to have all your holes filled."

I look up at him, mouth open, but a little unsure of my response. That's definitely not something I've done before, though I'm sure the blush on my cheeks is evidence of how much I'd be willing to try it.

And clearly August is a mindreader because the grin on his face widens, his arrogance growing by the second. "You've never been fucked in both holes, have you?"

"What gave it away?" I try to keep my voice flat, with a wry edge, but he laughs like I haven't succeeded. I don't want him to think the idea makes me nervous...even though it does.

"*Princess*, you don't need to be nervous. Do you think we'd hurt you? We've always taken our time with you, haven't we?" I shudder at the implication. "And the semester is almost over, so I'm sure we could find a day to lock you in our suite and, like I said, take our time. Think about it. With all that time, all of us will get a turn, and you'll let us since you're such a *good girl*."

I could probably come from his voice alone. His fingers against my slit pull a gasp from my throat, and when he shoves two of them into me, I'm nearly at the end of my rope right there.

But August doesn't get me off. He pulls his fingers free of my leggings and brings them to his mouth, cleaning them off and tasting me loudly.

"God, you're so wet just from the idea, huh?" he sighs ruefully, stepping back and leaving my body screaming for more. "But I don't want to get us banned from the library. Besides, Dorian is definitely back. And I'm sure he brought something for his *kitten*." When he's like this, August could charm the pants off of a statue.

I follow him back toward the table, nearly bumping into him when he stops and stares. "Huh," he murmurs, pulling his phone from his pocket. I look around him, surprised as well to see that Dorian *isn't* back yet.

"That's kind of weird," I agree. "Maybe he, I don't know, got lost?"

August shoots me a look, and brings the phone up to his ear.

It rings.

And rings.

And goes to Dorian's voicemail.

"Maybe he's with Foster," August adds, hanging up and calling his other packmate instead. Foster picks up on the second ring, but I barely listen.

This feels wrong. It's off, or something. Dorian should be back, and I can't bring myself to be surprised when August hangs up with a disappointed and worried look.

"He isn't with Foster." I walk back to the table in front of him, shoving my things in my backpack. "Where are you going?"

"Aren't we going to go look for him?" I ask, turning to glance back at August. "I figured, since we don't know where he is."

"I'm sure he's fine." But August doesn't look like he believes that either. He drags his own things back into his backpack, and after a brief hesitation, Dorian's as well. "But yeah. Foster's going to look for him by the dorms. I'm going to go to the smoothie and bagel place." He throws me a quick smile that's probably supposed to reassure me. "That's probably where he is, you know? Solid possibility of a disgusting line."

Except...he should've been back by now unless all of Winter Grove University is trying to get a smoothie.

"Where should I look?" I ask, having no idea where in the world Dorian likes to hang out. I barely know anything about him, honestly. Except that he's great at dirty talk and an asshole.

It doesn't seem like a lot, now that I think about it.

"The first floor? The campus center? I don't know why he'd be there, but..." August shrugs.

"But maybe he got tied up. Text me when you find him?"

"Yeah, and then we'll finish the study guides at my dorm, all right?"

. . .

We don't find him.

An hour later, even though Dorian isn't my *friend*, I feel... nervous. My heart pounds in my chest, and I walk back to my dorm with a frown on my face. I need to throw my stuff in my room, and I'm wondering if I can recruit Bri to the search. It seems reasonable, even if she doesn't like him, and I'm sure Zara would help as well.

I shove open the door to my dorm, Bri's name on my lips, only to find that the room is dark.

"Briella?" I ask, flipping on the lights. Is she sleeping?

Turns out, she isn't in the room at all.

"...Bri?" I murmur, more surprised than anything as I chuck my stuff onto my bed. She isn't here. Unless she's folded herself up in a box and decided to stay there until after finals.

Dragging my eyes over her things, I sigh. Well, there goes that. I could call her, yeah, but if she's not even on campus, she's going to take a little while to be of help.

But I decide to try anyway.

With my phone in my hand, I turn to look out the window, and my eyes land instead on the little bowl on her desk that holds a myriad of little metal pieces.

Right. It's Zara's pin that broke.

But what is Bri doing with it? Trying to fix it? I'd thought Zara had said that it was unfixable.

I dial Bri and put the phone on speaker, lying it down on the desk as I dump the pieces of the pin out on the wood. I know that I shouldn't, but if I can help her put it back together, why not?

There aren't as many pieces as I thought, and it's relatively easy to shove them back to where they need to be. The hilt is first, then two pieces of the blade that take me a minute to figure out.

Bri's phone goes to voicemail.

"Hey, Bri?" I still place with the other three pieces of the pin, trying to figure out what's left other than the tip of the knife. They're indented, like something small fit in them, and as I move them around, I'm finally able to fit two of them together and put them against the end of the knife. "I'm back in our dorm. Can you help me? Dorian's missing, and...just call me back, okay?" I hang up, the last piece of the pin still being rolled between my fingers.

I slide it into place a second later, confused. That was... rather easy, actually. And it doesn't look like anythings missing, except what's supposed to be in the little bracket that hangs from the tip of the knife. What had it looked like before? I remember the glittery hilt, the shiny silver of the blade, and there had absolutely been something there.

It clicks a second later, and I reach out and touch it as my mind conjures up the image of the unbroken pin. Hilt. Blade, the black bracket and–

And a small red gem that was meant to look like a drop of blood.

The door behind me opens, but I don't turn around. I can't. I'm too busy staring at the knife pin, my hands shaking as I do.

I've *seen* the little red gem, and I know why it isn't here. In fact–

"Sorry I missed your call." Bri's voice is concerned and quiet in the small space. "I was already coming in, so I just thought that I'd..." she trails off when she gets close to me, looking down at the pieces of the pin on the desk that I've slotted back into place. "Oh, you fixed it." She doesn't sound excited. Not even a little bit.

In fact, she sounds worried.

"Almost all of it." I can't help the way my voice sounds empty. Nor can I help the way I touch the empty end with my finger. "But there's still something missing, huh?"

"Yeah? I guess? I never really got a good look at it—"

"Why did Zara steal that newspaper article about the dead guy from the front desk?" My words are slow and deliberate.

"She *reads the newspaper*, Mercy."

"Does she?" I turn to look at her, and the look on Briella's face is confused and nervous. "Where is your girlfriend, anyway?"

Briella shrugs. "Does it matter?"

"I don't know, does it?"

She doesn't reply.

"You know, Zara was always really on board about my jokes of killing Dorian." My heart pounds in my chest, though I try to keep my voice empty. It doesn't work. I know it doesn't, but Bri is still standing here.

"Yeah? So were you."

"Was I? I just wanted him to leave me alone. And wasn't that last body found, the one that was mutilated after death, an alpha you knew?"

Briella tenses, her fingers flexing before curling into her palms. I glance down at her hands, then back up at her face. "Where's your girlfriend, Bri?"

"Is that...really what you want to ask me?" she whispers, the words almost too soft for my hearing aids to pick up.

It isn't.

But I'm almost too afraid to ask what comes next.

She doesn't offer a response, and I stare at her for too long before taking a breath around my pounding heart to ask, "Where is Dorian?"

27

I'm not exactly proud of threatening Bri, telling her that I'll tell the school and that I can't imagine how her parents will ever love her the same when they find that she's responsible for something happening to Dorian Wakefield. I add in that since his family is so important, repercussions will probably go beyond kicking her out of school.

In fact, I end up telling her, your parents will probably pay for the fuck up too.

After that, Bri tells me where they are, though it's a part of campus that I've never been to.

I *run* down the walking trail, out of breath as it leads me through sparse trees and lets out beyond the farthest dorms, on a stretch of the lakeshore that's used mostly by the scuba diving class and the biology department for water studies. The only things on this side of campus are a few benches, water, and a dock that looks out over the huge lake.

At first I don't see anything. There's no one running around, no Zara waving a *real* knife. Nothing that catches my eye, and I wonder if Bri lied to me after all.

Until my gaze lands on one of the benches that's occupied. It sits near the water, in front of a rockier part of the shore, and behind it is a small expanse of decorative trees. From here, all I can see is that it's a person. A figure, at best.

I can't even tell if they're alive.

My pace picks up, until I can't hear anything other than the wind in my ears and the pounding of my nervous heart. The bench is so far away, and I'm terrified that he's going to slump over, or Zara's going to run out of the woods and stab him or–

I slow down as I near the bench, my eyes anywhere but on the dark, short hair that has to belong to Dorian Wakefield, too scared about what I might see. He doesn't look up, but keeps his hands in his pockets as he looks out over the lake in front of him, barely moving.

Finally, I reach the bench, my heart hammering in my chest like I'm still running. His head tilts slightly, face turning as he frowns.

"You're not dead," I gasp, barely able to speak through my gasps for air. "Holy shit, Dorian. Why haven't you answered the phone?"

He blinks, eyes staying narrow. "You shouldn't be here," he says finally, still not moving. "Why don't you go home?"

"Why don't you go with me?" I demand, grabbing the edge of the bench and shivering in the cold, evening air. The metal is freezing under my fingers, and I take that moment to look over him once more. He doesn't look hurt...so why is he still *here*? "Why don't we call August and Foster? They can–"

"No." He cuts me off quickly, smoothly, and with a hint of worry on his face. "Besides, I don't even have my phone."

...Oh.

"Where..." I lick my lips, and try again. "Where is it? Are you all right?"

He tilts his head back, eyes sliding to the side as if to see something behind him, and my heart rate picks up yet again.

I don't want to look in the trees. In fact, I want to turn around and run the other way, but that isn't an option. Not without Dorian, and preferably his phone, though he could totally afford a new one. But when all is said and done, I have to look. I can't just keep standing here willing all of this to just be a dream.

Slowly I turn my head, the shadows from the trees are long and reaching in the rays of the setting sun, until my eyes fall on Zara.

Zara, who stands leaning against a willow tree, her arms folded over her chest and dressed in a bulky grey jacket with one pocket that hangs conspicuously heavy. She's already looking at me, waiting for me to make eye contact before the corner of her mouth crawls up in a small smile.

"The only reason he's not dead is because Bri told me you were coming," she tells me, unmoving. "She says you fixed the pin, and that somehow tipped you off. How did you know?"

"Because the cops showed me a red jewel they found at the scene of one of the crimes," I say, the words feeling like they're being dragged out of me. "Zara...what are you *doing*?" Dorian doesn't say anything, only leans back on the bench like neither of us are here and he's just watching the sunset over the lake.

But then again, what can he do? I'm sure if he gets up and tries to run, whatever's in her pocket is going to make a nasty appearance in Zara's hand.

Please don't let it be a gun.

"I only kept the pin because I didn't want them to find it. But I guess I should've been more worried about you finding it, huh?" ahe laughs quietly, her eyes dark. "Do you want to help me?"

A jolt of fear electrifies my spine, and I'm shaking my head before I can even think. "Help you *kill* Dorian? Absolutely not! Why would you even say that?" I lick my lips, feeling like they're suddenly too dry and about to crack. "Do you know what'll happen to you if you kill him? He's Dorian *Wakefield!*" This had worked with Bri. Surely it could work with Zara as well. "You'll...you won't have a life, Zara. You'll go to jail, at the very least. You'll–"

"What?" She reaches slowly into her jacket pocket, and sure enough when she lifts her hand, it's curled around a small gun. "I'll...die?"

I'm moving before my brain can make sense of my stupid choice. I lurch forward to stand between her and Dorian, who makes a noise of protest and lunges to his feet.

"Get out of the way," Zara orders, a second before Dorian snaps, "*Move*, Mercy!"

But I shake my head at both of them, my whole body trembling as I meet her eyes. "Move so you can *shoot* him? What the fuck, Zara? I'm not going to let you shoot him!"

"He hurt you," she says confidently. "Let me end it, so he can't hurt you again. I don't care about *dying*, Mercy." A smile stretches across her face, and for the first time, it hits me that Zara might not be completely sane. "So long as I can rid the world of some of the people like him."

"Like him?" I tilt my head to the side and take a small step forward. Dorian hisses a warning, but I ignore it, only looking back to make sure I'm still between them. "What does that mean? Like *him*? An alpha? Arrogant? Sometimes an asshole?" He's usually an asshole, but that doesn't feel very productive to say. "If that's your criteria, you're going to be killing people for the rest of eternity." She doesn't shoot or even point the gun at me, but it's so hard to take another step toward her.

I don't want to die.

My body screams at me not to do this. That I should run

and hope that Dorian does something to get away as well. But I know that if I do that, if I let Zara kill him, it'll be as bad as killing him myself. I don't know how I'd ever face myself again.

"You don't understand." She rolls her eyes like I'm a child and she's fed up with me. Like I'm missing some very obvious point. "You think you're the only person he's hurt? You think he'll ever be *sorry*? You think he'll *change*?" A scoff-laced laugh leaves her like a bark. "Or maybe you think you'll be the omega to turn him around."

"He doesn't need to be turned around." My words are quiet, and when I say them, I wonder where in the world they come from. Another step lessens the distance between us, but my body is starting to lock up. That gun in her hand stands out in stark contrast to everything around me, like it's the only thing that's real in a scene of surreality.

She could kill me just as easily as she wants to kill Dorian.

"You're not special, Mercy. No matter what he's said to you, or how he treats you in his suite. I've *scented* them on you, so I know you fuck him. I'm not an idiot. But he's using you, just like they all do."

"What makes you the expert?" I snap, and immediately wish I hadn't when her eyebrows jerk up in surprise.

"Because I wasn't special either. Not to any of the guys back in my hometown. Not to any of the *alphas* who promised they'd stop hurting me if I gave them what they wanted. You think Bri was special? She wasn't. And you aren't either. If I don't kill him now, you'll be begging me to in another month when he just won't stop hurting you." She lifts her finger and pulls back the safety, making my heart slam into my ribs looking for an escape. "So *move*."

I take a deep breath, eyes finding her and holding her gaze. "No."

"I said–"

"I know what you said." I chance a glance back over my shoulder, though my brain screams that I can't take my eyes off her. Dorian is rooted in place, and I feel slightly relieved that I'm still between him and Zara. "I'm not going to let you shoot him."

"Mercy!" She presses her free hand to her face, waving the gun in irritation. "You don't even like him! You *hate him!* You're the one that's joked about killing him before, so what's the difference now? Is it really just the sex?"

"I never would've killed him!" One more step puts me almost within arm's reach, but I don't have the nerve to grab for the gun. "Ever! I was irritated, I was upset. I was *hurt*. But that's life, okay? Maybe those alphas really did hurt you. Maybe they really hurt Bri. I can't judge them, or you, or whatever happened before. But Dorian doesn't deserve a bullet, okay?"

She hesitates. I can see it in her face, though when she tries to look over my shoulder at Dorian, I block her view by sidestepping to be directly in front of her.

"He doesn't deserve a bullet," I say again, my words slow. "Please, Zara. Please, just give me the gun." With one trembling hand I reach out toward her, my palm upraised and flat. "Let's figure this out, okay? It doesn't have to end with him dead."

She blinks, looking down at the ground as though my words are truly making a circuit through her brain and causing her to think. "It always ends the same way," she says, her words flat. "There's no other way for it to end."

"But there can be this time!" I'm pleading and frantic. I don't know what to do, and I'm terrified she's going to shoot me instead. "He doesn't have to die!" What else can I say to convince her? What else can I *do*?

"Mercy..." She closes her eyes hard. "God, I'm so tired. So *fucking* tired of this. Of them. Of being here."

"Then don't do this. Give me the gun, and it's over. We walk back together, and we figure things out." My hand inches closer to hers, though I'm not sure how much longer I'll have the nerve to do so. "Please?"

She looks up at me, eyes wide, and for a moment I'm sure that she's going to relent and hand over the gun. That all of this is going to be okay, and we're going to walk away from this.

"...I'm sorry," she says suddenly, and her eyes flick from me to Dorian, the gun coming down to point at him.

Again, I move before I think. I scream, knocking into her moments before the gun goes off and I feel a hot, burning pain in my left shoulder. It's not enough to push me off of her, however, and I drag her to the ground, hoping to God that I'm not dying and that Dorian is fine.

Zara is bigger than me and stronger, but I hang onto her arm with the gun as we roll in the grass, both of us trying to pin the other and fighting for the weapon. I scream again in her face, not able to hear what she's saying as my hearing aids ring in my ears from the discharge of a gun. Then my hand slips, though I'm not sure with what, and I lose my grip on the gun.

Zara rears back, the weapon in her hand and her eyes triumphant, but she's forgotten about Dorian. My alpha *slams* into her, knocking her back to the ground so hard that the gun flies from her hand to land in the grass. I lunge for it, grabbing it gingerly in my hands and wincing when the metal singes my palms.

"I have it!" I gasp, stumbling to my feet. "Dorian, are you okay?" I'm trembling all over, but when I turn, I see that Dorian has Zara pinned under his knee, and his phone is in his hand. He looks up at me, his eyes slightly wide, and when he starts talking, I realize that he already has the police on the line and is quickly telling them where to find us. When he hangs up, it's to call Foster and August, but by then I've sank to the ground, staring at the gun in my hand.

But also the fact that my hand is stained *red*. I flex my fingers, feeling no pain, and look up in confusion. "Is Zara okay?" She's remarkably quiet and still under him, but when I look at her face, I see that her eyes are on mine, and wide.

"What? Yeah, she's fine. Why?" Dorian demands, shifting to dig his knee harder into her back.

"Are you bleeding?"

My question draws a beat of silence between us. Even Zara looks alarmed, and when I lift my hand to show it to them, Dorian curses.

"Shit, Mercy...Where are you bleeding from? I can't exactly get up right now—"

"I'm fine," I promise, a little bewildered. "Nothing hurts. I'm fine."

"It's the adrenaline," Zara mumbles from the ground. "It's—"

"*Shut up.*" I've never her Dorian's voice sound like that, and I flinch back at the rage and the vitriol in his tone. "Shut the *fuck* up. You *shot her*, all because you wanted her to watch you kill me? You're such a piece of *shit*, Zara." I flinch again, and only then does Dorian glance up at me, that anger melting into concern. "The police are coming," he says slowly. "And so is my pack. Just don't pass out on me, okay?"

"I'm fine," I assure him, with my own quiet purr of reassurance. "Okay? I really am fine."

When his pack shows up five minutes later, I realize that was a bit of an overstatement. My shoulder burns, and as Foster peels back my hoodie, he hisses in sympathy at the source of the pain. "She grazed you," he observes, his eyes bright. "Are you all right?" Thankfully, August has already taken the gun, because I feel dizzy. There are sirens in the distance, and I'm grateful for that, but I manage a nod.

"I'm okay," I assure him, while cop cars pull up on the grass beside the trees. "Really, I'm fine. It probably doesn't even need stitches."

It *does* need stitches. The EMTs cart me off to the hospital, and if I wasn't so afraid of losing consciousness, I'd be questioning why August is with me in the ambulance, his hand clasping mine. He never leaves my side, even when I'm wincing and flinching at the feel of the numbing shot so that they can stitch up my arm.

Finally, however, he gets a chance to sit down with a sigh on the stretcher beside me, leaning against me. "Geez, Mercy," he murmurs. "Did you have to get shot?"

I'm about to respond to his teasing jibe when Dorian and Foster yank back the curtain of the hospital bay, both of them looking at me with varying expressions of alarm.

"Are you okay? Did the stitches hurt?" Foster leans forward to inspect my arm. "Did they numb you?"

"Nah," I lie, grinning shakily up at him. "I took it like a real masochist should. Without being numbed." August snorts, and even I have to admit that the look on Foster's face is hilarious.

That is, until Dorian pushes past both of them to lean over me, cradling my jaw in his hands as he stares at me with an unreadable expression.

"What were you thinking, little omega?" he asks, his voice barely loud enough for me to hear him. "What if she'd gotten a better shot? She's right. You don't even *like* me. And I've never been nice to you. Not really. None of us have, and you wouldn't have been in trouble for just walking away–"

I reach upward with my good arm and grab his hoodie, tangling my fingers in it roughly as I *yank* Dorian the rest of the way down to me. "Shut up, *alpha*," I mumble, my lips brushing his. "You're so dumb." But I guess if he's dumb, I'm dumb too. Before he can reply, I crush my lips to his, tasting every bit of him that I can reach as he melts into the kiss and leans down over the stretcher so that I can kiss him deeper.

A polite clearing of someone's throat makes me pull back, though Dorian just growls softly and chases my lips for one last brush before straightening to glare at the doctor over his shoulder. "When can she leave?" he snaps. "She's fine, right?"

The man nods a couple of times. "She can go home in a little bit. I just need to make sure she's not going to have any adverse reactions to the medicine we gave her and get her a pain prescription written up. Then she'll have to do some paperwork to get discharged." He stares at Dorian, unimpressed, before turning to look at me. "Are you feeling alright, Miss Noble?"

"Yeah," I say, flashing him a wan, tired smile. "As long as I can go home tonight and sleep in a real bed, I'm great."

He assures me that's possible, then starts to leave while promising the get the paperwork guy in here to discharge me, along with give me a prescription for painkillers.

"You need sleep," he observes, when I try to hide a yawn, and looks at Dorian pointedly. "Make sure your omega sleeps, all right?"

"He's not–" He's gone before I can finish the sentence, and I sigh, gazing up at him before looking from Foster to August. "You can't *make* me sleep," I point out, just to be difficult and prove that I'm fine. "Besides, I have movies to watch and studying to do. It's totally your fault that we didn't finish that study guide, Dorian. Who goes for a smoothie and gets *kidnapped?*"

He chuckles, and August leans in to brush his jaw against mine.

"Oh, little omega," Dorian purrs, pressing his lips to mine again. "You can be sure you'll be following every single one of the doctor's instructions to the letter. And I won't accept anything else from you." Gently he hooks his finger in the 'o' of my collar, and gives a soft tug while Foster chuckles in my other ear and August continues to scent along my jaw like they really are *my* pack.

And for the first time, I really wish that they were.

28

The fact that I don't see Briella for the rest of the semester isn't really a surprise. I only know that her parents took her home and that when I'm back at my dorm the next day, she's completely moved out. Even Dorian doesn't know the details, and only shrugs when I ask.

"Don't you care?" I'd asked him, staring at her empty side of the room while he sits on my bed. "Even a little?"

But he'd just shaken his head and gazed up at me in that way that made butterflies flutter around my insides. "I only care about one omega," he'd told me, and I'd immediately needed to change the subject.

I sigh at the memory, pushing myself to my feet as I walk out of my last final of the semester. It's kind of bittersweet, since I won't be seeing any of them over winter break, since I'm going home, and I'm not sure what we'll *be* when we come back. The collar still sits around my throat, but our deal had only been until now.

So, technically, I'm free.

Yet, I don't feel free.

Slowly I trudge down the campus center stairs, lightly mourning the fact that it feels like next semester I'll have to start all over. I won't have my friends, since one of them is in jail and the other is just *gone*, and Dorian's pack is...

Well, they were never *really* my friends.

An arm grabs me around the shoulders suddenly, being careful about my still-healing wound and I glance up into Foster's grin.

"Why do you look so *sad*?" he laughs, dragging me down the stairs and steering me toward the lakeside dorm. "Did you bomb a final? Though, for you I guess that means an A instead of an A+?"

"I'm not sad," I deny, grinning crookedly up at him as we walk. "And where are we going? The semester's over, so I'm not yours anymore." The words feel hollow when I say them, and Foster's brows jump upward in surprise.

Why am I so attached to them, it's only been a small amount of time I've spent with Dorian and his boys?

"Oh yeah? You think that's how this works?" He moves on to tell me about his own finals, dropping the subject as we get to his dorm and up to the suite he shares with the guys.

Upon opening it, he speaks before anyone else can, and says, "Guess what, Dorian? *Mercy* here says that you don't own her anymore, and that she's *free*. Can you believe that?"

Dorian looks up from the kitchen counter where he's cutting a pan of brownies, and his glasses slip down his nose a little as he looks at me. "Oh yeah?" A small grin curves over his features, and I can't help but feel something inside me warm.

"That was our deal?" I say, frowning. "I mean, unless I have brain damage from being shot in the shoulder and I can't remember?"

"Sure, but I don't think that means you're going to be rid of us," August says, falling onto the sofa with a groan. "Tell me you hated that bio final as well, please? It was shit, right?"

"It was pretty shit," I agree, walking to stand near the couch somewhat nervously. "What am I doing here, anyway?"

"I don't know." Dorian moves past me and drops the plate of brownies on the table, staring up at me as he sits down beside August. "I guess you can leave if you want to." I don't move, and he adds. "Do you want to?"

"Well...no. I mean." I sniff, trying to look bored. "I guess I don't have anything better to do."

"Or any*one*," Foster points out sweetly, swooping down to grab a brownie.

"Fuck you," I snap back at him, rolling my eyes, and his smile widens.

"Anytime. Really, I mean that. *Any* time, Mercy–"

"You may not 'belong' to us anymore," Dorian cuts in, his eyes on mine. "But somehow I don't think that's the whole reason you've been hanging around us so much."

I hesitate, frowning just a little as I think. "Then...maybe it's not the reason you *wanted* me to hang around you so much?" I ask, twisting my fingers together behind my back. It's the closest I can get to hinting at the fact that I want to still be around them, if only to get to know them better.

I don't love them, and it's not like we're *pack*. But to say that I don't feel something for Dorian and his boys would be a lie. Otherwise, I'd be crazy for taking a bullet for him, right?

"Maybe," Dorian admits, leaning back on the sofa and putting an arm around August. "But I think you should keep coming over, just so all of us can be sure. Don't you agree?"

With my heart pounding in my chest I sink down to the floor, grabbing a brownie after a moment. "I suppose," I say, with a long-suffering sigh. "I could even call you guys my friends, if we keep doing this. Since I have a few openings and the bar is incredibly low. Just don't shoot me, okay? And maybe don't leave any dead bodies around that I'm going to trip over."

August chuckles, and before Foster can say anything, it's Dorian who reaches out to drag me forward with the collar I'm still wearing. "No promises," he says. "But I guess we could *try* for you, Mercy Noble."

ABOUT THE AUTHOR

AJ merlin is an author, crazy bird lady, and rampant horror movie enthusiast. Born and raised in the Midwest United States, AJ is lucky to be right in the middle of people who support her and a menagerie of animals to keep her somewhat sane. When she isn't writing, she's probably watching something scary, witchy, or being swarmed by her pigeons.

Connect with her on Facebook or Instagram to see updates, giveaways, and be bombarded with dog, cat, and pigeon pictures.

Printed in Poland
by Amazon Fulfillment
Poland Sp. z o.o., Wrocław